Precious in His Sight

PRECIOUS
IN HIS SIGHT

M. E. Hughes

VIKING

VIKING
Published by the Penguin Group
Viking Penguin Inc., 40 West 23rd Street,
New York, New York 10010, U.S.A.
Penguin Books Ltd, 27 Wrights Lane,
London W8 5TZ, England
Penguin Books Australia Ltd, Ringwood,
Victoria, Australia
Penguin Books Canada Ltd, 2801 John Street,
Markham, Ontario, Canada L3R 1B4
Penguin Books (N.Z.) Ltd, 182–190 Wairau Road,
Auckland 10, New Zealand

Penguin Books Ltd, Registered Offices:
Harmondsworth, Middlesex, England

First published in 1988 by Viking Penguin Inc.
Published simultaneously in Canada

1 3 5 7 9 10 8 6 4 2

LIBRARY OF CONGRESS CATALOGING IN PUBLICATION DATA
Hughes, Martha.
Precious in his sight.
I. Title.
PS3558.U374P7   1988   813'.54   87-51649
ISBN 0-670-82401-1

Printed in the United States of America by
Arcata Graphics, Fairfield, Pennsylvania
Set in Sabon

To
Nell Salter

Jesus loves the little children,
All the children of the world,
Red and yellow, black and white,
They are precious in his sight,
Jesus loves the little children
Of the world.

(Traditional children's song,
Broadman Hymnal, 1940)

For their generous support and insight I would like to thank my editor, Amanda Vaill; my agent, Roberta Pryor; Richalleh, Nicholas Delbanco, Michele Orwin, Julie Houston, Joe Levine, and Freddie Greenberg. I also wish to thank Bennington College and the Millay Colony of the Arts, where the work came together, and Ray Hubener, who believed.

Precious in His Sight

· 1 ·

*T*hey married them young back then and always with an eye on adjoining acreage, so it was hardly surprising that Lizzard Patout knew, even before knowing who the female was to be, that he would impregnate her four times with four males in eight years—allowing a fallow year in between, which was sound, modern practice according to his agricultural course that came through the mail—one son for each farm bordering The Oaks, thus restoring the plantation to its original size. He never thought the small cane farmers on the north, south, east, and west might disappoint him by having only sons themselves. With church doctrine on his side and subtle hints as to his aim, they would, he knew, keep their wives in fold until the required daughters came, for he was, after all, of old family and the largest landowner in the parish to boot. He counted on Cajun greed. What he didn't count on was his wife.

Josephine Celeste Minville, the only child of Judge Minville, married Lizzard Patout in her sixteenth year and straightaway had three daughters, one of them with the harelip that ran on her mother's side of the family, enjoyed two relatively uneventful years as mistress of The Oaks, during which time the harelip died, which people said was merciful because how would you ever marry off a girl like that, got pregnant again and died herself, leaving her husband with two girls and a brand-new baby boy.

Old Man Patout was so put out with his wife that he swore he'd never marry again, and he was true to his word and never did.

For a long time after that we didn't know if the bearer of the Patout family name would survive. He was a sickly, weak child. Dr. Perkins said he needed his mother's milk. We'd just have to wait and see, which we did, and after a while, my, didn't he come around and develop into a fine, handsome little boy.

The three surviving Patout children—Clotilde, Janice, and Richard—were left to their own devices and on their own they stayed, as Old Man Patout sank more and more into an alcoholic blur.

"I didn't ax her for no girls," he would often say to his booze and bourré-playing cronies in the back room of the grocery shack where they played afternoons. There by the still, brown water of the bayou that snaked through town and the outlying environs he'd rant, "I never axed her for them girls, me, and the boy, he's a weakling, just like his mama."

In the beginning of time for those three young children, born in a house that was the envy of everyone living in Belmont, and with all the money anyone could ask for, life—with the exception of having no mother—was as near to perfection as any child could want.

As in most ancient houses, there were intriguing nooks and crannies for the children to explore and an attic overflowing with old clothes, books, and toys. The garden also lent itself to games. Bamboo grew in thick curtains along the edges of the garden proper and shut out inquisitive eyes. Elsewhere it formed massive clumps with secret chambers inside. Only the Patout children knew the way through the dense, green, snake-ridden walls.

Flowers filled the garden throughout the year, even spilling into the ditches in spring, but in winter the camellias—some as tall as the second-story balcony—outshone them all. Even the names of the camellias delighted the children—Purple Dawn, Pink Debutante, Prince Valiant, Pink Perfection—so drawn apart from the ordinary world of lessons to learn,

baths to take, and beets to eat twice a week for supper under
the watchful eye of Mattie Belle Wooten, the old black
woman who had nursed their mother and stayed on to raise
them after her death.

So the three children played in their garden, held trysts
deep within the bamboo, used the blood-red petals of fallen
camellias stuck with spit on their lips to play Ladies, on legs
and arms for Doctor and Nurse, and then one morning they
awoke and found they were nearly grown.

Clotilde, Janice, and Richard Patout—fate hung their
names together. Pronounced the French way, their names had
a musical sound and went right well on a calling card, too.
We were proud of our first family's next generation. Who
knows what they might have been if Old Man Patout hadn't
also noticed his children were almost grown, for he resolved
to mend his ways and take them under control.

About this time oil was discovered in East Texas. People
started pouring through town, coming from the East, heading
for the West, going to get rich on the soggy Louisiana-Texas
border. Just as in the days of the big migrations, some of
them that were going didn't make it, and settled down in the
little byways and outbacks along the way. Belmont got some
of them. They had names like Taylor and Davis, Smith and
Crabtree, and belonged to religions called Church of God,
Christian, Seventh Day, and Methodist. Up to then we'd only
had a small Baptist mission that met every other Sunday in
the back of the feedstore on account of Saul Robicheaux, he
was the owner, got mad at Father Blanchard and went and
joined the Baptists; an Episcopal Church, used as a stable by
the Union Army during the Civil War; and, it goes without
saying, St. Peter's Catholic Church.

All of a sudden Old Man Patout got himself involved with
a Seventh Dayer, and pretty soon she had him singing in the
choir. He didn't go near the bourré games or bourbon anymore, but the Seventh Dayer wasn't satisfied with that, no
sir. She was going to have those children in her church, too,

come hell or high water, those children who had been baptized Roman Catholic and didn't belong to her God at all. If she didn't have better sense, Old Man Patout should have. Growing up free and independent as they had, neither Clotilde, Janice, nor Richard were about to be told what to do.

Exactly what Richard did, no one ever knew, but one day his father beat him up bad. Richard almost lost an eye on account of it. As soon as he got well, Richard was packed off to a military academy in Virginia, told to stay there, and not to write home.

But it was the girls who fixed Old Man Patout real good. One of them got pregnant and refused to give out with the father's name. Of course, we didn't know about it back then. All we knew was the Patout girls had suddenly disappeared. At first we figured they were off on retreat—nice, respectable Catholic girls were always being sent off on retreat as soon as they got their figures—but when they didn't come back soon, we knew that couldn't be where they went.

Finally, about eight or nine months later, Janice and Clotilde reappeared. They said they'd been in New Orleans staying with their cousins, the Minvilles. Seems Molly Minville was expecting and the doctor had made her stay in bed the whole time. Somebody had had to cook and clean house for poor Charles.

Well, when most people heard the news, they said, "Why, how lovely for Molly and Charles. It's nice she named the baby after you all."

But when Hattie Leblanc heard about little Patout Minville, she got the funniest look on her face.

"Why," said Hattie, "I was in New Orleans toward the end of Lent and I saw Molly in Kolb's eating cabbage rolls with Charles. She didn't look the least bit pregnant. She should have been showing by then."

An ugly story began to circulate around town. In one version, Clotilde was the real mother of Patout Minville, in the other version, it was Janice. Whenever Molly brought the child home to Belmont for a visit, everybody would look real close to see which one of the Patout sisters he resembled, but with every passing year, Patout Minville looked more and more like his Uncle Richard, so we didn't learn a thing from his face.

(Janice Patout was crazy about her cousin's little boy. Patout Minville was a sweet child, but too easily led. The summer he turned eleven, he and Pugie Reaux, a bad local boy, got caught by the police for stealing hubcaps. They wanted to make a stink bomb and needed the money for supplies. After that, Clotilde and Old Man Patout wouldn't have him at The Oaks. Janice once went to New Orleans to see him, but after Molly died, she didn't go anymore. She didn't get along with Charles's new wife, but that's getting ahead of the story.)

Just about the same time, it must have been, when Janice and Clotilde came home, Richard Patout escaped from the military academy and headed south. He'd had no word from his beloved sisters in almost a year, a situation he must have found intolerable. He got within twenty minutes of The Oaks and was drunk or maybe didn't see the turn-key bridge open, drove off into the bayou and drowned.

The next day the *Belmont Crier* said the car was stolen. If that wasn't bad enough, they had to keep dredging the bayou for his body. It was nowhere to be found. Sheriff Breaux told everybody to be on the lookout for Richard, lest his body go on by.

"Look in the water lilies along the banks especially hard," Sheriff Breaux said, "because in our experience bodies often get tangled up in them lilies."

We looked and looked all week long, up and down the banks, but we never did find that body. It was hard on the children in town. They seemed to take a notion that Richard was going to turn up one day, just walk right out of the bayou dripping wet with an alligator-bonnet on his head, and try to touch them. You couldn't drive over the bridge to get to the other side of town without all the children in the buggy screaming their heads off. To this day there's more than one adult in Belmont who can't stand to swim in the bayou because of Richard Patout still being somewhere down there.

That was really the beginning of the end of the Patouts as a family. Clotilde, she took the news hard. She loved Richard better than anyone in the world. He was her baby brother. She blamed his death on Janice, and Janice, she blamed Clotilde. She said Richard wouldn't have been on the road that night if Clotilde hadn't let her disobey their father and write to him.

Old Man Patout didn't seem to know who to blame it on, but he never thought of himself. If anyone, he blamed the Seventh Dayer; he didn't see her anymore. He started drinking again and playing bourré and hardly ever left the vicinity of The Oaks, lest Janice and Clotilde got the chance to come within a mile of a man. It was only when he was drunk after that and walked home from the grocery store late at night that you'd hear him sing those Protestant songs. He favored "Onward, Christian Soldiers" and one about needing God every hour. He had a hard time getting through his days after his son was dead.

What of Richard Patout then? That was all Belmont ever knew. He was born. Lived about eighteen years. Stood five feet eight inches, just like his daddy. Had black hair, olive complexion, and black eyes that sparkled with life, just like his mama. Was double-jointed in his left hand, was fond of sticking out his tongue and making it touch his nose, which he did at all the birthday parties from the time he was six till he was nine. And he was gentle, has that been said? He was of a nature born sweet, gentle, and kind. Later on, after he'd been in the bayou some weeks and people got to grumbling because they still couldn't find his body—people will turn on you if you give them half a chance—people said all that sweetness had been nothing but show. Richard was already drinking and messing around with girls as soon as he reached puberty, but you can put that down to guilt. We all felt we had let him down by not being able to find him in that coffee-brown water.

In 1926 Lizzard Patout, the last male bearing the family name, died and was laid out in his four-poster bed. The whole town filed by. He left The Oaks to his daughters with the understanding that the old plantation home would be burned to the ground upon their deaths. He didn't want strangers living in The Oaks. He didn't leave much money, his drinking and gambling had eaten it away.

Being too entangled in their perpetual squabbles to run the plantation together, Janice and Clotilde turned the land over to a tenant farmer by the time the great block of ice had melted under the old man's four-poster. They kept two acres for themselves, upon which Janice grew vegetables and flowers, particularly day lilies, having a weakness for them, and Clotilde raised chickens and a cow. They continued to live in the main house—Clotilde on the left side, Janice on the right—but once business matters were attended to, they never spoke to each other again.

Shocked by their behavior, Father Blanchard, the pastor of St. Peter's Catholic Church, tried to patch things up. The week after Old Man Patout's funeral he went out to The Oaks and stood pivoting in the front hall, sending his appeal for rapprochement—on the grounds of their recent, mutual tragedy—into the right parlor and then into the left until the ancient Mattie Belle shooed him away saying, for she was a Baptist, "Father, Brother, whatever you is, you jus a lost ball in da high grass if you thinks you goin to change dere minds. Miss Janice, she say Miss Clotilde daid. Miss Clotilde, she say, likewise. Now, dat's da sumpshun I's goin by, and I 'vise you to do da same." With that she slammed the front door.

It was not long before Father Blanchard, the Belmont merchants, the farmers and Negroes on the adjacent farms, in short, everyone who knew the Patout sisters, realized the wisdom of Mattie Belle's words. A few days after Father Blanchard's visit, a truck rumbled out of town and took the dusty back road to The Oaks. It repeated the trip for the next three weeks. At the end of that time, the white-columned house was stuffed to the breaking point with furnishings, linens, and utensils for two complete households. Buford Wooten, Mattie Belle's son, added a lean-to kitchen on the back of the house to the left, installed a toilet and a claw-footed tub in an unused pantry on the right. Then he nailed shut the doors on either side of the long central hall. From that time forward, neither woman touched what the other had touched, walked where the other had walked, ate where the other had eaten.

It was said in town that the only thing the sisters shared for the next thirty years was the prayer for a bolt of lightning to split the house in two, but God never got around to it.

Clotilde, she was the big one of the two. She wore straight, no-colored cotton dresses and smelled of Lifebuoy Soap. Her hair was pulled tight in a knot on the back of her neck. She had one of those heads that's flat in the back, and she didn't have buttocks either. She looked more like a plank of pecky cypress than anything. And mean? She could make a hot pepper shrivel. But as mean-tempered as she was, she met her match in her sister.

Janice Patout didn't look a thing like Clotilde. She was tiny and, without the sour expression of her face, she would have been delicately pretty. Her hair was curly, thick, and black to the day of her death. She wore it in plaits around the top of her head like a crown. She patted it gently throughout the day. She had been the most beautiful girl in the parish when young, people said, and Clotilde, though never a beauty, had been charming.

That's hard to believe now.

In October 1960, Janice Patout died of the pneumonia that often kills old people during protracted illnesses. The death was a shock to no one. Janice Patout had been bedridden since August, after falling off the east veranda adjacent to her bedroom and breaking her right hip. The diurnal re-creation of the accident, attended by raging paroxysm, had carried the old lady through her last two months of life and into the grave mercifully self-recognizable. She died while her mind floated across the white chenille bedspread to that after-noon in August when she had been lying in her petticoat, face down across the bed, without bothering to pull back the spread, for Ruby, her maid, was going to wash it in the next load.

The day had been extraordinarily hot, even for Louisiana, and the bed had soon grown warm, causing her to turn her head restlessly from side to side, splaying the bedspread's popcorn motif across her cheeks. She had just begun to doze when she was awakened by the sweet voice of Ruby's child, Lily, coming through the screen door. The demented girl was singing "Tenting Tonight," the song into which she habitually lapsed while invading Janice Patout's prized day lilies, which grew in a crenulate border at the edge of the veranda.

The dreamy voice curled lazily on the ultima, emulating, to the old woman's horror, the sensuous arch of the petals over the child's hands, as she slowly worked from blossom to blossom squeezing their beauty into her palms.

By the time Janice got through the screen door and onto the veranda, ten blossoms had been crushed, and Lily had retreated to the safety of the backyard chicken coop where her father, Willie Wooten, was lopping off a chicken's head. The sight of her carefully nurtured hybrids bleeding and transparent in the sun so enraged the old woman that she forgot about the three rotten floorboards on the edge of the porch. As she leaned over to count the dead, the boards gave way. She fell head over heels into the day lilies where she was forced to lie all night until the farmer, Alphonse Romero, stopped by The Oaks the next morning on his way into town to ask if he could save the sisters the five-mile trip, and got

scared out of his wits by a white claw looming in SOS out
of a dewy clump of particularly brilliant "Fat and Sassys"
growing in the side yard.

At the time people said it was downright mean of Clotilde
not to have helped her sister. "Ain't dat jus like er," was the
way they put it. Although the more charitable noted, to the
intense irritation of those less so, that Clotilde had probably
been unaware of her sister's plight. They had not, after all,
spoken in over three decades.

In the end, even those who blamed Clotilde forgave her,
feeling she had atoned by having a stroke an hour after Janice
died.

"Well, well, so she loved her after all," they said. They
wondered what would become of Clotilde, all alone and sick,
stuck out there in that house with two kitchens. Her only
living relative was Patout Minville, but he hadn't been heard
of since he was a child. He'd be middle-aged by now. Even
if Clotilde knew where he was, she wasn't likely to send
for him.

While Dr. Rodriguez administered to Clotilde, Janice was
taken from The Oaks and driven into Belmont for the last
time. At Pellerin's Funeral Home, she was embalmed, made
up, and dressed; she went on view at suppertime. The next
morning, as the sun climbed the sky and only distant rum-
blings warned of the shower headed that way, Janice was
loaded into a long, silver hearse, and taken to the old city
cemetery on the other side of the Southern Pacific tracks. No
one was buried there anymore, but the Patout plot still held
two empty slots.

A small band of people gathered around the cut in the
earth and waited for Father Delcambre to arrive from the
neighboring town, where he had gone to record "The Rosary
Hour" at the radio station. Each man—there were no females
in the burial party—wore workday garb as though, on the
way home to lunch, he had suddenly remembered the funeral,

detoured off Main, dashed over the weed-grown tracks, and pulled into the cemetery with a glance at his watch.

They had arrived nearly an hour ago and stood, more or less quietly, their natural small-town garrulousness dampered by hunger and the prolonged, midday acquaintance with the coffin, a burnished mahogany contraption with brass handles and, according to old-fashioned practice, a color-tinted photo of the occupant on the lid.

Sheriff Stanley Mouton—known by the diminutive, "Te Mouton"—stood at the gravehead, hands crammed into the pants pockets of his uniform, a dark-brown-and-khaki affair. The sweat rings under each arm were outlined in white residue from bicarbonate of soda, which the sheriff tossed on his armpits each morning, standing nude before his full-length bathroom mirror.

"How could a man ax for anyting bettah?" he would often muse in the predawn hours, setting the orange Arm & Hammer box on the back of the toilet. "You can wash wid it, clean yore teeth wid it, gargle wid it; it stops armpits from stinkin, likewise iceboxes."

Upon returning from the bathroom, he would sit down on the edge of the bed, pull on his socks, turn to his wife, who lay under the pillows, and say, *"Mais, Sha-te:* Tell me, how could a man ax for anyting bettah?"

At this moment his mind was pleasantly empty. He stood at ease among his fellow men and waited, one foot planted on the piled-up clods, while his gun protruded over the cocked hip and aimed inadvertently at Alphonse Romero, standing on his right.

Alphonse Leon "Tutie" Romero stood unaware of danger, his arms akimbo, shifting a splendiferous stomach on stubby legs, breeches tucked into cracked leather boots on which a lyrical purple orchid and the name, "Tutie," peeked out through a layer of mud.

Next to him stood Jerome Xavier Pellerin, undertaker and

coroner, in shirtsleeves and a torn straw hat festooned with multicolored fishing lures. He was eager to get the funeral over because, as he told the young reporter from the *Belmont Crier* standing next to him, the fish were biting off Pecan Island.

"I *tole* Monseigneur to get his ass here by noon," he shrieked. The lures danced on his hat, heliographing south to the bay.

The reporter, to whom Pellerin delivered this reproach, grinned uncomfortably. Being Protestant and new to the area, he had not yet learned the proper response to the Cajun juxtaposition of sacred and profane.

"*Mais,* Pellerin, who you tryin ta kid, huh? You couldn't catch a Spanish mackerel waitin wid his mouf open in yore own battub," said Te Mouton.

The reporter laughed.

"No *way* you goin down for mackerel. We know bout you and dem Pecan Island gals. You goin after nooky," said the sheriff. He winked at the reporter.

"Shut up, Mouton," said the undertaker, laughing in spite of himself.

"Both of you shut up," said Alphonse Leon. He was attending the burial for the sake of his old-time pal, Lizzard Patout, and his position as closest family friend weighed on him heavily. Holy Mary, Mother of God . . . dey don't care, he thought. He finished the prayer, flipped to the next gutta-percha bead on his dead mother's rosary, and looked around the group. Yeah, dey jus come cause dey gotta, he thought. Only the presence of the man standing on the other side of the young reporter puzzled him, but Pugie Reaux puzzled everyone.

Dressed in a red polo shirt, black-and-white plaid slacks, Pugie Reaux chewed a wad of Dentyne slowly in the corner of his left cheek, causing the muscles of his strong, square neck to ripple down the jawline and into the body of his shirt. Men, no less than women, were aware of Pugie Reaux's exceptional good looks, which had only heightened with age, but he was a man of few friends. He lived in a wood frame house on the edge of town just past the dog pound and kept a collection of junk cars on his front lawn. It was whispered that Pugie had a second home, a shack on Pecan Island, and according to whom one asked, it was filled variously with fighting cocks, water moccasins, switchblades, machetes, erotic instruments, or poker chips. In town he was known as a self-styled detective. Nobody'd ever heard of a case to his credit, but his cold, handsome face was ever to be seen at fires and out on the parish back roads, where teenagers and cane trucks collided in bloody scenes each harvest. In short, wherever there was disaster, Pugie was sure to be there, chewing Dentyne and handing out crisp white cards with PUGIE REAUX, LICENSED DETECTIVE embossed in gold.

As he stood and waited, his eyes worked over the group, his mouth twitching every so often, but not saying anything, just listening, chewing, and waiting.

Lightning cracked. Thunder rolled over the cemetery. The air smelled of rain.

Tutie the farmer lifted his eyes. He must remember to give Monseigneur something for prayers. Last year his tractors had been mud-locked in the fields five out of every seven days. When grinding season closed, half his cane was still standing in the fields. Another rainy harvest would ruin him.

"Y'all hear if Patout Minville's coming back to live?"

"I was wondering why you showed up today, Pugie. Didn't cause Patout enough trouble when y'all were kids, huh?" Tutie said.

"Well," said Te Mouton, "if I was Miss Clotilde, all alone and ailing, I'd be ready to let bygones be. Wouldn't surprise me none if she sent word to her 'cousin' to come on home." He winked at the undertaker.

Pellerin guffawed.

The reporter looked puzzled.

Pellerin put his arm around the young man. "You see, son, Patout Minville ain't just her cousin."

"Shut up, Pellerin."

"Now Tutie, don't get your bowels in an uproar. I'm just trying to help the boy. How's he going to work around here without knowing some of our families' histories. Son, everybody in Belmont's kin to everybody else, sometimes in two or three different ways. That's why you got to be real careful who you're talking to when you call somebody a son of a bitch, you might be talking to his cousin." Pellerin jerked his head in the direction of the coffin. "Now you take Miss Janice here, or maybe it was Miss Clotilde, anyway one of them sisters was really Patout Minville's—"

"That's enough out of you, Pellerin. Tutie, keep your shirt on. Son, all you need know is Patout Minville is Miss Clotilde's last living kin and he's likely to inherit the place after she's gone, what's left of it anyways."

"Is that a sure enough thing to go in the paper, Sheriff Mouton?"

"Go ahead and put it in if you want, kid; just don't quote me."

"Well, lookie here," Pugie sneered. Monseigneur Delcambre was hurrying toward them, sidestepping graves.

"I'm sorry, gentlemen. Even men of the cloth have flat tires," he said with a smirk. His habit flapped, a black flag in the wind. He felt a drop of rain. "We'd best begin," he said, his head darting into the Bible. The mourners tightened silently around him.

The words were said; the coffin lowered. The group broke up. As soon as the white men had driven away, black men came out of the shacks on the edge of the cemetery. They carried shovels and one man a straw basket his wife had given him to collect flowers from the graves. A wind chime tinkled on somebody's porch. Quickly the men went to work. The last shovelful of dirt was in place before the rains came.

The grave sank in places, but not too bad, considering the speed with which the job had been done.

That night on the front page of the *Belmont Crier* there was a notice edged in black:

Janice Patout, daughter of the late Lizzard and Josephine Celeste Patout and long-time resident of this community, was buried today in the old city cemetery in the Patout family plot.

The Lizzards and Patouts once had wide holdings in this parish, the land in sugar cane and rice. Miss Janice Patout, along with her sister, Clotilde, who is recovering from a stroke suffered yesterday just minutes after learning of her sister's death, are the last direct descendants of Emile Lafayette Lizzard and Louis Henri Delcambre Patout, French explorers and first settlers in this area.

As stipulated by the late Lizzard Patout, the old plantation home where the Patouts lived for a century and a half will be burned to the ground upon the death of the last member of the family. Now, with the failing health of Miss Clotilde Patout, the fate of the old house, known as The Oaks (considered by Professor Ramos Quigley of the Department of Architecture, University of Southwestern Louisiana, one of the finest examples of early French colonial architecture) hangs in jeopardy. Reliable sources report, however, that Miss Patout may invite her cousin, Mr. Patout Minville of New Orleans, and his family to return to Belmont and live at The Oaks. It is to be hoped that the Patout Minvilles will be a comfort to Miss Patout, thereby speeding her recovery, and that the house may be saved in this manner.

Miss Janice Patout was a member of the Daughters of the American Revolution, the Daughters of the Confederacy, the Catholic Women's Aid Society, and former president of the Belmont Garden Club, though she had been inactive in recent years. She left her large collection of Victorian hair jewelry to St. Peter's Catholic Church.

Though noteworthy, the jewelry left to the most prominent church in town was not the cause of the avid newspaper reading that went on in Belmont that night. The managing editor of the *Crier*—a big, red-jowled man with perpetually sprouting nostril hair (golden hair, which supported the theory that a Scots regiment in full regalia had ridden down the bayou in confiscated pirogues during the War of 1812 and raped everything in sight on both sides of the bank—a spurious tale, no doubt, but revered for all that)—instructed his men to extend the run to three thousand on the day of the funeral, and he ran the obituary on the first page, to the right of the Levine's Shoe Store ad, and just under the banner head, consisting of a sheaf of sugar cane, a barrel of red peppers, a pile of rock salt, and the motto, "The Sweetest, Saltiest, Spiciest Spot on Earth."

Ironically, Janice Patout would have credited the biographical particulars listed in her obituary—daughter of a wealthy landowner, a descendant of original settlers—as the preeminent qualifications for her exquisite exit from town, but she would have been wrong.

She went out riding under the banner head because, as the managing editor knew, she was a fixture in a sleepy little town with not much to brag about. Since people cannot cluster around a gas pump without feeling that *they* somehow are not as good as *we,* the citizens of Belmont had long ago found that their greatest source of pride was not their pepper and cane crops—many other towns in south Louisiana could boast of those—nor their salt domes, which were actually nearer to another town (no, you will not find it on the map printed on the paper placemats that go down on the red Formica tabletops of Belmont's only restaurant before the waitress comes back and bangs water glasses on the table and sulks as she writes up your order). Their pride lay in the wealth of human eccentricity that thrived in their town. When Belmont's favorite eccentrics die, they are not forgotten. Death merely allows for the embellishment of tales told on dead souls.

So it was with Janice Patout. Let her die feeling superior, but Belmont knew a naughty tale about her. That was the real reason she got her obit on the front page. The managing editor knew it too, and by the time the last newsboy had flag-tucked his papers, put them in his bicycle basket, and pedaled away, every newspaper in town was either sold or spoken for.

· 2 ·

*I*t was early evening of the following day by the time James Rodriguez managed to clear both white and colored waiting rooms, get in his car, and head out of town to check on Clotilde Patout.

It had been a long, wearisome day, though no more than most of late, and the doctor was relieved to turn off the busy highway onto the lonely back road winding through the cane fields to The Oaks. When he had gone a few yards, he stepped on the brakes and looked back. No one could see him from the main road. The cane had swallowed him. Leaning over his bag, the mail, and a wad of shirts he had forgotten to take to the laundry again, he opened the glove compartment, patted around inside until he brought out what he wanted, slammed the compartment door once, twice, until on the third try it stuck, leaned back, and took a well-deserved swig of bourbon. It was harder each day to keep going. His wife nagged him to stop. He was the only doctor his age who had not retired. No one could blame him for needing a little snort.

He started down the road again, enjoying his prowess at keeping inside the mud tracks, the smell of the rich, wet earth, and the warmth of the liquor in his throat. How glad he would be to see his old friend. He hadn't had a person he could talk to all day. Of course, he would have to do the chatting for both. Clotilde Patout had the constitution of an ox. One stroke wouldn't kill her, but he mustn't tire her. He took another swig, stuck the bottle back between his legs.

On days like today he felt tempted to retire, but what would his patients do without him? Also, unlike most doctors, he needed the money. Throughout his career he had been too generous with time, sometimes seeing only one patient per hour. To his own regret, he could not be brief, even when summing up treatment for a cold. (It was also known throughout town that he forgave long-standing bills at the mere mention of hardship or tragedy.) More importantly, he could not imagine a worse hell than being penned up at home with his wife, even in semi-retirement, so he continued, though the joy long ago had gone out of the work. His drinking had worsened, his practice fallen off. Aside from a few loyal friends, such as the Patout sisters, most of his patients now were neither middle class nor white. The blacks of Belmont were keeping him going, though he wouldn't have admitted it to a soul.

He turned into a long drive. All the lights were on in The Oaks. The house seemed to float ablaze above the dark lawn, like a pleasure cruiser tied at port on the night of a festive occasion, but no music wafted his way, nor did he hear distant laughter, as he pulled to the brick veranda and cut the motor off. Clotilde didn't believe in wasting electricity. "Perhaps she's scared," he muttered. Physical infirmity often wrought remarkable change in a patient's personality.

Deep silence surrounded him, the silence of a small, rural community going dark. A dog barked far away. Rainwater dripped off the oaks and thudded on the roof of the car. It had rained heavily that afternoon. There was coolness in the air now. The breeze off the Gulf of Mexico brought him a whiff of burned leaves. Earlier that morning the farmers had begun to burn trash off the sugar cane. It was fall again. He would soon see the first battered bodies pulled from the wreckage of cars that went sliding out of control across roads slick with squashed sugar cane. No one had ever convinced the cane farmers it was their responsibility to keep the roads clean during grinding season, even when it was their own sons and daughters killed on the roads year after year. The local farmers never did anything that affected their pockets adversely.

He put his head back and gazed at the moon, striated in the trees. If he had had a child . . . He stopped and told himself that others might find the meaning of life wrapped up in a child, but he had never missed the presence of one. Medicine—with all the attendant responsibility it brought in a country town—had filled his life. As well, he reasoned, one didn't miss something one had never had. No, he didn't miss having a child, though he was sorry for Mary Louise's sake that she had never had one of her own. It might have made life easier for him. Living with Mary Louise meant sidestepping cautions hoarded for a child: Don't stay out late; don't work so hard; don't make house calls, nobody does anymore; don't get dog hair on your jacket, especially not if their owners can't pay; don't drive out of town to see patients; and above all, don't drink.

Damn her! He got out of the car and slammed the door. He ought to know who drank too much and who didn't. He kicked at the walkway, sending pea gravel across the porch. It pinged against a watering can sitting beside a fern.

"Is that you, Dr. Rodriguez?"

"No, Ruby, it's Spencer Tracy."

"Just a minute." The maid walked away from the door.

He sighed and looked down the front lawn to where the moon gleamed silver on the low-hanging moss. Something rustled in the flower bed. The previous week a coral snake had bitten a man on the neighboring farm.

"Ruby! Let me in!" he cried. "I'm here on serious business. Stop playing games!" No sound. He banged on the door. "Niggers are such children," he muttered.

"Only thing stopping you was yourself. It wasn't locked." Ruby held the door open with her foot. She led him into the front left parlor and pointed. Three fake logs glowed and crackled in the fireplace.

"I wanted you to see 'em lit up. They was in the back of Miss Janice's closet. She was hiding them from Miss Clotilde. I found 'em when I was cleaning out her things. Miss Clotilde, she says them's the only logs in town that make a noise. They's just like the real thing, only nicer, cause we don't have to clean up no mess after." She looked at him expectantly, but the doctor had already put down his bag and was opening the liquor cabinet.

"Damn it to hell, can't one of you darkies keep Miss Clotilde in soda?" He turned around. Ruby had disappeared.

He poured himself a drink in a tumbler upon which all the United States presidents' names were written in gold, presented to Lizzard Patout by the Southwest Cane Growers Association upon his hauling the most tonnage in 190 . The date was effaced by years of scrubbing. He drank it, poured himself another, and sat down.

It was a beautiful room, one he had always admired, with tall windows that rose from the floor and almost touched the ceiling. Antiques and Oriental carpets filled the room. Every table held a surprise to pick up and admire. He got out of his chair and roamed, picking up objects here and there, looking at the photographs encased in silver. On the piano at the far end of the room, a photograph of Clotilde Patout in a long white gown held his attention. It had been taken her first year at Sophie Newcomb. One year of college was all her father had given her, and he'd regretted even that. Made her unfit for most of the nice women she knew, he'd said, and he had no use for a daughter who could speak Latin.

He put the photograph down, walked to the liquor cabinet, poured himself another drink, and passed his hand over his face. "Not one living soul to talk to all day," he muttered, "a wonder I can still make polite conversation."

It was not that he didn't care for his Negro patients, but they depressed him with their weary, long-suffering patience. They would sit all day in his waiting room, brown bags of fried chicken and potted meat sandwiches next to them on the vinyl banquettes—hunger being the one thing blacks could not tolerate without complaint. They infuriated him. They were so unlike whites, of whatever class and no matter how poor or downtrodden, who would eventually get mad when he ran really late, storm out the door, go back to work or home, saying their time was of some value, not much perhaps—this was the South—but always more than the nickels and quarters knotted in handkerchiefs and carried with care by the people waiting in the room at the back. How they tired him with their shocking ailments, of the kind whites rarely had anymore. They were just like their cars, held together with spit and glue. By the time they came in for repairs, often there was nothing he could do. He seemed perpetually cutting into, or cutting off, pieces of rotting black flesh; being forced to give devastating news, which they accepted silently with bowed heads, until they got back in the waiting room and began to wail. Often he could not keep his mind on the next patient because of the soft moans and cries of their kin. (When sick, they brought the whole family in.) Lord, they tried his soul.

He drained the glass, picked up his bag, and, feeling fortified, headed for the stairs.

"You read it?" She tapped the newspaper smartly.

Dr. Rodriguez bent over his stomach and stuffed the stethoscope in his bag, noticing that the dye was coming off edges, showing cow-color underneath.

He stood up too quickly, felt a sudden dizziness, and reached for the side of the bed. He had been having these little spells lately. The lamp beside the four-poster cast a shadow over his patient's face. For a moment he couldn't recall her name. Three large, brown stains nestled in the lace of her blue flannel bodice. Coffee, he reckoned. With or without? With cream, he decided. That would make it hard to wash out. He counted the stains again, as though that might give him a clue to her identity. Her fingernails were certainly filthy. He had spent his life ministering to this woman and others not unlike her. He couldn't really think what for. As soon as the handle broke on his bag, and from the look of it that could be any day now, he was going to quit, but who the devil was she?

"This bag and me started out together sixty years ago. Sixty years. Why, that's a long time to practice medicine," he said to gain time.

"What's wrong with it?" she said.

"Why nothing, except the dye's coming off and the lock's—"

"The obituary, you fool!" Her eyes narrowed. "You've been drinking, Rodriguez."

Dr. Rodriguez smiled sweetly. "Only one woman in the world talks to a man like that. You get more and more like your father every day, Miss Clotilde. Now you just stay in bed. I'm having Ruby set up a cot in the kitchen tonight. Call out to her if you need anything. First thing in the morning I'll bring Françoise Fischler out. She's a foreigner, but she can tell you a thing or two about Shakespeare. Beats me what a woman with a fine education is doing out here." He glanced at his patient. Her color had risen. The eyes glinted in anger.

He suddenly felt sorry for the Fischler woman and hoped she could give as good as she got. He didn't know much about her, only having met her the previous evening when she came into his office without knocking and caught him taking a snort.

She was a large woman, unsmiling. She held no light of kindness in her eyes. No emotion showed in her face at all, but perhaps there was a trace of hostility in the voice as she had said, "Mildred, the waitress at the Greyhound terminal, said you might help."

Where she had come from she did not say, only explaining that she had been passing through Belmont, run out of money, and needed to work before pushing on. Would he recommend her to a young family as governess? She spoke French, German, Spanish, Italian, and Gaelic. No, she didn't have a Louisiana Teacher's Certificate. She was a Ph. D. in Comparative Literature, a university in Europe, no, not here.

"Ah," he said, regretful. Her diploma wouldn't count for much, her face would scare any child to death, but her clothes were worn and she was terribly thin, so he had asked, was she willing to sit with an elderly woman and do light housework? He knew Clotilde Patout wouldn't pay anybody just to sit.

"What illness has she?"

"Nothing contagious, a stroke. She needs help. Her sister just died, so she's living alone, though I'm hoping kinfolks will come live with her soon. Miss Patout won't pay much. Like all good Cajuns, she hangs on to what she's got, but you'll get room and board in a lovely old house and lots of good country air."

The woman hesitated.

"I'm afraid folks around here aren't fancy enough for governesses," he said gently.

"I'll sit with her," the woman said. "I'll sit, at least until her relatives arrive."

His left arm tingled. He looked down. Clotilde Patout had dug her fingernails into his wrist.

"I asked you a question, Rodriguez," she said.

He tried to back away, but she dug her nails farther into his flesh.

"Now, Clotilde, you mustn't excite yourself," he said. "There's nothing wrong with that obituary. I couldn't have written it better myself." His wrist was throbbing. He put his bag down with his free hand. He felt weak and nauseated. There was a fourth stain on her nightgown; he hadn't noticed it before.

"You're right, as usual, Clotilde," he said at last. "I am reluctant to discuss it. I didn't think it was my place to tell you what I thought, but since you seem to want to know . . . Honestly, my dear, if you don't let go soon you'll draw blood and then won't you be embarrassed."

"Not a bit," she said, but let go.

He sat down on the edge of the bed and held his wrist. She is an old woman, all alone in this house. She has coffee stains on her chest and her sister just died. She needs to bathe, to set an example for her Negroes, if nothing else. His wrist felt better. She hadn't broken the skin, but he'd better get Mary Louise to give him a tetanus shot when he got home.

He shook his head sadly. It was always this way when people grew old without anyone to love them. Patout Minville was the only blood kin she had left in the world. He doubted she even knew where the boy was. Oh son, come home, you're needed, he prayed. Tears welled in his eyes. Whatever would she do with an entire extra set of pots and pans? He felt under the covers until he came to what he thought was a hand and patted it.

God bless her, she had never betrayed by so much as a flick of an eyelash that anything had ever happened between them. Rumors had sped about, as they always did in a small town, some never died. All these years later it was still possible to hear old-timers say one of the Patout sisters had had a tragic affair which resulted in a child. Throughout it all, Clotilde had said nothing. She was like that, a woman of steel will and good breeding—a true Southern gentlewoman. She would go to her grave washed, scented—he must get the Fischler woman to dig out her toenails—laid in a snow-white dress, still bearing his guilty secret on her soul.

He took out his handkerchief and blew his nose. He loved Southern gentlewomen. It pained him that his own wife was not quite of that class.

"My dear friend," he said, blowing his nose again. "In sixty years of coming to The Oaks I have never told you, or any member of your family, what I truly thought about anything. Do you realize that? Not once. Oh, I'm sure you thought I spoke my mind, but I didn't. What's the price of sugar going to do this winter? We going to have more rain than usual this fall? How come we oughta tear down St. Peter's and put up a new church, when the old one is just fine? Your dad and I used to sit there on the front porch by the hour and I'd tell him right what he wanted to hear. The fact is, Clotilde, you and your family—your daddy, mama, and probably your grandparents before them—have always sailed through life giving everybody you came in contact with to understand that you didn't want anybody telling you what to do. Hell, your father wouldn't have died if he'd taken his medicine like I told him. But no, he knew how to doctor himself. If somebody was to ask me what the Patouts are like, this's what I'd say. For God's sake, don't try to tell them what to do."

"What's wrong with that?"

"Nothing, my dear, absolutely nothing. I admire the trait myself, only now you're the only Patout left out here at The Oaks, and you've had a stroke, together with the fact that I've been waking up with palpitations for two weeks—"

"That would go away if you'd quit drinking."

"—and I noticed that the handle on my bag was about to break when I picked it up off my desk to come here—well, all of that together, and then, of course, your poor sister's passing, made me think it was time now to give you my advice."

"I don't want it."

"I'm giving it to you anyway, Clotilde. I deserve it for all the years I've been taking care of you and your family and your servants—Ruby, Willie, and their poor idiot of a child, not to mention your field hands. I'm going to tell you if I have to strap you down to the bed to make you listen."

"What does this have to do with that obituary?"

"I don't see how a human being can lie there and ask her old doctor and family friend to admire a piece of writing describing how her sister just got put in the ground, when she's been pretending that same sister was dead for over thirty years. How can I talk about her obituary? You've forbidden me to use her name? Why do you care about her write-up? What, in the name of God, do you want me to say? They should have described the flowers better?"

"Was there advice you wished to offer?" She reached for the hairbrush on the nightstand and slowly began to pull it through coarse gray hair.

The room was hot and close and smelled of her oily hair. She lay back on her pillow, knotted in the blankets like an old, malodorous dog nobody bothered to pet anymore. His head hurt.

"I must be going soon," he said. "Mary Louise is expecting me home by dark. My advice is—and this is the first and only time you'll hear it."

"Come to the point. What a tiresome trait in a man."

"Yes, well, my advice is, call the boy home. It's long past time. I know, some people say you're a cold, hard woman without a hint of maternal instinct, but you don't fool me. I remember playing hide-and-seek a certain summer evening . . ."

"You always were a fool, James Rodriguez. When you bring the girl tomorrow, leave off the cologne. I can't stand a man who smells up a house. Now go away."

"There we were, lying in each other's arms in the moonlight. Voices called close by, but you paid no mind. 'Oh James, be quick about it, do. They can't see us through the pyracantha.' " He chuckled. "You always were a daring lass."

His voice droned on and on. Wasn't it natural he should have known? Even if he hadn't been a doctor long, he was after all a man, even then. Clotilde Patout stopped brushing. Her hand seemed to stick in midair. Her mouth hung open. The doctor went on. A married man, it was true. He couldn't forgive himself for having let her carry the burden alone. Men were selfish brutes. They'd do anything to protect their good names. He had never forgotten the look on her face when he told her he reported to the authorities any woman who came to him asking about abortions. It was a matter of self-protection.

Whatever is the matter? he wondered. She was fighting to get free from the bed sheets. "Ruby! Ruby!" she screamed and lunged at the needlepoint pull.

"My dear," he said, suddenly realizing he had been slapped. Forty years after causing so much shame she had, at last, slapped him, and he fell to his knees, overcome with joy, and tried to kiss the bony foot sticking out from the blue flannel nightie.

"Get up, James," she said. "Don't just stand there, Ruby. Go call his wife. He's not fit to drive home. Then you come back and help him downstairs."

She peered over the edge of the bed. Rodriguez, smiling blissfully at the ceiling, sprawled on the floor amid contents of his bag, knocked over in the confusion.

"You've got it all wrong, James," she whispered. His eyes came away from the watermark and looked at her, puzzled. "You didn't even get it in," she said.

"What! But whose . . . ?" He tried to sit up.

"That boy was Sister's kettle of fish. She passed him off on poor Molly," Clotilde said.

"Do you mean all these years I've been thinking I had a son . . . ?"

"Nope. Different pecker."

The doctor moaned.

She flopped back on the pillows and had a good laugh all to herself, while Ruby helped Rodriguez downstairs.

But later, when she had time to think, she saw he hadn't given her a bad piece of advice. It would suit her sense of justice to bring Patout back to The Oaks now that Janice was dead. She needed help with the work. Rodriguez said she'd live twenty years and more if she were careful, and that she aimed to be.

· 3 ·

*T*he next morning at 7:25 precisely, Dr. James Rodriguez drove toward Main Street in his two-door sedan, his face slightly puffy, the skin noticeably red under its camouflage of talc. As he neared the corner of Parkview and Allen, he glanced in the rearview mirror. Yellow streaked across the road. He slammed on the brakes, noted whose house he was passing, crossed himself, and drove on, grateful not to have hit a loose-diapered baby. With five cats, four dogs, and eleven children, the Broussards were continually spilling over their shallow yard into the street. (They held funerals in the backyard at least once a month, but, to his knowledge, had not buried a human yet.)

He stopped for the sign at Parkview and Main, made a right, and continued down Main to Latouche's First Class Hotel, where he drove around to the rear and parked in the owner's spot, knowing it was all right. Sam Latouche followed Jerome Pellerin around like a shadow. Both men were still on Pecan Island. They hadn't been back since the funeral.

Rodriguez got out of the car and walked toward the back entrance of the hotel. "How you making out, Frank?" he called to the darky peeling potatoes by the kitchen door, then frowned as he heard his wife's voice tell him not to use this out-of-date expression anymore. He didn't understand why life had to be made more difficult by not calling a spade a spade.

"Yes-sir-ree-bob," he called and smiled broadly at the black man, without the least idea of what he had said. It didn't matter. Never mattered what they said. Just as what he said made no difference to Frank. We don't want them interfering in our world, and they don't want us in theirs, he said to himself, and the screen door slammed shut behind him, cutting the connection in two.

"Good morning, Joy Rita," he called at sight of the fat proprietress behind the golden-oak desk near the entrance of the gloomy lobby. She was massive. Flesh hung from the body in folds. Her inner thighs were gray where the flesh rubbed together when she walked. He dreaded her yearly health examination, afraid his distaste showed, yet she always seemed glad to see him.

As though in proof of this, she said without pausing for a greeting, "How's about doing me a favor and picking out a nice, big cigar, Doc. The foreigner hasn't come down yet." Chihuahua heads tinkled on her charm bracelet. She leaned on the display case, looked over the monumental flesh of her forearm and into the glass-topped counter. Switching on the display light, she licked her lips at the stock. Cigars—some green, some golden-brown, some almost gray—sat in three rows of open boxes on blood-red felt. The display case groaned beneath her weight. She looked up, awaiting his command with a half smile. She was fond of this little doctor who picked up strays at the Greyhound terminal and paid for giving them a night's rest with breakfast thrown in.

"Give them lots of extra rolls and butter," he always tells her, "so they have something to steal when they leave. I'll pay for whatever they take."

If it weren't for the doctor, the hotel would be empty weeks at a stretch. No one in Belmont puts their visitors in the hotel anymore. It is filthy, roach-ridden. The odor of mildewed carpets is masked by rose-scented room spray that stings the eyes and nostrils when any one of the sixty doors upstairs opens.

"For God's sake, do they expect a palace?" the proprietress is always telling her husband. "Let them turn up their noses, I don't care if they stay." She and her husband run a Saturday night bingo game in the ballroom with dark green shades pulled over the windows. Sheriff Mouton warns her periodically to keep the shades down, or he will be forced by the Evangelical ministers to take action. The Latouches get by, but the doctor affords them the little extras of life—the permanent waves, the addition of another Chihuahua head for her, the girls down on Pecan Island for him, so she likes him, and now urged a cigar from her case.

He made his selection. She took it out, peeled off the cellophane skin, passed it back and forth under his nose, looking seductively into his eyes. She had not been to bed with a man since the Missouri Pacific train derailment brought a welder from Baton Rouge to town. She didn't think the doctor's wife did it anymore. The charm bracelet tinkled.

The doctor's mouth filled with saliva. He snatched the cigar out of her hand and turned his head, overcome with nausea.

"Keep your shirt on," she said, sticking out her little bottom lip. She ought not waste her time feeling sorry for such a man. There was a fly feet up in the left corner near the King Edward specials.

"Damn that girl. Ida Mae!" she bellowed. "Ida Mae! I told her to clean my case real good. They don't want to work now that nigger King's come along and offered them the promised land."

The doctor chuckled. "Well, I wouldn't want to be colored, now would you, Joy Rita?"

"That's not the point and you know it, James Rodriguez, so don't you go getting high and mighty with me. Ida Mae!"

A bucket overturned on the first-floor landing. A mop clattered down the stairs. The doctor looked up. The French woman picked up the mop, handed it to Ida Mae, then continued down the stairs.

"I'd be careful about what I picked up these days, Doc," Joy Rita Latouche whispered, loud. "You might have got hold of an agitator this time. They been passing through by the truckload, going to that march on New Orleans."

He shifted around. Françoise Fischler had reached the bottom step, put down her canvas carryall, and appeared to be waiting for him.

"What makes you think so, Joy Rita? I'd never forgive myself for putting something like that under Clotilde's roof."

"More to the point, she'd never forgive you." Joy Rita Latouche shot the doctor a knowing look, lowered her voice. "Dresses sloppy, wild-looking hair. That's the kind, all right."

"You'd look like that, too, if you'd been living out of a Greyhound for weeks." He walked away, nodding his good-bye. She shook out her charms and scowled at his back.

"Stupid woman," he muttered. Had the world gone completely crazy? Everybody scared, suspicious, wondering what would happen next. A state of siege. Nobody knowing the rules. This integration business was making it so nice black people and nice white people could hardly be civil anymore.

"Morning, Dr. James."

"Morning, Ida Mae. How's the bunion?" He walked on without waiting for a reply. But as he bent to pick up the French woman's belongings, he could not help wondering if a homemade bomb could fit in a bag that size.

"Is this all you have?" he said. She was carrying a jacket and books in her arms.

She nodded.

He motioned toward the back door, waved good-bye to Mrs. Latouche, who was too busy fussing at the maid to see. They went out. When he held open the car door, she seemed amused. It was a sign of the times.

Before long they were out on the back road to The Oaks. Scarcely ten words had passed between them. The woman was impossible to talk to. She sat in her corner of the front seat, her body pressed against the door, arms folded across her chest, hugging the bag. The doctor could think of nothing to say, so he talked about himself in endless fashion for the profound silence wrapped about her like a blanket was too much to bear in the front seat of a small car. Sometimes, hoping for a nod of encouragement, he glanced at her. She answered by lifting her eyebrows slightly, not unkindly, but with no expression he could read. She seemed almost transparent, the body an empty shell so still had she not, from time to time, lifted a strand of stiff black hair off her forehead and put it firmly back in place, he might have thought her dead.

So he talked. There seemed nothing else to do, noting as he talked that the leaves of the vines twisted around the barbed wire fence running alongside the narrow dirt road had fallen now, signaling the beginning of the empty time of year, when the landscape matched the sorrow of a heart in which there is no hope.

The sun broke through the grayness of the day and bore down through the windshield. She cracked the window. He smelled the dust billowing behind. A drop of rain hit the windshield.

"I love that smell," he said. "Always reminds me of home. I was all over the Pacific during the war, and it smelled just like that before a rain. Isn't that funny?"

She blinked sleepily, but she was listening to him now, for her hair had fallen once again into her eyes and she hadn't bothered to push it back. She looked over his left shoulder, beyond to the land, her mouth slightly open, her face relaxed at last.

"Yes, sir, even with the Japs crawling over us," he went on, "if a little rain fell in the dust, all I had to do was close my eyes and be back home. Funny, huh?"

"How fortunate you are, Dr. Rodriguez."

He glanced at her in surprise.

"It smells like that all over the world."

"That's nice."

"Yes, it's lovely," she said, returning his smile.

She was not unattractive. She might have been striking once with those high cheekbones and jet-black hair. He wondered if she was married.

"Too bad you arrived now," he said. "Most of the cane's already down. Outsiders think our winters are pretty ghastly. You can see for miles, but everything just looks flat and gray. We don't have real seasonal changes, not like you folks up North. I spec you going to miss that, eh?" He glanced at her, got no response, looked back at the road.

"Well, never having lived in a place where the leaves turn, I don't miss it, but take me away from south Louisiana and I'd have to come home every year just to drive out in the country and gawk at the cane. Look at that. Isn't that something the way it stands there waving in the wind. Makes me feel safe, all hemmed in by those green walls. You watch, this land'll get under your skin, too." He glanced at her. She was stifling a yawn. "Forgive me, I'm an old bore."

"Not at all. The fatigue of my travels. You must love it very much."

"I do. Sometimes I think I should have been a farmer instead of a doctor. Oh, well, people always think where they were born is the most beautiful place on earth. Don't you feel that way about your neck of the world?"

"The world of my childhood was destroyed during the war," she said.

He cleared his throat. "Well, perhaps I'm speaking from a man's viewpoint. I know my wife hates it here. She would've left years ago, but I wouldn't then. Now we're too old. I spec she might have felt different had we had children. One is always glad of one's roots when one has children, don't you think?"

"I wouldn't know," she said, cold.

Had he embarrassed her? Sterility affected some people that way. It was nothing to be ashamed of. His own wife wasn't able to conceive. He ignored the possibility of his own inadequacy, now that he knew Patout Minville was not his.

He could think of nothing to reply, so they drove on in silence, the pleasant feeling between them gone. He chewed on his bottom lip, tried not to think about the flask in the glove compartment, while she watched the flat countryside go by, wondering why he felt passion for the monotonous landscape. Without the huge trees and Spanish moss, it might have been Belgium. She hugged her bag. The doctor's questions were too personal. Since arriving she had also had the distinct impression of being watched. That might be from seeing too many newscasts. Nothing seemed to have touched this sleepy community. Perhaps her uneasiness was natural, a reaction to—her own sense of guilt, she almost said, but stopped this self-deception. She felt no guilt over leaving Stewart. Her feelings about Jeanne were more complex. She felt empty, but relieved. There was no need to feel responsible to anyone but herself anymore. She needed a chance to rest and forget. If only these people would leave her alone, not involve her in their lives. There would be solace in meaningless chores.

The car entered an avenue of oaks. Branches arched overhead, blocking the sun. The world inside was peaceful, green, like being under water. No strife was imaginable other than birds arguing over tree lice and worms. As they exited, the roof of a house loomed over treetops.

"What do you mean, eccentric?" she replied.

"Well, being a foreigner, you may find her ways a bit hard. For one thing, she sometimes speaks harshly to her Negroes, but it doesn't mean a thing," Rodriguez said. "She even speaks that way to me. She and Willie have been together on that plantation all their lives. They're almost family. You'll see. Just keep out of it, don't try to get involved." He pulled up and stopped.

"Don't worry, Dr. Rodriguez," she said, "I shall be careful what I say to *her* Negroes, but it's ironic, you know."

"What?"

She had already gotten out and slammed the door. The woman had actually laughed.

· 4 ·

*T*he beauty of the place was overwhelming, she saw at once. Tall columns stood in mute testimony to the passage of time. Shuttered windows opened to the floor. Moss crept over faded rose bricks. Too beautiful, she decided. Picking up her belongings—the carryall, one book of poetry, two novels, a black felt hat, and a mouton jacket, made in a style not worn since just after the last war—she crunched down the pea gravel walk, went up on the porch, rang, and waited. Dr. Rodriguez seemed to be having car trouble. She rang the bell again. There he went now, turning into the road. The door opened. The black woman stared at the jacket thrown over her arm.

"I'm Françoise Fischler," she said.

"I's Ruby. Miss Clo's having a fit. She's waiting on you upstairs. I'll take that." She took the jacket, stood aside. "This real?"

Françoise nodded.

"Ain't no use for it down here," Ruby remarked, caressing the fur.

And so she went inside with everything in the world that was hers—there was not even her name carved on the back of a bus-stop bench to say she had been elsewhere. She felt swallowed and ill at ease. After her new employer, a rather nasty old woman who leaned heavily on the black woman's arm, walked her over two stories and brought her down again, that was why she heard herself say, "I'll take this one," and point to the ugly cell next to the kitchen.

"Sister's sewing room?" Clotilde Patout motioned Ruby to take her back to bed. "Yes, I can see how beauty would make somebody plain as yourself uneasy," she said. They moved toward the hall door. "Well, you've made your choice. Now stick to it. I don't believe in letting people change their minds. Never could stand wishy-washy people." Her words were slightly slurred.

In late afternoon after finishing her chores, Françoise walked out upon the grounds. On the other side of an old-fashioned cistern, she came upon a black man hoeing. He was the only person she had seen for hours. He did not stop or look up as she approached, though the rhythm of his hoeing broke.

"My name is Françoise Fischler," she said. "I'm taking care of Miss Patout."

He rested one hand on his hoe, took off his brown felt hat. "I's Willie," he said, looking down at her feet.

She offered her hand. He giggled.

"Yessim, I's Willie," he said. He put his hat on and began to hoe again.

"You come to work here often?"

"Whenever you hollers."

"Do you live nearby?"

"Out beyond the chicken coop, me, Ruby, and Lily."

"You're Ruby's husband?"

"Yessim."

"I haven't seen Ruby this afternoon."

"Nome, I don't spec you has," he said.

"Have you and Ruby lived here long?"

"All my life and my mama and daddy before that and my grandmama before that."

He looked at her then—quickly—hardly long enough for her to get a good look at his face, but she saw that his eyes were blue. He bent over and hoed furiously.

"Go on off now, lady, leave me be. I's got work to do. I

can't stand around talking to no white lady all day. Besides, Miss Clotilde, she looking out the second-story guest bedroom window."

Françoise looked up. Clotilde Patout stood with her face pressed to the glass. She was staring in their direction, but did not seem to see them. Tapping on the glass absentmindedly, as though in time to music, she was obviously lost in thought.

"She doesn't see us, look."

"Don't need to. I done seen her stand like that a million times looking off into vacant space. She looks like she jus got up and left her body leanin against the window frame, but she's there, miss. You watch. Tomorrow she goin to tell you not to stand in no herb patch talkin to no nigger man at dusk." He began to work the soil harder than before. "It ain't ladylike," he added.

Françoise watched him work. He was extraordinarily thin. His body seemed all points—elbows, kneecaps, cheekbones— and then there were those blue, blue eyes, which had only looked once at her face.

"You aren't much of a man, are you. No matter. I'm not much of a lady, so we'll get along," she said. She walked away, disappearing around the corner of the house, into the dusk that lay on the front lawn under the massive trees.

When she was gone and the old lady was no longer at the window, Willie threw down the hoe and listened, following the sound of a cane truck grinding into gear somewhere on the other side of the wall of sugar cane that bordered The Oaks on the east.

"Mr. Tutie is hauling cane late tonight," he muttered.

Certain he was alone, he knelt.

"Lord, make me a better person," he prayed. "Don't let anger carry me away. And while you're at it, Lord, tell that woman not to talk to me, cause it's only goin to get me in a heap of trouble and that's somethin I can do without, leastways until I find that money. And Lord, tell Miss Janice, if you see her up there, I'd appreciate a little hint if I'm gettin warm. I won't give none of it to Miss Clotilde. I'm just goin to use it to get Lily and me away from here. Amen."

He picked up the hoe and walked home then, shutting his eyes as he passed the chicken coop, for it wouldn't do to see nasty things right after talking to God. He groped along, letting his feet carry him down the worn dirt path, holding on to the fence as a guide. The chickens clucked softly in the shadows on the other side.

He stopped and faced the fence, his teeth hitting the chicken wire. "Tomorrow I'm going to put what's what right. Y'all hear me?" Willie hollered.

"Go on. Have fun tonight. It's your last chance. I's got me some lumber and a can of black paint now. This time tomorrow night we's goin to have us a Him door and a Her door. I'm goin to stand right here and see to it myself that none of you hims goes into Hers. Y'all hear me? Last chance. Better cuddle up good tonight."

The chickens clucked softly.

He ambled off, eyes still closed, stumbling over a tree root now and again. He didn't open his eyes until his foot hit the first step of the shack. He looked up. Ruby was standing at the screen door.

"It ain't right the way they sleep together like that," he said.

Ruby opened the door.

Willie shivered. Lord, protect me and Lily, protect Your faithful servant and his child throughout the night, amen and praise His name.

He mounted the stairs, moaned softly as he passed the body of his wife. The screen door shut. A light rain began to fall. It was night.

· 5 ·

*S*he switched on the lamp by the bed.

"Françoise Fischler?"

There was no answer.

"Miss Fischler?" she called again. "Come in here. I want to talk to you."

The old woman listened to the house, her eyes growing wide. She thought she heard a noise again and called out, but there was no reply. The back of her neck tingled.

Stop it this instant, you fool, she said to herself. You've had a stroke, you're not going crazy. Don't let your imagination run wild. She pulled the covers up.

Rain hit against the windowpanes.

"Of course, that's what it was," she said, reaching for her shawl at the foot of the bed. She climbed down from the four-poster, went to the window, and looked out. It was too dark to see. Down the back in the distance the lights of Willie's shack twinkled through the shining trees.

I'm going to have to speak to Françoise Fischler, Clotilde thought. I have no intention of letting her put ideas into Willie's head. One can't be too careful these days, with the Negroes acting peculiar. The young ones walking around with chips on their shoulders, just hoping to find the slightest excuse to act sullen and rude. Thank goodness the older ones still have some sense. I won't have anyone ruining Willie.

She jerked at the curtains, made sure they were closed tightly, and started back to bed, but her reflection in the dresser mirror caught her attention. She stopped to peer in.

Although the French woman had only been in the house for two days, Clotilde could already see signs of change. Her appearance had improved. Her hair was combed and powdered to hold down the grease. (French women did that when they were sick, the Fischler woman said.) She had on a fresh nightgown. Her fingernails were clean. Even the sheets on the bed were pressed.

Clotilde thought for a moment of going downstairs to see if the woman had carried out her orders in the rest of the house, but she decided to wait until day. She was tired. She shouldn't be out of bed. She glanced at the four-poster, almost with dread. She had not slept well for days. No matter how exhausted, she seemed to lie there, turning from side to side, thinking things over, rehashing the past.

The house certainly feels empty tonight, she thought. Ruby had gone home early to see about her child. Lily had whooping cough now. She'd just gotten over the measles.

"That child always has something. She'll be the death of me yet," she said.

The French woman was still outside, prowling around in the rain and the dark. There was something rootless about her, as though she had no connection to anyone or any place in the past. She wore no wedding ring, but Clotilde felt she was married. Women who had never married had a certain weightlessness to them; they moved more quickly, almost in staccato.

I suppose it comes from not having had our spirits crushed by males, she thought. Pitying all married women, she sailed back to bed, slipped and almost fell. More slowly, she proceeded to the four-poster, climbed in, pulled the covers up, and closed her eyes.

In the past she had often put herself to sleep by thinking up ways to torment her sister. She might still have done so, even with Janice gone, but the house was too quiet. Her anger had always been fed by the racket Janice made, rattling around downstairs in her half of the house, long after she knew Clotilde had gone to bed. Now there was nothing. No sound at all in the house.

She turned on her left side. She had not forgotten what the doctor said about asking Patout Minville to come back to Belmont. If she did have to let Françoise go, because of her influence on Willie and Ruby, it would be very smart to have Patout and his family already living at The Oaks. Although she could scarcely believe it was true, she couldn't live alone anymore, even for a day. Her days of independence had passed.

She turned over, banged on the pillow, and lay down again, smiling to herself as she remembered the doctor's last visit. There was only one person in the world who could appreciate the joke on Rodriguez, but poor Adeline was dead.

"Why of course, why didn't I think of it before," Clotilde said, sitting up suddenly. Instead of lying there hour after hour to no avail, she would visit with Adeline Delahoussaye, as she often had before when she could not sleep. She looked around her bedroom, searching for the best spot to stage the visit with Adeline.

There, by the window overlooking the back, she seated Adeline in the rocker with the gooseneck arms and faded tapestry cover. Near to it, on the other side of the window, she put the rosewood piano she had never seen Adeline play in thirty years of friendship, never seen her play, with Adeline's husband's picture in a gold-colored frame from Woolworth's on top—Jim Bob Delahoussaye, who had died of a heart attack in his corn patch out back of their house one summer day when the temperature reached 102 and he had forgotten to wear his straw hat. In the picture he was a young man with the brightness in his eyes that wears off after twenty-five, and a carnation in his buttonhole. He never wore a suit without a flower in his lapel; the men in Belmont had made fun of him for that. He didn't have one on him when he died. Adeline loved him.

Over her own, more somber wallpaper Clotilde placed Adeline's pink-and-white cabbage roses. They'd picked that paper out together just after the last war, 1948, to be exact, on a trip to New Orleans when Jim Bob bought his first Beltone hearing aide. The cabbage roses matched the bloom in Adeline's cheeks; also her bosoms, Adeline's husband might have said, had Clotilde not forfended him with a look. (Clotilde laid the blame for Jim Bob's near lapse into vulgarity directly at Adeline's feet; she had continued to wear low-cut dresses and rouge her breasts even after turning sixty.) At the end of one lovely day of shopping on Canal Street, Clotilde was forced to endure the French Market with the elderly Jim Bob leaning across the wrought-iron table to blow powdered sugar off his doughnuts onto his wife's huge chest. Adeline laughed so much that her creamy bosoms shook on top. (Were they not unlike congealed cream cheese and pineapple salad turned out dancing on a plate?) Clotilde had to look away.

"Now, let's see, where were we?" Clotilde said, shutting the door on that unpleasant scene. She looked down the length of the bed and across to the rocker where Adeline sat waiting; her friend did not look entirely happy this evening.

Poor, naïve Adeline, all alone and scared after her Jim Bob passed away. Trying so hard to do what was right for her always-unsatisfactory son and his wife.

Adeline wrote to him. "My Dearest Jimbo, Please bring your charming wife and come make your home with me. I am so alone. Think how happy we could be, here in our old home, all together again except for our sweet, departed Daddy. Your Loving Mother, Adeline."

"You know, Clotilde, I have decided, if Jimbo comes home—no, I'm not going to force him; I want him to do what's right for himself. If he can find another job in St. Louis that would, after all, be the best—but if he does come home, then I've decided to put the house in his name. He'll have it one day when I'm gone anyway, but in the meantime, I want him to be able to hold up his head in public. A grown man can't live openly in a house held in his mama's name. Men's egos are such delicate things."

So she changed the title to his name. Soon after, when she developed a slight palsy in her right hand which made it difficult to hold a pen, her son and daughter-in-law suggested it would be easier if she put her bank accounts in their names. Six months later they moved her into the parish nursing home.

Clotilde shifted restlessly in the bed. The visit was not going according to plan. This was all ancient history. There was no use going over it. When people made their own beds they had to lie in them.

"I always said so, Adeline, even to you. I told you. I said, 'Adeline, you haven't got the brains you were born with if you let those two walk all over you,' but you wouldn't listen to me. I'm not going to talk about this anymore. Now listen, I have something funny to tell you. I said to myself this evening, 'Clotilde Patout, there's only one person in the world who'd appreciate the joke on Rodriguez as much as you, and that's Adeline Delahoussaye.' You were out here that night when we played hide-and-seek in the dark. You, Jim Bob, and Rodriguez. Was Richard here then? Sister, of course; she always had to butt in on my parties. Can you believe the vanity of the man, thinking all these years he'd fathered that boy?" She laughed, but this evening Adeline Delahoussaye wouldn't stay in her rocker, where the cabbage roses of the wallpaper matched the bloom of her complexion. The nuns in the nursing home kept pushing her down, tying her arms to the metal tubes of a potty chair, and then going away.

"Did you ever think it would come to this for me?" she said.

Clotilde shuddered. In spite of herself, she reached out and opened the double doors of the parish nursing home.

"Why are outside doors in all nursing homes double?" she asked.

"Because you can never tell when you might have to scoot a coffin out," said the director.

"I'm terribly sorry, Madame, I'm a busy man. We've already provided services for four of our dearest old souls today. The next is due up at eight. I'll have to leave you here. The information desk is straight ahead."

Clotilde walked down the shiny waxed hall. Why? she wondered. Don't they see the connection between slippery floors and old people's broken bones?

She walked to the nursing pen. The people in white, protected from her by a high Formica counter, continued to talk and laugh among themselves. A man came in and deposited a broom. One of the women leaned on the switchboard and scratched with a pencil under her French bun. They seemed not to see Clotilde. No one would answer.

I'll find her on my own, she thought, going to the center of the cross where four long corridors met. To the north, south, east, and west, shining linoleum floors and door upon door upon door, were linked by lines of old people sitting in wheelchairs, lined up and wainscoting the walls with gray hair, toothless grins, faded print nightgowns, blue-veined bones.

These are Adeline's new neighbors, she thought. At least *I* shall treat them like human beings while I'm here. She plunged in.

"How do you do? How do you do?"

Clotilde came to the first door on the north corridor, read the number, realized she was going the wrong way, and turned back through the line of gaunt faces and eyes. Reaching the center of the cross again, she saw the sign: ROOMS 100–150. She took the east corridor.

A woman gurgled at her.

"How do you do," Clotilde said and hurried on. Down at the end of the hall she spotted an old gentleman with a baby in his arms. The baby was wrapped in a cozy blue blanket. The old man cooed and tickled it under the chin.

A newborn, she thought. His first grandson. How nice.

She rushed up. His eyes were blank. He drooled. Spit fell into the face of the doll in his lap.

She cried out and rushed on, flinging herself at last against the door to Room 148. Inside Adeline sat in soiled pajamas, tied to a potty chair. Tears poured down her cheeks.

"They won't let me up. They say I'll fall. Did you ever think it would come to this for me, Clotilde?"

When she left that day, Adeline said, "I don't know what's in store for you, my dear, but don't let anyone do this to you." Then she kissed Clotilde, who wiped the kiss off as soon as she got out—she never was able to stand other people's bodily effusions—and swore to herself no one would ever do the same to her in old age, the idea. She never visited again.

Clotilde threw the extra pillows on the floor, switched off the lamp, and lay down. I'm not going to see Adeline again. She always winds up in that horrible home, she thought. Her eyes closed. She drifted to sleep.

If I do ask Patout to come, she thought, awaking for a moment, I've got to be careful how I do it. I have nothing to offer him. He has no reason to come, but he would if he thought there was something to gain.

Yes, that's it, the old woman thought, snuggling down in her cover. I won't tell an out-and-out lie. A hint of money will do. After he arrives, I'll set him straight. Once here, he'll stay. He was crazy about this old house when he was a boy. He won't be able to tear himself away.

But suppose Patout didn't believe her. If he thought she was lying about her financial condition, he would never stop pestering her, like Adeline's son, until he gained control of her bank accounts, the house, and the land. Once that was done, they would put her in the nursing home and leave her there, waiting to die.

It wasn't such an outrageous thought. There were always people in Belmont who were convinced with a house like that she and Janice had money. They said anyone with that house and those servants must be made of money.

First of all, she was going to have to get rid of those Negroes. When there was sugar cane on the land, there was some excuse for Negroes. That day was long gone, and now all keeping Negroes did was make people think you had money. Kept niggers. She shook her head. Kept niggers. What she got for it was a demented child, a health hazard—ringworm, tapeworm, impetigo; a maid, her mother, who was deeply superstitious, psychotic, and had filthy habits—spit on her hands to crease sheets and napkins. Might kill her husband one day, if she didn't get to him first. And Willie! Digging all over the yard for buried treasure, ruining the St. Augustine grass.

"Sister used to get so mad when Willie let the cow eat her day lilies. Sister."

The sibilant sooed across the room. Suddenly the sister with whom Clotilde once shared life hovered in front of the dresser.

"I got on your best nightgown," Clotilde said, and fell asleep as quickly as a baby.

· 6 ·

Three weeks later a man, a woman, and a little boy came riding into town in a turquoise two-door Studebaker with two pillows, a teddy bear, and a corn stick pan laid up on the back window ledge. They stopped at the police station, swerved in too fast and almost jumped the curb. The woman reached behind her in the backseat and felt of the boy's legs.

"He's not a china doll, Sophie," Mrs. Lester Thoreau of the dry goods Thoreaus heard the stranger say, as she walked by the beaten-up car that had once been a flashy model.

"I do always think it's a mistake not to stick to white in a car. Whoever do you think that is?" she whispered to her friend, Mildred Gonsulin. Mildred turned around and stared.

Patout dipped his hat good morning to the ladies, winked at Sophie in the car, then disappeared inside the police station to ask directions.

Sophie Minville returned her husband's smile, relieved to see him enthusiastic about something again; it made him look much younger.

"Gypsies. They look like gypsies to me." Mildred Gonsulin sniffed.

"Bitch," Sophie said to the retreating back, pulled the potty from under the seat, opened the door and emptied its contents on the pavement.

"Mama, not here," the boy shrieked.

"Okay. We're in business," Patout said, climbing back into the car. "Cheer up, you two. We're almost home." He started up. They went on down Main Street and got caught at the traffic light.

Sophie said, "It sure isn't New Orleans."

"It sure isn't New Orleans," the boy echoed, peering over the corn stick pan at a closed movie house and a gas station where the pumps had been pulled out of the ground.

"It reminds me of that one-horse town I grew up in. My poor mama was always raring to get out of—"

"Don't start tearing it down, Sophie, when we haven't even gotten here yet."

"I'm just stating a fact. It isn't much of a place, but what do I care how the peons live?" she said.

"We're going to live in a castle, and the horses and dogs get to sleep in their own room in the middle, and at night we pull up a little bridge so nobody can get us."

Sophie laughed. "Hush, Cato, you're embarrassing your daddy."

"What kind of nonsense have you been telling him?"

"Nothing much. Just that his father is from a wealthy family and we have decided to go home to live with them in their big house. Just what you told me, in fact."

The light changed. They went past the Farmers and Merchants Bank, the hotel, and the post office. After a stretch of Victorian homes, they emerged out of town, drove for about a mile, then tunneled through the corroding relics grazing on both sides of the road in Big Boy's Junk and Salvage Yard like a mute herd of black and bleeding beasts. The highway contorted violently around two live oaks and an abandoned cane derrick, then settled down in another straight stretch.

Patout turned off the highway at last. They went down a dirt road running through a field, an avenue of oaks, and she thought, how foreign this place looks to me, so different from Mississippi, and how strange that a man I never knew all the early days of my life is now sitting beside me, saying this is home, and I have a child in the backseat, who will grow up taking this place for granted. "Yes, Pat, I see it."

The roof of The Oaks was visible over the top of the sugar cane.

The car slowed. She took out her lipstick, smoothed her hair, and braced for the turn, but the car went by.

"Wasn't that the drive?"

"I want you to get the full impact of the place you're going to be mistress of someday."

He stopped the car in front of a crumbling brick post that had once supported an ornamental gate. He and Cato hung out the windows.

"Thar she blows!" Patout said.

"Thar she blows," said the boy.

"It's just the way I remember. Talk about beautiful, huh, Sophie?"

"Are you sure your Aunt Clotilde was expecting us today?" she said very coolly.

"Poor old soul can't wait to see us anytime we get here, day or night. Can you imagine living out here all alone?"

"I don't want us to arrive while she's having dinner," Sophie insisted.

"What's the matter, don't you like it? Hey, son, what do you think. Pretty grand, huh?"

"It isn't a castle, is it?"

"For Christ's sake, what's the matter with you two? I get you out of that dump in the city and all you can do is gripe."

"Pull your body back in the car, Cato. Not on the floor, sit on the seat like a gentleman. That's a good boy."

Patout stared at her.

"Okay. Now what have I done?"

"You might have gone on in the drive like we belonged here, instead of stopping in front to gawk like poor people out on a Sunday drive." She studied the cane field on the other side of the road.

"I see. Ruin it all for me, just like you always do." Patout turned the motor off.

"I'm not trying to ruin anything. I just think you show a lack of judgment at times. What will Clotilde Patout think of us, sitting out here in front."

"What difference does it make. I'm her own flesh and blood. For God's sake, what's come over you? You want me to turn around and drive back to New Orleans? Is that what you want?" He started the car, swung around in the middle of the road, and slammed on the brakes at the entrance to the drive.

"What'll it be, Belmont or New Orleans?"

Sophie put her arm over the backseat and felt the top of the boy's head. He had gotten on the floor when his father began to shout. He's so sensitive, she thought. Surely life is going to be better for him here.

"Don't be an ass, Patout. Turn in," she said, filled with foreboding. The avenue of trees was dark. She thought someone was standing at a window on the second floor as they pulled up to the front.

"Pat, I hope she'll like me," she said.

"Is that it?" He laughed. "Why, honey, I never met anybody who didn't like you." He leaned over and kissed her. "Now come on you two. Where's that boy? Cato? Oh, Cato, where are you?"

"Here I am, Daddy," said the small boy, jumping up from the floor.

Sophie smoothed his hair, checked herself in the mirror. Patout went around and opened the door for her.

"See, I can be a gentleman too, just like Cato," he said. "Oh, Sophie. It's going to be wonderful living here with you and the boy." He kissed her again in full view of the house.

They walked across a gravel path, mounted the steps of the porch, and rang the bell. The door opened immediately.

"You Mr. Patout?" The black woman eyed them suspiciously.

"Yes, ma'am. I'm Patout Minville, and this is my wife and my son."

"Miss Clotilde, she says y'all go around to the side porch over yonder. That's your place for now. There's a foreign woman here goin to bring you y'all's supper on account of my Lily's took sick again and I got to git on back home. I already done made up the beds." She started to close the door.

"Don't we get to see Aunt Clotilde this evening? We drove all the way out here from New Orleans—"

"Yessir, I knows. Miss Clotilde says to tell you her doctor done told her she can't see no visitors today. Maybe tomorrow. She hopes y'all be real comfortable." The woman closed the door.

"That was downright rude," said Sophie.

"Well, let's do like the woman told us. Let's get on around to the side. I'm starving. Maybe we can eat a little supper, take a little nap, get you-know-who to take one, too, so we can do you-know-what, huh, Soph?"

"Stop it, Patout. Someone might be looking."

Patout shook his head. "Do you never stop thinking up something else to worry over? Didn't you hear her say the old gal is sick in bed? Come on now, you, too, son, come on, let's get around to our quarters."

When they reached the corner, Sophie realized that Cato was not with them. She turned around. The boy was standing by the Studebaker looking at a window on the second floor.

A few days before the Minvilles arrived, Clotilde Patout suffered a second stroke, which left her slightly paralyzed on the left side of her body. This time, with Françoise Fischler's help, Dr. Rodriguez managed to keep the old woman quietly resting in bed. Within a week and a half she improved remarkably, and that being the case, Rodriguez no longer saw any reason to keep her in seclusion. He told Patout Minville he might visit his kinswoman for an hour the following day.

"I'm sorry to have limited you and your wife to only a moment with Miss Clotilde until now, but I feared the excitement of seeing you after so many years would have been too much of a strain," the doctor said in the somewhat stiff manner he seemed to fall into whenever addressing the younger man. "She has been asking for you, Patout. Perhaps this first time, you should go alone. Mrs. Minville and Cato can see her later in the week, don't you think?" The doctor glanced at Patout Minville's wife, a pretty young woman with an unfortunate disposition to nerves, he rather thought. Then he drove away.

Early next morning before the interview, Patout Minville left the house. He was feeling slight misgivings about seeing Clotilde Patout. Her invitation to The Oaks still surprised him. She hadn't cared for him as a boy.

No wonder! I was practically a juvenile delinquent back then, he thought, settled on a clump of live oaks about a mile away as his goal, and set off across the lawn.

"I never thought she'd let me near this place again," he

said under his breath and jumped the ditch. He knew better than to ask why she'd changed her mind. It didn't matter. Nothing would make him happier than a chance to show her he was a different man. "For Mother's sake, if nothing else," he muttered. His mother had always wanted him to love them. Too bad he hadn't come while Janice was alive. He couldn't picture her. Only snatches of the past remained, except for the house and the land. These he'd never forgotten. They looked the same, only a bit worn down, diminished by the sale of the land. He looked up, tried to gauge the distance remaining to his trees. In all likelihood, they no longer stood on The Oaks. He crossed the road, jumped the ditch, and entered the cane field, wondering who it belonged to now.

While he plodded through the field, behind him in the house Clotilde Patout was waking to the sound of laughter in her sister's half of the house.

"Françoise?"

The old woman listened. Someone laughed again, a door slammed, then silence.

"Françoise?"

There was no answer. Tears came into her eyes. She collapsed on the pillows and feebly called out again, "Françoise!"

The stairs groaned. Someone was coming slowly upstairs. "Did you call me?"

"You know I did. I'll have a bowl of chili and crackers, a glass of buttermilk, and my bills. I've got to tend to them now, before my cousin comes up. No telling how long he'll stay. Don't argue with me. And open the window curtains. No, not when you come back, now. Who was that laughing?"

"Mrs. Patout is playing with her child. They just went outside on the front lawn."

"Don't they know I'm sick? Tell them to go inside and shut up. I can't rest with all that racket."

"No, I will not," Françoise Fischler said. "You ought to

get up and look at them, Miss Patout. It would do you a world of good to see them playing. They're charming together, those two." She walked toward the window and stumbled over a wicker table in the dark room.

Clotilde Patout laughed.

Françoise Fischler opened the curtains, then pushed the shutters out. Light flooded the room. She returned to the old woman in the bed.

"You're plainer than I was at your age," Clotilde Patout said.

The French woman did not respond.

She struggled to raise herself on her elbows. "How you doing this bright little morning, Miss Françoise? How you fixing to pass the time? Going out on a picnic with your young man? If you had one, you'd take him over to the cow pasture where the grass grows out the color of emeralds, and you know what, Miss Françoise, you'd set him down in a cow pile. That's the kind of luck you have. I also want a cup of coffee." She flopped over and faced the wall.

Françoise stared at her back, shrugged, and left the room. When she returned from the kitchen, she set a glass of orange juice and a bowl of oatmeal down on the bedside table, walked to the opposite side of the room, pushed aside the heavy velvet curtain that concealed the door to Clotilde Patout's dressing room, and opened the door.

"This doesn't look like chili and crackers to me," the old woman said.

"It isn't. You can't have that yet, so you might as well save your breath."

The old woman let that pass.

"Who was that turned in a while ago?"

The French woman stopped, half hidden by the heavy curtain of the dressing room door.

"Alphonse Romero."

"What'd he want?"

"He took some flowers to the grave. When he got there, he decided you might want some, too. He brought some back."

"What am I suppose to do, press them in a book?" She cackled.

The woman made no reply. Her face was in the dressing room.

Clotilde asked, "What kind?"

"A red carnation, a yellow rose, and some mums." Françoise began to shut the door.

"On my tray. Stick them in water on my tray, Françoise. Do you hear me? Send me Ruby."

"Ruby's not here, Miss Patout. Lily climbed up a fig tree and ate ant poison out of a tin. They had to call Dr. Rodriguez. He's over there now trying to get her to vomit."

"Then send me Willie. It doesn't take three grown people to make a Negro child vomit. Did you hear? I'm not going to have him loafing around here anymore. There're going to be changes now." There was no answer from the dressing room.

When she finished cleaning the dressing room, Françoise opened the shutters in the tiny room, leaned against the window frame, and looked out across the front lawn toward the flat cane fields, where the green sea was growing smaller each day.

Black Velvet, Clotilde Patout's Angus, was chewing her cud over the fence that kept her off the front lawn. Gazing fondly at a clump of day lilies, she stuck out her tongue. She had been trying to reach them all her life. She cried a soft, low, mournful moo.

The day lilies had magical powers, or so Ruby warned Françoise the day after she arrived at The Oaks. Ruby came to the kitchen door to collect the leftover chicken feet and head, to which she was entitled whenever chickens were killed. She held out her apron to receive the parts and said, "Willie showed me them day lilies once, and then I got a daughter. I catched that one in the lily patch. I don't want another one of that, me. You watch out, Miss Françoise, and don't go near them things. You do and you're done for. Not even the traitteur going to help you get that baby out your stomach."

Then she gathered up her apron and trundled off home to the unpainted shack in the backyard behind the chicken coop, where Lily raked an old tin fork in the creamy dust, making dead-end roads till dusk under the chinaball tree.

Lily was insane, or brain-damaged. Nobody seemed to know or care. She just was. And since her mother was in no mood to catch another one of those things, whether from Willie or Demi John, the young black who drove a tractor on the neighboring farm up and down the furrows giggling like a fool until he got to the end of a row, where he'd yell, "Sho nuff, praise the Lord," before turning the chugging machine around and starting down another row, it didn't look like there would be another like Lily coming along to keep her company under the tree.

When Françoise was new at The Oaks, she tried to keep a diary, tried to write what she felt about Clotilde, Willie, Ruby, Lily, the boy on the tractor. She'd known what she wanted to say: That she was living on a pie-shaped wedge of land that had been removed from the rest of the world. That she didn't know exactly where she was. That all the people, in that land where she was, went through days and nights, seeming to be alive, but were not real. That she wasn't real either. How could she be, when everything told her she was living out some kind of nightmare.

There was Lily, scratching roads, growing impatient at the shallow chinaball roots, pulling back her gums to show green, rotten teeth, biting at the roots of the tree until her teeth broke in half. She must be dreaming when she looked out the kitchen window and saw Willie Wooten, whom she thought not lacking in intelligence, leaning over, blowing the mucus out of his nose, and then licking his fingers.

Even with her eyes closed, there was no escape. The land was so quiet. Belmont on the north, Lizzardville just to the south, Highway 90 on a half mile beyond the chicken coop, but still so quiet she could hear, "Sho nuff, praise the Lord!" and the insane, endless giggles of the madman on a tractor in the field next door.

Her diary lay buried in the bottom of her dresser drawer. She was not able to express what she felt in words. She never wrote down that Lily, mostly—because the girl reminded her of her own daughter's existence—but all of them, made her feel the hopelessness of life.

Black Velvet twisted her head, trying to knock a fly off her back.

Françoise had been staring at the moving figure for a long time before she realized it was a man zigzagging across the cane field and heading that way.

She closed the shutters of the dressing room and went into the bedroom next door.

"Mr. Minville is back from his morning walk. Are you ready to see him now?" she asked.

"Yes, send him up," Clotilde said.

The French woman went to the door.

"And don't forget to send me Willie Wooten."

"I'll see if I can find him." She went out the door.

He sat down on the Victorian settee under the window while she said, "There isn't any money, Pat. My father didn't see fit to leave any for daughters. His only son was dead. He never recognized my capabilities. Of course, he was perfectly correct in the case of my sister. Janice would have been through her money in a matter of days, but I?" She patted the back of her flat head. Money had been left in trust for the bare maintenance of the house; there was rent from a tenant farmer, which paid for whatever taxes were due. She had a small income from oil mineral rights left to her from the Minville side of the family, which would, of course, pass to him on her death, but there was little to count on from that—at most, twenty-five dollars a month.

"Still, I am very proud of that. My mother, you understand, believed in me, from my very earliest days." She paused to let it sink in.

Patout nodded.

He wasn't what she expected. His looks were adequate— brown hair and eyes, nice nose, olive skin—not a face one remembered. No personality in it. Kept who he was well hidden in the back of his head. He couldn't be more different from Richard, she thought. Still, he was serious, respectful, and solicitous. She could hardly fault him, but in his choice of a wife.

"Other than that," she went on, "there is nothing, Patout. I shan't have you living here with false expectations. It has always been my greatest sorrow that my father, instead of conserving his wealth for his daughters, ran through his money before his death. Oh, you'll hear rumors of his having actually saved some money, even through those last horrible years, when he would drink anything but gasoline, but if he did, he didn't see fit to leave it to his daughters, his own flesh and blood."

"I am sorry, Aunt Clotilde." He had always called her that. It was a sign of respect; she was so much older than he.

"Willie thinks it's buried in the garden." She giggled.

Patout smiled, looked down and blushed. "I thought you were laying in new sewer pipe."

"For heaven's sake, Patout Minville. What's the matter with you. I'm not going to eat you, man."

"No, no, Aunt Clotilde, I'm just sorry. I'm sure Uncle Lizzard wouldn't have wanted you to take it like that."

"You're mistaken."

"Aunt Clotilde, I came here with no money. It took most everything to get here."

"Well, you'll just have to get yourself a job, won't you. It's the only way of avoiding starvation I know of."

"Yes, ma'am." He smiled and rose to go. "I expect you're tired now."

She looked at him, standing there at the foot of her bed, hat in hand. She supposed he'd been through a lot—Molly dying when he was young, Charles losing every penny. There was something hangdog about him and just a little too sweet for her taste. He definitely wasn't a tooter.

"It's going to be a while before I have enough money to build down by the road and move my family out of here," he said.

"That's all right. I didn't expect you to do it soon. Just tell your family to stay on their side of the house and your wife to quit dropping those pans, and we'll make do all right. Dr. Rodriguez tells me they're hiring out at the factory and the discount dollar store is looking for a new manager, perhaps you ought to go on down there now."

"Yes, ma'am," he said, smiled, and shut the door softly behind him.

He'll do, the old woman thought, for she had seen the sweet smile. She fell asleep, content with her plan.

· 8 ·

*H*e closed the door behind him and headed for the stairs, feeling like a man whose worst suspicions have been confirmed months after noticing, and trying to ignore, the first signs of an incurable disease; in short, he was both frightened and relieved.

For an impecunious family man to be relieved, when told his inheritance has disappeared, might seem irresponsible to some, but when this incriminating thought wafted across Patout Minville's mind, it went in one door and out the other as quickly as the odor of cabbage cooking in a rural house open front and back.

No one could seriously believe he didn't want to give Sophie and Cato a better life, but to come into money based on the happenstance of a name would have made a travesty of his life until now. It could have made him bitter. There was nothing worse than bitterness in life.

Something crashed in the kitchen on the other side of the wall. "Damn it to hell!" Sophie said.

He looked up, expecting Clotilde to shout, but there was no sound from upstairs. His wife and son moved away from the wall. Their muffled chatter faded. The grandfather clock ticked in the parlor. Years ago he had spent an entire afternoon in there crouched behind a love seat. Someone—it must have been the dead sister, for Clotilde didn't strike him mean-spirited in that way—told him the grandfather clock played, "She'll Be Coming 'Round the Mountain," whenever no children were there. It was pleasant to think he might have the clock for his own someday, but not wanting Clotilde to feel they had descended upon her for plunder, he already decided that neither he, Sophie, nor their child would ever ask her for anything. Sophie hadn't liked that, having already picked out a sterling silver tray, two candlesticks, and a porcelain shepherd holding a dog she couldn't live without, but that was the least of his worries. He had spent his last dime to haul them out here. They couldn't even return to New Orleans; there wasn't enough money for gas.

There was never enough money for anything Sophie really wanted. He'd never been able to afford anything that delighted her as much as Clotilde's letter inviting them to live at The Oaks. He had never seen her as excited as the day it came.

He had spent the previous night on the Gulf Coast, caught while trying to sell vacuums to poor whites during a hurricane watch. (His supervisor said you could count on poor whites to fill your quota during hurricane season; they never got out in time.) A family in Bay St. Louis had taken him in—a man, his wife, six kids, and a grandmother. They had stayed behind to protect what they owned from the looters who blew in with swarms of mosquitoes after every big storm on the gulf. Lord knows, they didn't have much to protect—a few sticks of furniture, wall-to-wall matted shag, some religious stuff hanging on the walls, lamps, and a coffee table made out of cypress knees. The Ralph Joneses. He wasn't like to forget the name after sharing a night like that, nothing between them and the elements but white asbestos siding and a three-by-nine screened porch.

Throughout the night while the house shuddered under the hurricane's attack, Mrs. Jones spray-waxed furniture. She said it kept her from thinking. Mr. Jones sat cursing softly, nursing his last cigarettes. They did not blame each other for wanting to stay.

Sometime after midnight the wind intensified. A pine near the house snapped in two and fell on the roof. The grandmother got down on her knees, began to pray. Mr. Jones turned to his wife, his face gray with strain.

"Wilma, are we going to get out of this alive?"

"No, dear."

"Then I'll have my last cigarette," he said.

They laughed. The incantation of Hail Marys emanating from the corner of the room sent them off again. Patout joined in, surprised to learn death could be taken jolly.

At dawn the wind subsided. They opened the door and went out. There were no houses standing within half a mile, but everything on the Joneses' land seemed miraculously intact. Even Patout's Studebaker still stood in the drive, though the wind had driven a dinghy through the rear window. They helped him pull it out. He got inside; it started right up.

"Well, I guess that's the last time any of us'll get caught in a hurricane," he said, shifting into reverse.

"Hell, mister, we've worked too hard to get nice things to risk losing everything on account of a little wind. Next time it blows, just come on by. We'll be here."

How relieved he had been to open the door of his own home at last, only to find Sophie and Cato jumping up and down in the middle of the bed, screaming, "We're going to be rich!" They hadn't even taken their shoes off. He made them come down at once. He'd like Sophie to see those poor bastards on the coast, dillydallying while the sky changed from navy blue to black, torn between leaving their possessions or losing their lives, waiting until the sky hawked down, seized the water, and rode across the shoreline on the backs of waves. Now that's what he called taking care of what you owned.

But Sophie said, "Too bad the water didn't wash up higher. I bet their house would be a whole lot cleaner with a lot less junk," then she poked the letter under his nose.

"My Dear Patout," the letter began, followed by inquiries about himself, his family, and the words, "If you'd consider coming out here to live, you wouldn't regret it. You and your family would wind up being a whole lot better off."

The letter said nothing about money, but Sophie assured him Clotilde was talking indirectly about inheriting so, since Sophie was always better at interpreting people than he, a week later he had found himself driving one hundred fifty miles across a washboard road to an outpost of five thousand souls perched on the edge of a swamp. Belmont. What a joke.

Family photographs lined the stairwell. Faded men and women with pink-tinted lips and cheeks, they stared at him out of tarnished, oval frames. Though paled to insignificance by light and time, the proud manner in which they carried themselves (even the rubbery newborns seemed to sit up straight) said Money, Privilege, Rank. He looked down at his shoes, mud-splattered, cracked, the sole coming off the left. Feeling like an intruder, he hurried to the foot of the stairs. The setting sun came through the fanlight and illuminated the hall. Admiring the color of an étagére by the door, he lost himself once again in thought. If only Sophie could be content with what they had, he knew he could make her happy. Happiness was simply doing right by those one loved, but Sophie had a different idea.

"Poverty does terrible things to people," she would often say in her rather breathless way, her eyes growing wide with fright. She had been counting on the inheritance to make a great change in their lives.

Having lived without money since his mother's death and his father's remarriage to a woman with a fondness for betting on cockfights and dogs, he told himself he was not afraid of living without it. When other young men of his class were preparing to go away to university, he, his father, and stepmother had been forced by debts to sell their house and move from New Orleans, eventually settling into a deserted camp far from the water in the woods north of Waveland, Mississippi. There his father had sat for the next three years drinking gin, keeping a diary of imaginary slights. One day Patout and his stepmother, Hattie Harriet, were eating boiled crabs on top of the *Mobile Register*. (Patout liked her. She smoked like a French movie actor, a cigarette stuck in the corner of her mouth while she talked. She didn't even take it out to suck crab claws.) His father walked in, said, "Son, get your elbows off the table," and fell over dead. He wasn't quite fifty. In Waveland he lay under a blanket of sand mixed with pine needles and beer bottles, crickets sawing the still, dry heat. No headstone. No money and, as his stepmother said, "What for? All he had was a birthday. Seems like a headstone deserves something else on it." She didn't waste compassion on the man who blamed her for his troubles.

It was not poverty, but that kind of bitterness that ruined people's lives. Wherever he went, he found people wasting the precious days of their lives longing for what they didn't have. It wasn't realistic to expect life easy. People should accept conditions as they found them. The important thing was to accomplish something, something that would last through the ages.

By the time he was nineteen years old, he had dedicated his life to this end. When his best friend wrote from his university in North Carolina—"My Dear Patout, Concerning your gift 'to the ages': Do you realize only a few old broken statues, a Dead Sea Scroll here, a cracked vase there, are all that is left, after three thousand years and untold numbers of artists working night and day to create something lasting? Think again before you place your life on this single-minded track. It will destroy any chance you might have had for ordinary human happiness."—he never answered his letters again.

Saying good-bye to his stepmother, he set out for New Orleans to become a painter. For the next three years he painted with zeal, pleased with himself for starting from noon, even on Saturdays and Sundays, but having little training and no means of supporting himself, apart from a series of mediocre and debilitating jobs, he grew discouraged. He couldn't maintain his enthusiasm when no one admired the results.

And then one day he met Sophie serving overcooked eggs and grits in the back of a café, and his ideas about what was important in life began to change.

Now four irreplaceable decades of life had gone by with nothing to show but a wife, a child, a broken-down car, a squashed D. H. Holmes suit box of poems on yellowed paper, a portable easel with a missing wing bolt (it no longer stood up), and a box of dried oil paints, but to his own surprise, his lack of accomplishment was no longer painful.

He had learned to take great pleasure in his wife and child and, on those occasions when he did need solace from the pain of his wasted life, he would go to the balcony over-looking the street, lie down on a lopsided chaise longue left by the previous tenant, and enumerate all the ordinary plea-sures he would have missed, had he become rich and famous. (Lying on the balcony in full view of the general public was one of these.)

He took out a cigarette and stuck it in the corner of his mouth, just like Hattie Harriet. What had become of her since his father's death? She was young then; she might still be alive. If she wasn't, he hoped she'd at least gotten herself a nice coffin. Everyone deserved a container for decaying in private, instead of being stuck in the sand like a dog.

"Well, Patout, enough gloom," he muttered. He wasn't such an old man; in time, everything would work out. According to Clotilde, the discount dollar store needed a new manager. He was overqualified, but the job was a start. Soon he'd be able to take advantage of Clotilde's offer of free land down by the road. He'd build a nice little two-bedroom house—they'd never have been able to afford that in New Orleans—and maybe they'd have another child.

Why, next thing you know, I'll be calling up to order the

brick. Sophie would like a brick house; only doctors have them. "Yes, sir, no point in not trying to make a go of it now we're here," he said to himself.

On the other side of the wall Cato coughed. The boy was puny, always catching colds. Living in the country was going to be good for him.

The grandfather clock struck the half hour. The light in the front hall began to fade. He felt peaceful, as though he had always lived here. Perhaps the situation they now found themselves in was partly his fault. He may have exaggerated the wealth of his mother's people when he told tales about them to Sophie. He loved to tell stories to her. The more he elaborated, the more excited she became, as easy to charm as a child.

Bacon was frying; its smell seeped under the padlocked double doors of the right front parlor. Bacon was his favorite food. Whenever Sophie cooked it, she said it was for him. Shutting the front door softly behind, he went out and rounded the corner of the house, glancing down to the spot where he would one day build himself a house. Mounting the side porch and going in by the screen door off Janice's old bedroom, which was now their living room, he called out, "Sophie, is that bacon I smell?"

"Just for you." With a tablespoon in her hand she came out of the kitchen and grinned.

"It's dripping," he told her.

She shrugged and threw the spoon from the door to the sink.

"Sophie, don't!" Came the sound of glass shattering.

"For heaven's sake, Pat, don't look so devastated; it's only a jelly glass."

"Do you have to make so much noise?"

"Noise? That's a new one. Now look, Patout, I'm willing to put up with a lot of shit, but I'm not going to tiptoe around here. If she's going to start laying down rules, we're going to pack up and go right now, even if she does have fifty million dollars." She giggled. Just saying fifty million made her feel good.

"My cousin has nothing to do with it. I only wish you'd be more careful," he said, mild, sat down and knocked an antimacassar off. He picked it up and smoothed it back over the arm of the overstuffed chair.

"So how did it go, other than her making snide remarks about me."

"She didn't say anything about you. I heard you myself just now coming down the stairs, you'd be amazed how much goes through—"

"Pat! Do you want to drive me nuts?" She leaned over him.

"It went fine." He kissed her absentmindedly and reached for the *Belmont Crier*.

"You don't look like it went fine."

"Didn't I hear Cato coughing?"

"That's just the tail end of his cold. Oh!" She rushed from the room.

"Bacon's burned. Cato? Wash up. We're going to eat in a minute. Pat? Come talk to me in here. I can't leave now."

He turned the *Belmont Crier* over and slowly read the help-wanteds. The columns were blurred and still damp with ink. The *Times-Picayune* never ran classifieds on its back page. A posthole digger, an experienced shoe salesman, a man with a truck for hauling dirt, and a 7-Eleven nightshift clerk were the picks of the day. "It's twenty-six days till Christmas," said a box in the lower right-hand corner.

"Pat?"

Damn the woman. She never let him get things out in his own way. He wiped ink off his fingers on his shirt. It didn't matter what he told her, by now she had already concocted her own version of what happened upstairs with Clotilde. Sophie was like that. If he didn't move fast enough to suit her, and who could move fast enough to suit Sophie, she would punish him by going off and getting it on her own, some substitute, that was never, ever, she let him know, as good as what he could have provided, had he gotten off his ass.

There she was right now on the other side of that wall, turning bacon. He sniffed. She had put on a new batch. The other must have burned to a crisp. There she was turning bacon, he hoped she left the ends soft, pushing hair out of her eyes, he hated hair in his eggs, yelling at him to come tell her what happened, and all the while her little head was just swimming in made-up details. He could already tell Clotilde was going to come out a villain, that poor, sweet old lady, but once Sophie made her mind up, that was the end of that.

Well, she can wait for once, he thought. He was not going to be bullied and manipulated into telling her what Clotilde had said before he was good and ready. Besides, he was hungry. You'd think Clotilde would have offered something to tide me over till supper, he thought.

"Cato?" Sophie said.

"Cato! Your mother's calling you," he bellowed.

A small boy came out of the room on the other side of the stove and stood, peering anxiously into the living room. He had the blue eyes and mahogany curls of his mother.

"What were you doing in there?"

"Playing hotel."

"You stay out of there."

"Françoise doesn't mind. I asked her."

"Well, I mind. You don't have any business in somebody else's part of the house. That door is always supposed to be closed. You act like this place belonged to you. Go wash your hands.

"Yes, sir."

"And she's Miss Françoise to you."

The boy's face puckered.

Sophie appeared at the door. "Go on, darling, wash your hands."

The boy wimpered toward the bathroom, steering clear of the overstuffed chair.

"Your daddy's not that bad." He held out his hand, but the boy wouldn't have any part of him. He shrugged.

"Why do you have to act like a beast?"

"Someone's got to teach him manners."

"Pat, what's wrong?"

"I thought we were about to eat," he said.

They ate through the meal in silence. When he was finished, he excused himself and went on the porch. He could hear her talking to the boy. She was always giggling with him, telling him stories, making him excited just before bed, and then he couldn't sleep, so she'd lie with him in the bed and rub his forehead until he quieted down. Sometimes that went on for hours, night after night. He had not been raised that way; his own parents would not have permitted him to invade their time together after the evening meal.

"He's asleep now," Sophie called from the dark of the living room. Patout couldn't see her, but the sound of her voice startled him with its softness. She was tired; she wouldn't fight him now when he told her what they would have to do.

"Will you come out for a while?" he said. He wanted her to hold him in her arms there in the dark.

"Coming out?" he repeated.

"No. I've some chores to do yet," she said. "Come in when you're ready."

He heard her move away from the screen door. Yellow light fell upon the porch floor. She had turned on the floor lamp on the other end of the sofa.

Now came *tinkle, tinkle, tinkle, tinkle*. He grinned. "Autumn Leaves," was it? But she had turned the Zenith down before he could catch it. The more flamboyant the pianist, the more Sophie thought he was an artist.

He got out of Janice's rocker and went to the screen door. She had picked up some handwork and was sitting on the far end of the sofa under the lamp, still in her blue apron, stitching a guest towel, it looked like. Embroidering, he guessed. He liked that about her. She was always trying to pretty up the place, though once finished, she never treated things right.

"Mind if I come in? We got things to talk about."

"Whenever you're ready."

He switched on the overhead light.

She grimaced and pointed to the corner of the room, where the four-poster was pushed against the wall to make room for their pile of suitcases. The overhead light was shining through the lace canopy, illuminating the sleeping boy.

"He won't wake up. I can't see a thing in here."

She appraised him for a moment in the steady way she had of looking through and beyond, then lowered her eyes and stuck the needle in the eye of the daisy.

He switched the light off again and stumbled on the corner of the sofa. "There isn't any money," he said.

He hadn't meant it to come out that way; he meant to say what an opportunity it was going to be for them to live here in this small, quiet town. A place where one could bring one's children up without fear. And think how much happiness they could bring to Clotilde, that sick old woman, all alone in the world except for them. He didn't really see how they could go off and leave her. Wasn't it true that if one did the right things in life, goodness would out, that sort of thing? Not his whole life plagued by ill luck, that wouldn't do for a man with his heart in the right place. But that wasn't what came out.

"There isn't any money," he said, as though that were the point. One didn't base life's grand decisions on a small matter like money.

She said, "None?"

"Not a dime."

"How come she can afford this house?"

"Mineral rights."

"There, you see."

"Sophie, it's twenty-five dollars a month. Her tenant farmer pays a little rent, but that goes for taxes and repairs. I went over all this with her. She doesn't have anything."

"You said she was rich."

"She was. When I was a kid, she and her sister were always pushing money in my hands. Maybe I miscalculated a bit. You know how kids are, give them a quarter, they think you're a millionaire."

"For God's sake. You make us give up the only decent place we've ever had, quit your job—the only one since we've been married that made any actual money—based on a child-hood fantasy. How could you, Patout."

"There was nothing about money in her letter. You were so certain, you convinced me."

"Since the day we met you've been going on and on about what refined people you came from. Now it's my fault for believing your aunt would be too much of a lady to mention money outright? Sure, it's my fault, the whole thing." She reached behind and unfastened her bra.

"You used to like my stories," he complained, half ashamed. It was pointless to go on. They could get a fresh start in the morning. "Don't worry, Sophie. We'll work something out." He reached for her.

"I'm not supposed to think anymore, right, just lie back and fuck."

"Sophie, stop! He'll be screaming in a minute."

"What if he does. Maybe then you'll notice you have a child and wife who are totally dependent on you. Year in, year out, never enough money to go anywhere, do anything, living on nothing but your dreams of the way life should be, not the way it is. I've had it, Pat. I can't go on like this. What are we going to do?"

"Clotilde says the discount clothing store needs a new manager."

"Great. Just what I wanted. A husband who clerks in a nigger store."

"I know I'm overqualified."

"Overqualified?" She laughed.

"I've had sales experience."

"Oh, I forgot. You sold vacuums. Three in four months?"

"You're just upset and saying anything that comes into your head, Sophie."

"She's lying to you, Pat. You've got to stand up to her."

"For the last time, there is no money. Maybe she'll leave us the house when she's gone, but that depends on how we treat her in the meantime. She's scared, Sophie. She's sick and alone. Sophie, please believe me. There is no money."

"None?"

"Not a dime."

"Pat, that's impossible. What about them kept niggers?"

He shrugged. "They don't cost anything. It's not like you think, honey."

Her eyes filled with tears. "Do you mean I'm going to stay in this rathole for the rest of my life and take care of you and that whimpering brat and that old bitch upstairs. That's going to be my life?"

"For God's sake, Sophie, you're waking the whole house." He gestured toward the kitchen door. The refrigerator door opened and shut; a pot scraped against the kitchen wall as it was taken down from its hook. Cato whimpered. Patout went to the bed. The boy began to cry.

"Sophie, please come here. I just make it worse."

There was a knock at the door.

"Who is it?" Sophie called. By now the boy was screaming.

"Françoise."

"Get rid of that woman, Pat." Sophie went into the bathroom and slammed the door.

Patout opened the kitchen door. The French woman stood

in the doorway, barefooted, hair in shambles, wrapped in an old bathrobe. Does the woman never smile? he thought.

"Miss Patout needs her sleep. Shall I give it a try? I'll make us both some hot milk and rock him awhile."

"Yes, please. Whatever you can."

She held out her arms.

He put the crying boy into her arms and closed the door. In a moment the house was quiet again.

"Sophie?"

She was standing in front of the bathroom mirror with her nightgown pulled down to her waist, crying. He took her into his arms. She cried out with pain as he touched her.

"I think I'm pregnant again. Look at my breasts. They're so swollen. I can already feel them pulling out of shape. What are we going to do?"

"I'm sure you're not pregnant, Sophie. She took Cato for a while."

"Nosy bitch. Softly, Pat. It hurts so unless you're gentle."

He grabbed her buttocks and lifted her up, pushing inside her. He had read a scene in a book once, a man making love to a young girl that way, but in real life it didn't work very well. She kept slipping through his hands; he hadn't given her time to take off the nylon nightgown; he bumped her head against the linen closet, which she didn't like. Now, at last, he thought, thank God, she's quiet, now at last.

"Damn it, stop!"

"What?" he said. His penis slipped out; he came on her leg.

She said nothing, only, "How convenient to do it in the bathroom," reached out, took a towel off the rack, wiped herself, and went out of the room. He heard her go into the kitchen to retrieve the boy. Cato was crying again, damn him, demanding her attention. She was singing to him now, a song about a fox.

He retreated to the porch, lit a cigarette, sat down and rocked. Bungled again. Got to get it first try, he told himself.

Not like before the kid. They'd spent hours in bed. How did married couples do it?

The crying ceased. The bed squeaked. She was standing at the screen door, just inside.

"I told her I didn't appreciate her eavesdropping."

"She was just trying to help."

"No, she wasn't, Pat. I don't know why she did it, but it wasn't to help us out. There's something wrong about her."

"What do you mean? Mysterious?"

"I don't know. I haven't figured it out yet, but I feel uneasy around her. She gives me the creeps."

"You aren't used to servants," Patout observed.

"That's not true," she cried. "If you really want to know, she looks like she's got nigger blood in her."

"I don't understand how you can be such a lady about some things, but when it comes to this—"

"What?"

"Stop saying nigger. You use it all the time."

"Why?"

"It sounds common."

"Now he's worried about my being common in front of his aristocratic family."

"Let's not start again."

"I'm not starting; I'm finishing. Do you really intend for us to stay here?"

He sighed. "I had thought so, but if you're dead set against it, we'll go back to the city as soon as I've got enough for the trip."

"How long?"

"Maybe five, six months."

"No, not me, Pat. I can't wait that long. Your six months have a way of going on and on. Next thing you know I'll be an old woman with half my life gone, still sitting here in the boondocks without two nickels to rub together. I'm not going to live that way, Pat. I've seen too much poverty in my life already, I know what it can do."

"Have you got a better idea?"

"I think I do. Don't worry, Pat. You leave it to me. I'm going to have a nice home, well-behaved children who go to all the nicest parties in town, and I'm going to have a husband who is a good provider. Oh, sweetheart, I'm going to be so proud of you." She moved away from the door.

Alarmed, he half rose from the rocker, but she had already climbed into bed. He heard the four-poster squeak.

My darling wife, he said to himself. No one could change so quickly from despair to hope. During their marriage, almost always brought on by his failures, there had been times she succumbed to despair, refusing to dress, barely speaking, shuffling back and forth from the bathroom to their bed, and then, just as he grew frightened and began to watch her, she would suddenly return to herself, exuding confidence, broadcasting her hopes for the future to anyone who would listen— the deli man in the back of the A&P, the oyster woman around the corner; they had few friends of their own. At such times she seemed to believe she could fix anything, make it come right.

And the truth is, you and Cato think so, too, he thought. Overcome with tenderness, he got up and went to bed, pushing Cato between them, for Sophie was afraid for the boy to sleep on the edge.

9

Sophie awoke the next morning at a quarter of nine to the touch of her child feeling her face. She groaned and rolled over, eyes shut, and waited for the tiny finger to come back to her face.

First he touched her eyebrow, petting it carefully, letting his finger follow the curving outline. Then she felt it move to her earlobe, down her cheek to her lips. He tickled her under her nose.

"Boo!" she cried.

The boy curled like a roly-poly bug, giggling delightedly into her face.

"Where's Poppa?" she said.

"Gone."

"Gone where?"

"I'm not suppose to say."

"Oh," she said. "I see. Well, suppose we get up and have some breakfast. Are you wet?" She rolled him half over and felt of the bed. "Good boy." She pulled out the waistband of his pajamas, reached in, and spanked him playfully, then let it pop.

"Ow, Mama!"

"Mama was only playing, Cato."

"You hurt me."

"No, I didn't. Come on now, be a big boy. Cato, please don't cry."

The boy wailed.

"Cato, listen. Do you want to play a game? Let's play 'Where's Daddy?' "

"I don't want to play. I know where he is."

"Will you tell me?"

"No!"

"I tell you what, if I guess where he is, you don't have to say anything, just laugh, okay? He went into town to see about a job?" She tickled the bottom of his foot.

He giggled hysterically. "That's not fair, Mama."

She tickled his feet and then under his arms. He thrashed about in the bedclothes, trying feebly to ward off her attacks, struggling to poke under her arms. At last they fell back exhausted in each other's arms and lay still.

A ray of sun painted a bright stripe across his chestnut hair. She reached out and took up a curl, rubbing it between her thumb and index finger. What beautiful hair he has, she thought. His complexion looked a bit pasty. She worried about his health. He was frail and too small for his age.

Goodness knows she tried, but what could she do if his father didn't bring home enough money to feed him right. Cato would be starting school soon. Perhaps she should keep him home another year. She held her right hand high in the air and counted on her fingers. Nine months. Just time enough to present him with a new baby sister.

Oh, God, don't think about that, she moaned.

Cato's eyelids fluttered. "There was once a big tree in a big, black forest," she whispered, "and one day a woodsman came and cut her down. He went chop! chop! chop! and the big tree went round and round." She glanced at the boy. He was asleep.

Slowly she climbed out of bed. When she was dressed, she slipped out, making sure the screen door didn't slam, tiptoed across the porch, and went around the corner of the house to the front door.

She tapped gently on Clotilde Patout's bedroom door. There was no reply. She opened it and poked her head in. Clotilde Patout's eyes were fixed on her face.

"Who told you to come in," she said.

"I'm Sophie, Patout's Sophie," she heard herself saying in a high-pitched, silly voice.

"I know who you are. State your business."

"Oh! I have none, that is to say, I didn't come up here to talk business, I wanted to see if you might want a little company. I woke up early, you see, only not early enough for our Pat. He went on downtown, just like you told him, to apply for that job at the store. I didn't even know he'd gone, but when I woke up, there I was, all alone in the bed, but for the boy, and I got to feeling lonely, and then I thought, Why, I bet Aunt Clotilde's feeling lonely too, and so I got dressed and came up right away." Her voice trailed off.

"I see," the old woman said.

Sophie pushed the door open. Gently, gently, feel her out. Don't make sudden moves. Approach her like a bad-tempered dog, she told herself and slipped inside the room.

"I understand your child caused some trouble last night?"

"Oh, no, Aunt Clotilde. Cato's never any trouble . . . Oh!" Sophie blushed. The closet door opened. Françoise Fischler came out.

"I didn't mean to startle you," she said.

Sophie turned her back on the woman. "Yes, I had forgotten, Aunt Clotilde. Cato had a nightmare last night and woke up crying."

"I hope he doesn't make it a habit. Rodriguez says I need my rest, now more than ever."

"We wouldn't dream of disturbing you, Aunt Clotilde."

The old woman shifted in the bed. "How old's the boy."

"His name is Cato."

"I know his name. I asked you his age."

"Six."

"Why isn't he in school? When children that age miss a day of school, they never catch up. Stunts them for life when they fail."

"He won't really be six till January fourth; they wouldn't let him start in New Orleans. You had to be six by the start of the school year."

"So he won't begin until the fall?"

Sophie reached the foot of the bed. She eased herself down, remembering how her grandmother, when she was old, had loved to have visitors sit on her bed to talk.

"Well, I suppose if you think it's better, I could go down to the school board and ask—"

"Françoise, pull over that chair." The old woman motioned Sophie off the bed.

"No need to go. I can tell you right now the answer's yes. Children start here at five and a half. Personally, I think it's a good idea. Doesn't do to coddle them. We'll enter Cato right after the new year. Now, what else is on your mind?" the old woman said.

Sophie glanced behind her.

"If you're looking for the servant, she's gone. Speak up. I knew from the minute you walked in you had something on your mind."

"Aunt Clotilde, I grew up in a small town in Mississippi. People didn't have much there. My family had even less. On my first day of school, I had to wear a dress my mother cut down from one of her own."

Clotilde Patout laughed. "That must have been some cutting."

"You've got to promise me, if we stay here with you to live, you've just got to promise me that you'll help us out. Patout says I'm not to ask you for anything, but it's not going to be that way. I can't let Cato—"

"I don't see why I'm obliged to promise you anything, Mrs. Minville. You aren't any kin of mine."

"But Pat and Cato—"

"Any kin of mine knows how to take care of himself; he wouldn't be a relative otherwise. If you ask me, the only reason you've come up here and told me this sob story is because you're after something for yourself. Now out with it, what is it you want?"

I'm going to be sick. I've got to get out of this room, Sophie thought.

"Let me tell you something, young woman, so we understand each other straight off the mark. I don't like you. I don't think I ever will. I don't like redheads, for starters. Yours isn't the most glaring kind of red, but even so, you look like a redhead to me, and redheads mean trouble. For another thing, you ought to wear dresses that cover you up like a lady, not have your top button unbuttoned, with your bosoms hanging out. Patout ladies always wore whole slips, not half slips, especially not when they were wearing georgette.

"I don't like most women. They're sneaky, unreliable, and apt to lie. How do I know you're in such a strained situation? You had enough money to get here, didn't you? If you need money, you should have told your husband to tell me so, instead of sneaking around here to butter me up, using your son as excuse. If you're threatening to leave The Oaks if you don't get your hands on some money, then all I've got to say is go. I don't need you here. I've got that foreign woman to look after me. I don't need you half as bad as you think I do, so go."

"Please, I didn't come here to start an argument. I wanted to make friends and tell you a little bit about our lives. I didn't mean to—"

"Don't tell me what you meant. You think you smell money here in this old house, don't you, Sophie Minville. Maybe you ought to take a lesson from Willie Wooten. He thinks there's money here, too, so he went out and bought himself a shovel. Now if you think I've got money hidden somewhere hereabout, why don't you ask Willie if he's tired of digging yet. Maybe he'll sell you his shovel." Clotilde Patout laughed.

"Why are you so hateful to me? I haven't done a thing to you," Sophie said.

"But you would if I gave you half a chance. You came here thinking you were going to be some kind of millionaire. Well, take my advice. If you think there's money here, go out and find it. I won't stop you. I'd be glad if somebody in this family had money again. Now go away. You've tired me."

"Please, can't we be friends?"

Clotilde turned her face to the wall.

"Patout will never forgive me if I've upset you. Please, I wouldn't have come up here if it hadn't been for Cato."

"The boy is not my responsibility. There's only one responsibility I have and that is to God. You can hardly argue with that, unless you aren't a God-fearing woman." She looked at Sophie. "Well, it was unrealistic to expect that much from my nephew, I suppose."

"Nephew?" Sophie said in surprise. "I thought Patout was your second cousin."

The old woman sat up in bed. "Get out of here," she screamed. "Françoise Fischler!"

The hall door opened immediately.

"How dare you eavesdrop on my conversation with Miss Patout," Sophie said.

Françoise shrugged. "If you need to believe that, go ahead," she said, weary. She put a tray down beside the bed.

"Get her out of my sight, Françoise Fischler. Out! I want her out!"

"I think she wants you to go now, Mrs. Minville," the foreign woman said with what seemed to Sophie like an obvious smirk. She escorted Sophie to the hall and shut the door.

"Why is she so angry?" Sophie said.

"She's very sensitive since the last stroke. She doesn't like to be corrected, Mrs. Minville."

"Well, I see you've already figured out how to get around her." She walked downstairs and slammed the front door.

10

*P*atout Minville took a job as foreman at the chicken slaughterer's, out on the edge of town where the broom factory used to be. The job paid almost nothing—two-fifty an hour more than the Negroes got—but with a steady income he was able to get a bank loan and build a house on Clotilde's land. Down front by the road, almost in the ditch, it was as far from the main house as he could get his wife from his aunt, for the feeling between the women was a strong, vibrant thing, which fed on the smallest offense.

There was a palpable detachment of that corner of Clotilde's yard with the first stake driven into the ground. Of it, Patout was unaware, but the cold, incurious gaze of The Oaks, standing behind its screen of trees, made all who passed by see at once the inappropriateness of the paltry, two-bedroom affair, while yet no more than four pine sticks and string.

Into this house he put his son, a small, frail-looking child of six and a half, his wife, pregnant with their second child, and various cartons and packages of yellowed notebooks and canvases, mementos of the years he had spent trying to be an artist in New Orleans. He couldn't bear to part with his boxes of worn-out dreams (although he could neither look at the canvases nor read what was written on the yellowing papers without cringing in shame), so he pushed them into the back of his closet, concealed them with dirty underwear, and closed the door.

He had built in the house side-by-side closets, one for him and one for her. Perhaps at no other time did he feel so aware of himself as a grown-up man as when he stood in front of those closets. Coming in from the late shift at the slaughter-house, he would tiptoe into the dark bedroom and see in the half-light of the plastic night-light shaped like a hand, the closets standing side by side like a man and his wife. Ecstasy would overcome him as he went to hang up his shirt and pants. He felt like a man in a gallery, mind anywhere but what's on the walls, until a painting catches his eye, and unaware of the journey, he travels down the length of a neck, lost in the wonder of human flesh.

Nor were the closets the only wellspring of joy. Even the line of the gutter thrusting off the roof into the rain cistern pleased him. This old-fashioned cistern served no useful func-tion, town water having reached The Oaks twenty years be-fore, but Patout insisted on installing it, over the objections of his wife, who wanted a modern dishwasher instead. They argued about it for days, until one morning at breakfast he announced, "It's not for me, Sophie. The cistern is for Cato. The use of old-fashioned technology breeds old-fashioned, high morals in a boy."

"What will you think of next," she said, dropped a cast-iron skillet into the sink and splashed soapy water on the floor.

"The bank gave me the loan. You want a dishwasher, go get a loan yourself." He got up from the table and left the kitchen, surprised at his anger, gratified by his wife's aston-ished expression. It was the first time he'd stood up to Sophie about money, and it pleased him extraordinarily that he left her that morning speechless.

Remembering the scene, he leaned over, kissed his sleeping wife, and quietly left the house. She couldn't even sleep with-out messing up the bed.

It was early yet. Felt more than seen, the cistern stood nearby at the back corner of the house. The wood gone black and spongy with moisture, profound in its silence and size, the huge cask seemed a reassuring old friend, too heavy to disappear.

Stepping high over the silvery network of wet crabgrass, Patout went to the Studebaker and got in. The sky was beginning to turn gray. He warmed the engine and slowly backed down the drive. The house appeared out of the gloom. There was not a nail, bolt, or screw that didn't satisfy him. Sophie felt she had come down in the world by moving from The Oaks into what, by comparison, could only be called a shack, but to him the new house was a triumph.

How could I, he asked himself for the hundredth time, cause eight grown men to stand about in their carpenters' aprons, full and bulging with nails—that symbol of male activity—waiting my order to build. The pleasure of being in control changed him. He longed to feel that sensation again, certain only good would come were he, one day, to lead men. He had not given up his ideals, but only found self-respect and pride, qualities he had always lacked in sufficient supply, he told himself. But to Sophie, he had shut a door.

He stopped for one last look. Inside, his wife and small son were sleeping. Another child was on the way. Six months before he couldn't afford gas, now he had a job and a long-term mortgage. Life is extraordinary, he thought.

Behind The Oaks a light went on in Willie Wooten's shack. A girl in a dress too tight came out on the porch with a fork in her hand and watched Patout Minville drive away. She started the truck in her throat and drove off the porch into the dirt under the chinaball tree, making roads with the fork in front of her truck, which nobody else could see.

It was early when he got to the slaughterhouse. The workers had not yet appeared. He liked arriving earlier than the black men and women, a sweet, good-natured lot, who worked the line day after day without complaint. It gave him time to make a fresh pot of coffee, sit in his tiny office overlooking the huge, empty room, and reflect on life.

Had Clotilde Patout money to provide for him and his family, he might have gone back to writing poetry or painting full time, but he told himself it was all right the way things worked out. Most men, by the time they reached middle age, had to provide for families. Responsibility almost made him feel glad. He turned on the hot plate and spooned coffee into the drip pot, adding one tablespoon extra for the pot. This job, despite Sophie's disparaging remarks, suited his needs.

Often, as he stood by the conveyor belt making a quality check, he felt free to use his mind. He had only to lift his head, look through the cargo doors past the piles of broken crates with white feathers stuck to the slats, focus on the field that stretched behind the plant, and the carcasses of chickens going by went right out of his mind. Within a week of taking the job he'd composed a new poem, "Across the Road, into a Park." He smiled to himself. It was one of his best. The following week came another. At that pace, he'd double his output of a lifetime in ten months. On days he did not compose, he silently recited to keep the poems fresh in mind. None had been written down. He was waiting for time to perfect them.

Having composed a new poem the previous day, Patout planned to work on it this morning. Something was not quite satisfactory about the rhythm, and in spite of "garden" in the title, he hadn't yet worked in a reference to flowers, cornflower blue being the only image that came readily to mind.

He glanced through the window overlooking the floor. Workers already manned the stations. The machinery was beginning to roll. His poem would have to wait. He washed out the demitasse cup, restored it to its hook over the sink, and left the office. His head man, Big Jim Dominique, waited below. Patout went down the metal staircase, enjoying the hollow clang.

"Good morning, Mr. Pat," workers called. He stopped every so often as he went down the line and waited while

Big Jim took a chicken off the belt and held it out for inspection. Pin feathers gone from the legs? Giblets packed neatly inside? Company's tag properly knotted, left wing? This morning, every question answered yes.

"Everything seems fine this morning. Carry on, Jim," Patout said. He stepped away, lips moving, and wandered toward the cargo doors, groping for the opening.

"My home is a beautiful . . . No, that's not right. My home is . . ."

The workers standing nearby poking wings and legs back on the long, black belt jerked their heads in his direction and winked. Big Jim, a tall, handsome man, raised his hand and gave the all-clear. Ten rows away, another man raised his hand and made an "O," which stood for, "Mr. Pat's off again." Another worker farther back passed the signal, another and another until everybody down the length of that vast tin shed knew what was going on. (This communal action led by her husband thrilled Delia Dominique, who drew in it a parallel to the handsomest rooster always leading the morning crowing, followed by his nearest neighbor, then his neighbor's neighbor, and so on until the news of dawn spread from one side of Belmont to the other.)

Now some of the workers departed for the sunlight and a quick smoke. Others sat down, took off shoes, massaged toes. Rachel Mae Whitney asked Florina Robicheaux if she thought he'd be out long enough to grab a Coke. "Go on, honey. He ask, you in the ladies'," Florina replied. The scattered few left for appearances on the conveyor belt amused themselves, too, flopping chickens over, raising the Pope's nose, seeing whose chicken could make the loudest fart, while the white man stood in a trance, looking out the door.

"My home is a garden," Patout murmured,
"into which I creep at the close of the long work day.
I open the door, step on the cool, plank floor,
Sniff the delightful aroma. My wife is baking a cake.

My little son stands by the window looking out,
Dreaming of what, he does not say,
Shy of pressing, I steal away
To greet the one who tends my garden
While I am gone all day.
Hello, my darling wife, I say.
She gives me a kiss from her warm, parted lips,
And I drink, as thirsty as any plant
Not tended as well as I."

11

*I*n the beginning Cato was not a worrier. In the beginning of his life, when he was very young, he appeared cut from new cloth, and if not completely in looks, at least in spirit he greatly resembled his mother. High-spirited, adventuresome, gay, these were qualities marking them both.

Bang on the piano she used to do. By the hour, bang on the piano, and with him, too. Seated by her on the bench with the lid that flapped open—you could hide things from burglars underneath—he would sit beside her and wait till she shouted, "Now!" over the crashing of the keys, and he'd jump down and depress the loud pedal and hold it there till she yelled, "Let up!" when he'd get back in his seat by her side.

And they sang together, lovely songs. Things from old wars and old times when men *did* court women, as his mother said, not like *this* pedestrian age, when women didn't wear lace and men didn't bring them flowers, or get to pick them up when they fainted on the floor.

And she would rock him by the hour.

But after the move to Belmont, his mother no longer had that excess of energy and high spirits that had made her at times resemble a young colt in a pasture on a bright spring morning. All that changed. She who was before had disappeared and left in her place the one with the huge stomach who stood at the front window, looking out at the empty road, or lay in the dark in her bedroom, one arm flung over her eyes, dreaming of her beau, Walker McDonald, who had gone to New York and left her in New Orleans, because she was afraid to go, and now was a big, famous movie star, only his father was not supposed to know.

"God damn him, we don't have enough to get by on," he sometimes heard her mutter. He liked the words—get by on. It sounded like his family was a big new sedan on a two-lane highway with another car in the other lane trying to pass. His father drove very fast. He was sure the other car would land in the ditch.

Sometimes at night he now awoke sweating profusely and tearing off his T-shirt, the bed soaked with his sweat and urine and the sheets twisted in long ropes around his legs like the coiled ropes of the wisteria turning again and again on itself with each passing year until, one would think, the life would be choked off, only to find it was the only way it could flower.

In the dark then, in a room not larger than a closet, where his plain single bed was pushed against the wall near the corner where the window broke through to the outside in a lopsided, deliberately ugly manner without forethought to beauty or proportion, he would awake, panic-stricken, caught in the vestige of a dream. He was terrified then, in those years, of death, anyone's death: mother's, father's, Willie Wooten's, anyone's but his own, for his own was not ever coming, but he was terrified, since he could not die, of being left entirely alone.

And in those first moments of waking, when he lay wet, sobbing, causing more wetness to gush from his face and crash against the bedsheets in ever-widening pools, when he thought surely he would have drowned, or at least lose a leg from gangrene the way the sheet was twisting around and around his left leg, had he been anyone else but himself, who could not die, or suffer as ordinary people, he would say to himself, go away, dream, and push away the pictures of the swirling water undercutting the bank on which their house stood. No matter how hard he tried, the water rose, for the coulee had gone wild in the night. The dry bed of the coulee cracked open. Water burst out. Boiling up from the center of the earth and from the banks where the oaks grew, milk began to trickle down faster and faster. The white ribbon snaked down the root-torn banks and merged in the bottom of the ravine with the brown bayou water, rushed forward, and swirled brown and white under the foundations of their house.

"Mama!" he screamed.

The bed creaked. He heard his father groan. He heard the bed creak. A pillow slammed against their bed. She padded across the bare wooden floor. He heard her. Bare feet padded across the wooden floor. She was scratching her head. She was coming to him. He heard her yawn in the doorway.

He pulled the soaking blanket up to his chin. "Mama?" he whispered.

"Just a minute, damn you."

Her presence went away.

She tinkled. He heard her. She dripped in the pot. Paper scratched against her place down there. He waited, his eyes growing larger in the dark until they verged on the sockets, like green grapes held in a pucker as he felt their backs with his tongue. A soft, solitary fart. The toilet flushed.

"Move over," she said. A shiver ran over his body. She flung down the rubber pad. A sheet, a new sheet, a clean sheet for her side fanned the night air over his wet body.

"Now this way."

He rolled over.

She got in beside him.

"Now go to sleep and shut up," she said.

She was not there in the morning when he awoke. The yellowed window shade flapped against the sill of the window set lopsided in the wall. His skin felt hot and stuck to the rubber sheet under his body. Someone stood in the doorway. Without moving his head, he looked up.

"Your mother's in the hospital. I've come to take you to The Oaks for a few days."

"Is my mother going to die?"

The foreigner shook her head.

Later, they told him he stayed with Clotilde Patout for several weeks, but he remembered nothing of it. Later, it seemed he had always had his own room in the big house, on the first floor, behind the left parlor, with a bathroom of his own, and the secret stairway to the second floor.

When they finally let him return to that other house where he had lived with his mother and father, he found twin boys lying in wicker bassinets in his room. They moved him into the living room, where he slept in front of the fake fireplace on an army cot. When company came, the cot folded in a hurry. He called out to her no more after that in the night, when he awoke twisted and wet in his sheets.

Later he found his bed at the bottom of the dried-up coulee, where his mother burned trash since his father, she said, wouldn't dig her a proper pit. The headboard was burned off. A spider had made a web in the top left circle of the box springs.

His mother seemed older, her body drained of life. She nearly died when the boys came, they said. She needed to rest, but the twins cried ceaselessly, long into the night, began again early in the morning, and kept at it throughout the day. His mother had headaches now. She cried every day. She said, if only I could get some sleep. His father did not hear the twins cry. He lay on his stomach, his right arm flung over the side of the bed, his mouth open and snoring bass in the symphony of cries.

Cato could see from his cot into his parents' bedroom. From a bracket on their bedroom door, clothes dangled from hangers and eclipsed his father. The view of his mother was unobstructed every night, he made sure by jerking the offending garment down, twisting it into a knot, and throwing it out of sight on the twins' closet floor, where it lay for months forgotten in the dark.

She never missed the articles he disposed of in this way. She said, when her husband accused her of squandering money on things she said she needed, but obviously did not judging from the way she treated them, that that was not *it* at all. Patout missed the most charming attributes of her character, she told Cato, those that made life bearable, such as this one.

"It makes life a continual Easter-egg hunt, Cato, don't you see? If I lose something and forget it completely, then when I find it, it's like having something new all over again. It's my way of having new things, since your father can't give me the money to buy them."

Cato saw that she extended her charming attribute, as she called it, to people as well as things. Sometimes, in a moment of reverie, he saw her start when he came into the room and struggle to identify him. Was this boy really hers? She was not quite sure for long moments on end, the great eyes of his mother told him, and he felt at such times such terror that, although unlike his father, he saw her point and admired the charming attribute, he was careful never to misplace things of his own. He developed a positive mania for neatness.

It was this helplessness in the face of the external world that made him watch over her at night until she was safely asleep. He carried her there in his arms, a phantom hovering over her frail body under its thin bed sheet, struggling to cross over into her own dreamlike realm, where people didn't question her motives. Not until he was sure she was gone did he turn over himself and fall asleep, the rough canvas scraping his skin through the bedclothes, reminding him even now on the verge of parting from life for the day that he was alone in the tight, boxlike house of the snoring man and his screaming children, but it did not, in the end, matter. She was asleep. He was certain. And now he was falling asleep, too. And he would smile to himself at the pathetic fears of the boy on the cot. The next thing he knew, it was morning.

On other nights, however, she fooled him, rising up suddenly on one elbow, pushing the hair off her face, and grabbing the bars of the headboard, just as he was about to turn over and go to sleep. She would sometimes stay like that for hours, staring out the window behind the bed, as though looking for something in the distant sky over Belmont.

Tonight her husband's snoring was unendurable in the hot, close room with Clotilde's magnolia fuscata sending its sickly sweet smell across the yard and into the open windows. Driven from her bed, she yanked her slip straps up, padded barefoot across the hall to check on the twins, and went into the living room where her son lay. Matthew and Andrew began to cry.

"Why don't they shut up?" she whispered. She sat down on the floor beside him and rested her head against the side poles of the cot.

He smelled the Lady Esther Cold Cream she wore on her face and neck every night. His father said she thought she wouldn't die like the rest of humanity as long as she slathered on cold cream. She didn't like him when he said that. He didn't notice. He said it once a week, regular as clockwork. Cato wondered if he oughtn't tell his father she didn't like it, though he liked to hear his father say it. It was a source of deep satisfaction to know his mother had something to keep her from dying. It helped him believe in their strength, for he felt they could get through anything in time, if she just wouldn't go off and die, like Sally Delcambre's mother last year, and before you knew it, the whole family had disappeared. It was horrible what could happen when your mother had no cold cream.

"I don't know what's worse, him and his foghorn, or his damn, screeching babies. Why don't they shut up? If they don't stop, they'll make me cry."

He patted her head gently. She was still sitting on the floor, her head resting against the cot.

"Know what I was thinking?"

He shook his head.

"We're going to get that house someday. They think they're going to set fire to it like it says in that will, but I've figured a way out. You've got to make that old woman love you, Cato. Then she'll write a new will and leave everything to you. As soon as she dies, we'll move right in. We weren't meant to live like this. I can't understand your father, his coming from nice people and all, putting his wife and children in a shack. That's what this nothing of a house amounts to. Why, Willie Wooten's even got a better house than this. You've got to get her to love you, Cato. Understand?"

"Yes, Mama," he said.

Then it was morning. He awoke to the stench of eggs being scrambled in the iron frying pan inherited from Janice Patout filling the house and sending him flying to the toilet to retch.

"Why?" she wanted to know.

"Bodies smell like that when they burn," he told her. His father appeared at the bathroom door.

"When did you ever smell a body burning?" his father shouted. He was red in the face.

His mother put out her hand and pushed her husband out of the bathroom.

A roach crawled out of the dirty clothes hamper and scurried across the pink linoleum. Cato stepped on it.

"Answer me, son!" he was shouting, like a man falling backwards off a cliff.

Cato, the bony version of the man in the body-building ads in the back of comic books, hung his head and prayed his father would go away.

His father shook his head. The floorboards in the hall groaned under his weight as he passed into the living room.

"Cato, you must try not to vomit," she whispered. "Least of all on Sunday morning."

"I don't see what Sunday's got to do with it," he said. They giggled hysterically, but he did see. She was scared that without his day of rest, the red-faced man would collapse on the floor and die and then where would they be—three children, no salary in the house, nothing but Clotilde Patout to rely on. And yet, he didn't think Clotilde Patout was so bad.

· 12 ·

*T*here was among other things her garden. He didn't think a thoroughly bad person would have such a place.

Sometimes he would sit under the ancient fig trees that grew along the side of The Oaks. It was his favorite spot, also favored by the chickens, and with the heat beating down on the fragrant leaves, and the smell of the soft dust left by generations of chickens scratching the hard soil to make nesting places for summer siestas, and the soft clucking of the contented chickens squatting in the lower branches away from the hot sun, he sometimes felt that strange sensation of belonging, of having his hard, human outlines erased, smudged like a charcoal line in a drawing, so that the person inside escaped, just ran off into the background and became part of all things in the world.

The fig trees, the patches of sunlight inching back and forth the length of the afternoon, the gentle breeze, the chickens softly clucking and he, all became indistinct from one another and were at peace and very still, as though they were waiting for something and afraid to think too hard about what it was lest their world go away. Way off in the distance he could hear Alphonse Romero's tractor chugging up and down the fields. A barge went by on the bayou, rammed the earth going around the curve too fast, and made the earth shudder, and all were one.

This is what he believed death felt like because rocks were dead, his mother said, and he felt at such moments exactly like a rock.

"What you doing in there?"

The voice shattered the moment. He lost the paradise in the dust under the figs with the white and red chickens. A black hand thrust through the cloven leaves, slapped the air both ways, latched onto his shoulder, and dragged the boy out roughly.

"Miss Clotilde ain't going to like that. Look at them elbows, boy. You ought to be ashamed. Hup, two, three, four. Hup, two, three, four." Willie Wooten marched him toward the back porch.

"Don't y'all think y'all's escaped," he yelled back over his shoulder. "I'm coming for you in a minute with a broomstick in my hands, y'all hear that?"

"Why don't you like the chickens in the figs, Willie?"

"Ain't clean, honey. Miss Clotilde don't want them chickens shitting on her figs. Now march. Hup, two, three."

He found her precise, exact, and sure of knowing how to do most anything.

"Take ferns," she would say to him as soon as he arrived on the gallery and sat down in the swing at the end. His mother could not see him there from the windows of their house. Tall green shutters and a thicket of banana trees shut her out.

"Are you listening?"

"Yes, ma'am.

"Now ferns . . . Don't fidget. If she wants you, she'll holler. Ferns, especially these maidenhairs, they're delicate things, you got to give them exactly what they want or they'll just refuse to grow. You gotta water them every morning early, before the sun comes well up—it's death to a fern to put water on it with the sun shining on the leaves—and you got to water them from below. They won't tolerate water on their roots—makes them rot out—so you put it here, in this little tray underneath and watch how much you put on them, just a tad too much and they'll rot out anyway. They don't hold with being drowned, you see. Whoa! That's good now, that's enough. Now this is a succulent. Succulents like . . ."

And down the row of plants on the gallery they would go, him watering from a rusty Maxwell House coffee can dipped now and again in a big bucket of water she filled from her own bathtub first thing in the morning, her lecturing as they went around, watching him every second to make sure he didn't give the plants too much or too little, putting out her hand and pulling his and the can back when the plants had had enough, steering him on to the next pot she wanted watered. She had a very deliberate ranking system whereby she gave them water and it had something to do with whether she liked that particular potted plant this morning, or whether she had decided she did not.

She didn't, he noticed, hold with plants that got sick and refused to get well. She was tenderness itself when a plant first got sick, looked a little limp, a little brown around the edges of the leaves, but watch out if it stayed low-down too long. Clotilde Patout didn't like plants that gave in to their sicknesses. He even suspected, though he couldn't prove it, that she withheld water from a plant that had let its sickness go on too long.

"I spec that tap water's not doing it any good," she would say, and the next day the ailing plant would have vanished. Sometimes it would reappear in another two weeks, full and green with new leaves, a convalescent plant, and he would be amazed and ask her how she did it, got them well.

"When a plant turns honery, the only thing to do is put it in the flower bed, child. If it wants to get better, it will; if it don't, it won't. Nothing in the world like rainwater to make things well."

But he still suspected she did it as a way of punishing the plants, hoping the rains wouldn't fall in time, and in such a way, he knew his mama was partly right.

· 13 ·

"Give it to me," Sophie said, squatting down.

Cato stuck out his right foot and nearly fell.

"Put your hand on my head," she said.

"Sophie! What's holding him? We won't make the bell." Cato looked over his shoulder. His father was pacing up and down on the porch.

"He's coming. Rev up the engine," his mother shouted. She patted Cato's shoe. "Now the other."

Cato gave her the left, being careful as he did not to press too hard on her head for, unlike the babies, she had a lot of hair and he couldn't tell where the soft spot was.

"For Christ's sake, Sophie. He's still got to pass muster with Clotilde."

"Sweetheart, did you hear the motor start yet?" his mother said.

Cato shook his head. His father cursed. A few moments later, the car door squeaked.

"Done!" his mother said.

Cato looked down. Encased in the new brown shoes with unbroken laces gliding in and out of the round holes, the feet seemed to belong to somebody else.

"Do you like them?" she said.

He nodded.

"Here." Her voice shook. She handed him a nickel. "Put this in your pants pocket. If you can't stand it, go to the little store in front of the school. Mr. Delcambre will let you call. I'll come get you, even if I have to crawl down that gravel road."

He nodded. The nickel felt nice in his hand, but he stuck it far down in his pocket.

"Now, let me look at you." She stood up. "My grown-up boy."

As she leaned over to kiss him, he threw his arms around her neck. She lifted him, new brown shoes, old satchel, long pants, nickel, and all. Their chests clung together like the two small magnets in the bottom of the cigar box where he kept his marbles. He could feel pain sucking them flat against each other.

"How I wish I could go with you today," she whispered. Slowly their bodies turned, then dipped and turned again. She began to hum.

"This is the First Grade Waltz," she said.

"Damn it, Sophie. Let go of him." His father's face was pressed against the window screen.

She put Cato down. "Scram, before your father has a hissy."

He walked to the screen door and turned. She was sitting on the bed next to the twins, folding a clean diaper.

The Studebaker honked two-toned, high, low, as though it were losing its voice. Once it made Cato laugh, but his father got angry and said it was just one more part he couldn't replace. The car would soon have to go.

"Mama?"

Her head jerked. She looked up, surprised to see him still there.

"Will you be all right without me?"

"For a little while, pet, but be careful. Remember, I couldn't live without you in the world. Go on now, honey. It's late."

She bent over the baby on the left, took the pin out of its diaper, and pulled the cloth away from the body.

"Pee-you!" she said.

The baby dimpled. Its mouth flew open in a soundless laugh.

Cato ran out the door.

"I wish *I* could afford new shoes," said the old woman in the big, black bed.

Cato backed up and ran into his father's legs. A hand came down and held Cato by the shoulder.

"Sophie spoils the boy, I'm afraid," his father said.

"No doubt," said Clotilde Patout. "Turn around."

Cato obeyed.

"Come here."

Cato hesitated. The old woman's silver-colored hair hung down the sides of her face. She looked like a piece of Wrigley's Spearmint Gum minus the silver wrapper, but unlike the gum on television, she couldn't get up and dance. She'd had another stroke. Cato hadn't seen her for over a month.

"Come here! What's the matter with you, Boy? Don't you remember staying with me while your maw was having those babies?"

"I expect he's just overly excited, Aunt Clotilde. It is his first day of school." His father gave him a push.

Cato inched closer to the bed. There was a honey-colored gun propped against the headboard.

"He looks right like Richard at that age," Clotilde Patout said. She lifted a bony finger, took aim, and shot Cato between the eyes. When she laughed, Cato saw there weren't any bottom teeth in her head.

"Doesn't have my brother's personality," she said.

Cato knew he was a bitter disappointment.

"Well, we'd better be moving along," his father said.

"Not so fast, Patout. Now you listen. You take him straight to Vera Wall. That's who's got the first graders in that new school over yonder. Vera Wall was my best friend's first cousin once removed. You tell Vera this boy is part of my family. I expect her to teach him something. Make sure he does his work, and if he misbehaves, she's to let me know." The old woman looked at Cato. "She's an old goat, but she can still make little boys jump."

"Yes, Aunt Clotilde. Come along, Cato."

"Don't rush me, Patout Minville. Come closer, Boy."

Cato's eyes darted to the gun.

"Give me that." She yanked the satchel out of his hands, threw it on the foot of the bed, and reached under the pillow next to her. "Here." She handed him a red leather satchel.

He took it from her shyly.

"Touch there," she said, indicating a tiny button on the shiny lock.

He put out his finger and poked it. The lock flew open at once. He looked up. The old woman was staring at him.

"What do you say, Cato?"

"Hush, Patout. Sometimes grown-ups don't have much sense, do they, boy."

He smiled.

"Well, I'm glad to see you're pleased," she said. "Never let it be said that I let a member of my family go off shabby to his first day of school. Here!" She kicked the brown satchel. "Better take the old one along. You can transfer your pencils while you're riding in the car."

"Thank you, Aunt Clotilde," he said.

"Nanan, not Aunt Clotilde. Where is that foreign woman. She ought to have been here with my coffee by now." She reached for her gun.

Cato jumped away.

The old woman laughed. "You scared of guns? Lord, I was shooting water moccasins with a twenty-two by the time I started first grade. As soon as I'm up and about, I'm going to teach you to shoot. Where is that foreigner anyway?"

"I'll get her for you, Aunt Clotilde. We're on our way out."

"No need. Go on. The boy is going to miss his bell. She'd have to be dead and buried not to hear this." She picked up the gun and gave the floor three hard whacks.

"I wish you every success in school," the French woman said, gliding past on the stairs.

"Thank you, Miss Françoise," Patout said.

The door to Clotilde Patout's room slammed.

"What's the matter with you, Cato. She's a nice woman. She likes you. You listen too much to your mother. Hurry up. Get in the car."

They traveled down the drive in silence. When they reached the dirt road, Cato turned around in the seat, got on his knees, and watched the little house by the ditch recede. There was no sign of life in the windows.

His father slapped his leg. "Get down. Start transferring your stuff. We'll be there in a minute."

"There's nothing inside," Cato said. The satchel lay flat and sad on the seat.

His father glanced at it.

"Why on earth are you carrying it then?"

Cato shrugged.

"Speak up. I can't hear you nod your head."

"Mama said everybody has to have a satchel when they go to school."

"Your mother." His father shook his head. "Paper and pencils might have been more to the point."

"Do I have to carry it?"

"You're darn tootin you do. Aunt Clotilde went to considerable trouble to get that for you. She must have arranged with Mary Louise Rodriguez to buy it. You're going to carry that bag and be proud of it."

"It's red," Cato said.

"That has nothing to do with it," his father said.

They were going around a bend in the road now and Cato was imagining his mother sticking herself with a diaper pin, when his father called out, "Thar she blows."

Cato looked out the window. A squat yellow building hugged the ground in the distance. An American flag danced on top. All the windows were square.

"That's Landry Elementary, son. The newest school in town. There was nothing but cane growing over there last year."

Sugar cane surrounded the school on three sides and as his

father drew up in front of the building and stopped, Cato saw that the school ground was still wavy, as though the neighboring fields had gotten tired of growing cane and run out from under the plants. There were no swings, no seesaws, or jungle gyms. There was nothing in the yard but sun-faded gray dirt and a red mongrel with his tail tucked between his legs, waiting in the heat at a side door for his child to come out.

"Cato, I don't care if the rest of them stand on their heads and scream, I expect you to stay in your desk and be quiet. They're just rough country boys and girls. You're a native of New Orleans. You know how to behave."

Cato saw the little store across the street. It had a sign that said SUNBEAM BREAD, HOMEMADE GUMBO. GROUND MEAT, 39 CENTS. It stood next to a house with a blue door.

The bell rang.

"Come on. You're late," his father said. They got out of the car and ran.

From the beginning, Cato did well in his schoolwork, except when it came to art. Miss Wall and his classmates made fun of his drawings—huge birds with great yellow claws and feet coming in for landings on tiny houses that could not support them, a giant mosquito captured in a mayonnaise bottle with an A&P label left on, held by a boy so small he could fit in the insect's eye.

"It's a matter of proportion, Cato. Don't you see?" said Miss Wall. She held up his picture in front of the class. "Joan Marie, what is wrong with Cato's drawing?" she asked.

Joan Marie Boudreaux lived with her grandfather in the bridgekeeper's shack next to the turn bridge downtown. Her legs were covered with mosquito bites and scratched-open scabs. None of the children would talk to her because, on the first day of school, Miss Wall had told the principal in their hearing that Joan Marie, who lived on the other side of the bayou, had no right to be in their school.

"Mr. Boudreaux insists on placing his granddaughter here," the principal said, "and technically, he's right. Since his kitchen hangs out over the water, he has the right to send Joan Marie to our school, along with the other children who live on the better side of the bayou." The principal touched a bruise just under his eye. He'd run into the new bookcase installed in his office in the dead of summer, but every child in the room thought, because they knew the bridgekeeper was a drunk—their parents always said so while waiting for Old Man Boudreaux to weave to the center of the bridge and turn the key for a barge to pass—Joan Marie's granddaddy socked the principal in the eye. She has no right to be in our room.

"Joan Marie Boudreaux? I asked you a question," said Miss Wall.

Joan Marie reached down, scratched her ankle, and smeared blood up her leg. "I never seen no purple mosquitoes," she said.

"But I suppose living that close to the bayou, you have seen mosquitoes that big?"

Miss Wall and the children burst into laughter.

One day just after the bell, Miss Wall entered the room, marched up the aisle nearest the inside wall, swatted Johnny Lefkowitz, and ripped September off the wall. As if by magic, the suffocating heat and gnats in their mouths disappeared. October came with clear, blue skies and a gentler heat, softened by a breeze off the gulf. Now Cato's birds, insects, and flowers grew smaller, until they were the size of boys and girls, but everything he drew was shrinking day by day. He could not stop it, though Miss Wall fussed. "You're going to put my eyes out," she said. She stopped inspecting his work. It was so small, she said, she couldn't see to comment.

Every day Cato carried the nickel in his pants pocket. Sometimes he longed to use it, but when he thought of his mother's knees torn and bleeding from crawling down the gravel road, he put it right out of his mind. Still, it was nice to know he could call with that nickel in his pocket.

The other comfort of his days that fall was the thought that he was a native of New Orleans. He had not known it before he started to school.

In spite of this distinction, Cato sometimes wished Clotilde Patout had left them alone. He felt like a boy in a box cut in two by a saw whenever he asked himself, who am I. There was his early childhood in New Orleans, and there was everything that came after Clotilde Patout had plucked her fat, black pen out of its marble desk holder and summoned them to Belmont. He would gladly have lived all his life in one place.

He thought the other children in Landry Elementary could close their eyes and see a long, unbroken tunnel going backwards until, reaching the edge of the void, All That Came Before I Came, they plunged off the earth's flat surface like the toy ships of Spanish explorers that sailed across the top of Miss Wall's mimeographed sheets. It distressed him that his own life was chopped in two, and he couldn't see any connection between the earlier boy and the one who came later. Cato could not remember New Orleans well, but he thought of that time with a happy ache.

One Saturday morning, not long after starting school, he asked his mother to tell him a story about when he was a boy in the city.

"Well, climb up in my lap," she replied. "Doesn't this feel like old times. What shall we have today?" she asked. "You want to hear about the time you crawled up in my lap and the cat jumped on top of you and the rocker went, plop! Or the day you fell into Audubon Pond trying to catch a duck? Or the time you went behind the counter in the glove department in D. H. Holmes and took off all your clothes?"

"The crayfish story, please," he said.

She began. "Once upon a time it rained all day and night

and the next morning a crayfish happened to be walking down Poydras when the rain started up again. 'Dear me,' said the crayfish to himself. 'I have forgotten my umbrella at home.' So pushing his big feet in front of him, for he didn't want them chopped off by the screen door, he scurried out of the rain and into the nearest house, where he crawled under the nice, warm blanket on Cato's bed and bit him. And that is how a scar shaped like the new moon came to be on the end of Cato's big toe."

When she was done, he went off by himself to ponder the adventure of the boy in the story, being careful not to stray beyond the new clothesline into Clotilde Patout's part of the yard. His mother said Nanan shot at dogs who wanted to use the bathroom in her yard.

He went to a thick clump of bamboo growing in the side yard. Listening for a moment, trying to decide if the rustling he heard was bamboo leaves or snakes, he dropped down on all fours, crawled and squeezed through the stalks, keeping one eye on the sharp-pointed daggers of the plant. Reaching the inner chamber at last—he believed he was the first white man to go inside this secret place, he didn't know about Indians and Negroes—he took off his right shoe and sock and touched the scar on the end of his toe. Feeling the crescent-shaped dent made his childhood in New Orleans less of a phantasy than his mother's vivid tale made it seem.

In the beginning of his life he had not been a worrier, but the coming of his family to Belmont, coinciding with the arrival of twin boys, not only transformed his mother, but changed him as well, until the days and months of his life ran together in one long somber note.

He tried to break loose from his serious moods and play lightheartedly, as he saw other children on the hard-baked clay of the schoolyard do, but his attempts to mimic them failed. He was stiff, wooden, and shy. His classmates frightened him, when there was not an adult nearby. When Miss Wall came out on the playground to supervise—Red Rover,

Red Rover was her favorite game—arguments broke out over who had to hold Cato's hand. Joan Marie Boudreaux would have been his friend, but he was terrified of catching the sores on her legs.

One evening when his father came home from work, he quizzed Cato about what he'd done that day.

"Who do you play with, Cato? You never mention any names."

Cato hung his head.

"For heaven's sake," his father said, "they've got so many kids in that school there aren't desks enough to go around. Every time I drive by I must see twenty boys sitting up on the sill. Don't tell me you can't find one little boy to play with."

"No, sir, but I'm just so tired all the time."

"Boy, how old are you now, six?"

"I'm six and a half, Daddy," Cato replied, regarding his father with his puzzled, solemn air. Patout burst into laughter.

"God help you, son, if you don't have fun now. Get out! Play with other boys."

"How can he when he's stuck out here in the country every afternoon after school?" His mother and father started to argue, and Cato slipped out of the room.

One night after a similar argument not long before all saints', Cato was lying on his cot in the dark, when he heard his mother go into the hall and ask the operator for the Mallard number.

Mrs. Mallard was the mother of one of his classmates. Her husband was dead. The previous winter Mr. Mallard had crawled into the grinders at the sugar mill to rescue a stray dog, when his supervisor came back from a coffee break and turned the motor on. Soon after Mrs. Mallard had joined the ranks of white women in Belmont who would baby-sit.

"Mrs. Mallard? This is Sophie Minville. I'm going to just have to go shopping tomorrow. My clothes are in shreds. Could you take Cato home with your boys after school?"

Cato put the pillow over his head. He hoped Mrs. Mallard would die in the night for demeaning her children with her job.

The next afternoon Mrs. Mallard took him and her boy, Bob, by the hand and waddled off the schoolyard. Her two older boys, Eric and Stan, lingered in front of the little store to throw oyster shells at classmates hiding in the ditch, screaming, "Eric and Stan have a sugar daddy. Eric and Stan have a sugar daddy."

"How'd you do in school today, children?" Mrs. Mallard's voice had a funny, tinny sound.

"I made a hundred on my spelling test," Cato said.

"Shut up, you," said Bob Mallard.

They walked in silence the rest of the way.

When the widow woman stepped off the sidewalk at last, taking him and Bob Mallard in tow down a worn path in the grass and around to the back of a small, weathered house on brick pilings, Cato's heart sank. I bet Mama doesn't know Mrs. Mallard doesn't paint her house, he thought, eyeing the peeling paint. The house looked like it had been rolled in white chocolate curls.

Reaching the back door, the Mallard boys pushed inside the kitchen ahead of their mother. They went immediately to the refrigerator. Eric, the oldest, opened the freezer, reached up, and felt around in the ice. Smoke curled down his arms. He took out three Eskimo Pies, handed them to his brothers, and slammed the door. They began to eat.

"Boys, mind your manners," the widow woman said in her weary voice.

"It's all right, Mrs. Mallard. They're just rough country boys," Cato said.

"Seems like somebody's too big for his britches," Mrs. Mallard said to her boys. She pulled open a drawer, took out a box of crayons, and slammed it on the table. "Y'all go on," she said, still talking to her boys. "Mr. Cato here probably likes to paint."

They ran.

She gave Cato some paper, went into the living room, pushed up the window, and yelled, "And stay on the sidewalk." Cato began to draw.

At five o'clock, when his father drove up, Cato was watching a green lizard try to decide whether to go up or down the downspout in the Mallards' backyard. He ran to the Studebaker, got in, and rolled up the window.

A few minutes later his father came out of the house, shoving his wallet into his left rear pocket. Mrs. Mallard followed him to the car.

"What do you say to Mrs. Mallard, son?"

"Thank you. I had a nice time," Cato said. He stared straight ahead through the windshield.

"I'm awful sorry, Mr. Minville. My boys are a little too rough for Cato. I thought it better to send them outside to play."

His father drove slowly through the street full of boys and girls on bikes, tricycles, and skates.

"Was Mrs. Mallard nice to you, son?" he said. His voice had a sad sound.

"She showed me her husband's tooth. He got it knocked out when he was a boy about my size. He forgot to put it in on the day he went to the sugar mill and died. She said that's all she's got left of him that wasn't squashed. I hate her. She has to baby-sit to feed her fat face."

Cato was sent to bed without supper as soon as they arrived home.

"Sophie, what I want to know is where he gets his high-and-mighty ideas from?" his father said. He was talking to his wife in the kitchen.

Cato couldn't hear what his mother said.

"So much for buying him playmates," was his father's reply.

After that, his parents allowed him to find his own friends. He withdrew himself now, he and his disproportionate body sprouting with its awkward limbs, as one does who feels he doesn't quite fit, even in the bosom of his family.

He bolted his food, got up, and left the table within five minutes of sitting down each night.

"Do you think we have rabies!" Patout would shout at his son's retreating back. He had noticed a change in his son, but thought it only natural. Boys need time to be alone, once they start to grow.

"You watch him start locking the bathroom door as soon as he finds his private parts," Patout said to Sophie one night after Cato had gone into the living room.

"Don't be filthy, Patout." She got up and cleared the table. "Cato should have more privacy, so should I." She sighed. She couldn't worry about her son's troubles. She was preoccupied with her own.

For hours at a stretch Cato would lie upon his back on the cot in the living room, which still served as a temporary bedroom against the time when his father could afford to add on an extra room. Knees crossed, kicking one foot continually in midair, he would read his well-worn Donald Duck until someone came into the room, then he would rise and leave.

His home seemed now all aclutter. The tiny prefab house down by the road was filled to overflowing with people, both large and small, and an enormous number of possessions each collected there. Whenever he tried to be alone, moving from one tiny room into another, some other presence had already beaten him there. He hated to be reminded of people, even when they weren't there, by stepping on their possessions. There by the back door on the pink and white linoleum lay a panda no bigger than his foot, its soiled red ribbon fraying on the ends. The double doors off the twins' plastic filling station seemed to say, please smash me to smithereens and grind my splinters into the rug. That blocked the entrance to the hall. In the bathroom his father's paperback mysteries and news magazines spilled over the sides of an unwinding basket and lay upon the floor, getting wetter and wetter with each bath and shower, printing the bottoms of the family's damp feet. Once Cato found a picture of a naked woman in cowboy boots stuck inside a *U.S. News and World Report,* and felt ashamed of himself, as though he had been spying on his father. And, wherever one went in the house was an endless procession of his mother's shoes, bracelets, earrings, and blouses.

When he complained, his mother cried out, "I know it's a rat's nest, but you find me one square inch where I can put another closet. This house wasn't big enough when your father built it, and now with the twins, it's hopeless."

Afternoons after school he often weeded the flower beds alone, handling Janice Patout's prized day lilies as tenderly as though they had souls, or trudged back to the chicken coop where, depositing his schoolbooks outside the flimsy gate, he would go inside and sit on a log with Flossie and Gertrude, until Willie Wooten wrung their necks.

And sometimes Cato visited with Clotilde Patout; his mother made him call.

· 14 ·

*H*e called her Nanan. She called him Cato, Boy, sometimes Butthead, or Stupes. Early on he learned she didn't take to fools.

If he said something silly like, "Nanan, why do gravel roads have nails?"

"They fall off trucks, Stupes," she'd say and cuff him on the back of the head. Stuff like that. That was the way it went between them.

Nanan said he had lots of things wrong with him, but she never mentioned nervous.

"How in the world," she was always saying, "did a kinsman of mine get to be almost seven years old without learning . . ."

How to shoot, ride a bike, skate, swim, shell peas, tie shoelaces, thread a needle, peel sugar cane, hold a machete, add and subtract like lightning, wash out his own underwear. These were some of the things wrong with him, and, there never was a dwarf named Rumpelstiltskin.

"Never in the whole wide world, Nanan?"

"Not even in Belmont. What kind of trash does that woman put into your head?"

That was another of Nanan's favorite sayings.

Every other Sunday when Cato and his father went to see the old woman in the bed, Cato waited for her to call his father by another name, too, but she never said anything but Patout Minville, Patout, or sometimes simply Him, when she was talking to the boy. Cato believed his father felt bad about that, for something came over him when he stood with his son in that room.

Holding Cato by the shoulder with his hat in the other hand, Patout Minville passed what he felt through his hand into the boy's body. Suddenly Cato felt himself fixed to the spot where they stood just inside the bedroom door, unable to turn his eyes away from the eyes on the pillow surrounded by lace and silver hair. Then the bedposts, already looming over his head, seemed to grow taller and inch toward the ceiling, while he and his father grew smaller. Startled, quiet, waiting, they stood, only a twitch in his left eye showing they were alive and not statues of rabbits in the middle of a field standing high upon haunches, blinded by the glare of a hunter's torch, a man shooting rabbits in a field after dark. Not fair, not fair, Cato wanted to shout, but the room was so silent.

His father would try to speak, to say what would release them unharmed, so they might go back into the Sunday afternoon sunlight to his mother waiting with the twins on the porch. But often, his father could not find what it was that would let them go, and Cato would know his father had failed when he heard the old woman laugh in her gasping, crackling way.

That Christmas before he turned seven, his mother fell sick and was taken to St. Joseph's Hospital in Belmont. After the ambulance drove away, his father called Mrs. Mallard to ask her to sit with the twins for the next several days. Then he rang the big house and asked Françoise Fischler if she could stay with the twins until he returned. When he got off the phone, he told Cato to pack.

I'm going to stay in the hospital with Mama, Cato thought.

When he and his father drove up to The Oaks, Françoise Fischler was waiting on the veranda.

"All right, get out, Cato. Here, don't forget this." Patout

reached behind him and pulled Cato's suitcase off the back seat.

Françoise Fischler stepped off the veranda and sat down in his place in the front seat. They drove away.

I guess he's going to take her to our house and then come back and pick me up, Cato thought.

"Ain't you coming in, Mr. Cato? The mosquitoes will get you," Ruby called through a crack in the front door.

"Thank you, Ruby, but my father's coming back for me. I've got to stay in the hospital with Mama."

The front door slammed.

A few minutes later it opened again. "Miss Clotilde, she say for you to come up and see her a minute. You can leave your bag right there. She says I'm to watch it for you while you go up. She'd be obliged if you'd go up cause she's been out of bed all day, and Dr. Rodriguez is going to be good and mad if she gets up one more time."

Cato looked down the long front lawn. His father had stopped in front of their house. Françoise Fischler got out. His father turned the car around in the drive and drove back into the road.

"Tell Nanan I'm sorry. My father's coming back for me right this minute. I've got to stay all night with my mama . . ." His voice trailed off. The turquoise Studebaker went past the long drive and disappeared.

"Cato, get in here, Boy."

He turned around. Clotilde Patout was standing in the doorway in her long white flannel nightgown. He walked toward her slowly, his feet sinking into the pea gravel.

"He forgot me. I packed my suitcase like he said."

"Ruby, you get his suitcase," Clotilde Patout said.

Tears ran down his cheeks.

"You're going to be staying with me for the next few days."

"Mama's expecting me."

"Get in here, Boy, no she's not."

"I hate you. Let go of me, you old bitch."

His face stung. He was being dragged down the hall running alongside the staircase. She is going to murder me and cut me into little pieces and put them in a hole in the ground like Mama said happened to her girl cousin when she was my age, he thought, imagining the coffee stains on the old woman's chest were blood.

"Miss Clotilde, you hadn't ought to be out of bed."

"Nonsense, Ruby. I've listened to that stupid Rodriguez long enough. The idea, a child saying that word. Doesn't even know what it means yet." Clotilde Patout pulled him into the bathroom and turned the faucet on.

"Go on, Ruby. Make the bed. I'll tend to this myself. The idea, not telling the boy, just dropping him off and leaving it to me. He ought to be horsewhipped."

Cato's head went under the faucet. Water poured across his face. A bar of green soap slid into his mouth. It tasted of perfume. His tongue suddenly seemed to fill the inside of his head.

"Eat," she said.

He took the ice cream meekly from her and spooned it into his mouth. It was good after the first bite washed the soap out of his mouth.

She sat down on the edge of the bed. The light from the lamp shaped like a horse fell on her chest. The stains were something else, but not blood.

"Cato, didn't Patout tell you anything?" the old woman asked.

Tears came into his eyes.

"Stop it. I won't have a crybaby in my house, sleeping on my clean sheets. Shall I tell you about your mother?"

He nodded.

"She had a miscarriage. Do you know what that means?"

He shook his head no.

"She was going to have a baby, but her body decided not to. When a woman's body won't hold the child, she has to go into the hospital for repairs, just like a car. Do you understand?"

"Why did she want a baby? We have two."

"Lord only knows. If she didn't know better, your father should have."

"Can I stay with Mama tomorrow night?"

"St. Joseph's Hospital doesn't allow children in under nine."

"Why?"

"Stop that sniffling, or I'll take you over yonder and let Mrs. Mallard deal with you. You want that, Boy?"

He bit his bottom lip and crossed his toes, until the feeling his tears would spill over stopped. He did not want to stay with Mrs. Mallard and her tooth.

"That's better. Because children under nine have no discipline. Now, what else do you want to know?"

There was a little girl sitting on a mushroom in the bottom of the bowl. A spider was about to touch her. I must warn her, Cato thought.

"Well, then, I have a question for you, Cato. What's a bitch?"

The boy looked up at her eyes. They glittered like those of the spider.

"Bob Mallard said it's somebody who doesn't get money from the rat when he puts a tooth under his pillow."

The old woman turned away. Her body was shaking. He reached out to touch her. She jumped.

"A bitch, Stupes, is a female dog. Now it's time for you to go to bed. Do you want to sleep with me?"

"No," he cried out.

She yanked the bowl out of his hands and walked to the door. "I hope we can be friends one day," she said and flicked off the light. The room was dark. A shaft of light from the hall fell on the bookcase.

"Help me, Ruby," he heard the old woman say.

"He didn't mean nothing, Miss Clo. He just miss his mama."

"He's got me, hasn't he."

"Now Miss Clo, that ain't the same thing and you know it."

The stairs groaned. The light went off in the hall. His room was dark. The long arm of the oak outside seemed to be reaching for the latch of the screen. The loud, slow ticking of the grandfather clock in the parlor said, "Ca-to, Ca-to."

The next morning he awoke to a knock on the door. He couldn't think where he was for a moment in this room by himself, silent and orderly, instead of the well-trafficked living room.

"Cato?" the foreign woman called. "Miss Clotilde is waiting for you at the breakfast table. Do you need help dressing?"

He pulled the sheet under his chin.

"She doesn't like to be kept waiting." Françoise walked away.

The following day Dr. Rodriguez came to get Cato and took him into town. He stood next to Cato in the parking lot of the hospital and pointed to a window on the fifth floor. Cato saw someone wave. The doctor said it was his mother.

"Satisfied she's alive?" Nanan said when Dr. Rodriguez deposited him at the front door. He did not like the way Nanan spoke when she mentioned his mother, but he didn't know how to stop her.

His father called from time to time and spoke to Nanan. He did not ask to speak to Cato.

As the days passed, he asked less about his mother. He missed her, but she was safe inside the hospital where he could not go. He was still frightened of the old lady, but trusted her enough by now to know that she told the truth. His mother was in the body shop for repairs. She would be home one day soon. He did not miss his father or the twins.

For one thing, he loved his room. "My own room," he slipped into conversation whenever he could.

"Nanan, was that horse lamp in my own room yours when you were little?"

"No, Cato. I thought I told you before. That lamp belonged to my baby brother."

"Did he sleep in my room?"

"He did."

"And did he like it as much as me?"

"What? The room or the lamp?"

He considered. "Both."

Clotilde Patout sighed. "Richard loved his room. . . ."

"You mean my room," Cato said.

"That's what I mean, your room. Richard loved the room that is now your room. He was proud because it has its own door leading off the back porch like that. He used to say"— the old woman closed her eyes and put her head back as though she were pulling it out of the air from a long time ago—" 'Clo,' he'd say, that's what he always called me. 'Clo, you don't even have a door to the outside in your bedroom, and you're the oldest. Do you want to change rooms?' "

"Why did he want to do that?"

"Because even though he loved your room, he loved me even more. Richard was a sweet, loving boy."

"I'd never give up my room to anybody," Cato said.

"And he loved that horse lamp because he won it in the parish horse show, the year they started the sugar cane festival. It was a statue, but daddy turned it into a lamp for Richard and put it by his bed one Christmas morning. When Richard woke up, it was there. Course, it was an oil lamp back then."

Cato had never heard of an oil lamp. He thought Nanan must have been very poor when she was a girl even though, his mother said, she had lots of money now and wouldn't share it with anyone.

When he began to feel more at home, he began to explore

beyond his room. One day hearing the grandfather clock rasp and strike the hour in the front parlor, he crept into this room where no one went, closed the mahogany sliding doors behind himself quietly.

Ruby, who had been taking a break to enjoy the logs, jumped up from the love seat, dust rag in hand. They stared at each other. Sweat glistened on Ruby's top lip. For all that they were fake, the logs did make the room feel warm. Then cool as a cucumber Cato said, "Nanan wants you, Ruby."

"You didn't come in here looking for Ruby."

He backed away.

Ruby flicked her rag over the sewing cabinet to the left of the fireplace. Taking her time, she worked carefully and moved slowly toward the door. "No, sir, no little white child going to fool me. Why'd you come in here, Mr. Cato?"

"I told you, Nanan's calling you," he said, backing into a table. A porcelain figurine fell on the floor.

Ruby clicked. "Now look what you gone and done," she said. She bent over and picked up the broken halves. "If I heard her once, I heard her a million times. Miss Clo, she say, 'Ruby, that shepherd boy and his dog is my favorite thing in the whole house.' "

The black woman was watching him out of the corner of her eye. He squeezed between a wing chair and the wall. She gave him a brilliant smile. "Now, Mr. Cato, I'll tell you what I can do for you. This here we're going to put right back like this, see?" She took the gum out of her mouth and stuck the dog back on the shepherd's right foot. "Lucky for you it broke that ways. Now I'm going to ax Miss Clo what she need, but if I was you, I'd keep out of here. One thing she don't forgive and that's somebody messing with her things. Miss Clo, she don't like a sneak."

Ruby put the figurine down, slid the doors back, and disappeared.

For a while after that, he confined his hunting to his own room. He wanted to go in the parlor and see if the shepherd

and the dog had come unstuck. He didn't like to think what
the old woman would do to him if she found it. He tried not
to think about it. His mother would tell him what to do when
she came home. Sometimes he discovered odd things in the
cabinets running along one side of his room. He found cards
of funny-looking boys dressed in shorty nightgowns, some
of them worn over pants that stopped at the knees, and high-
topped shoes. All the children in the pictures were doing
strange things with sticks in their hands and great O's in the
background. Some of the little girls held cats. The girls all
had big, shiny curls and blue eyes. The cats were always white
with pink inside of ears and ribbons around their necks.

He found bottles with lids screwed on tight and dust inside.
A top. A dozen of the funniest-looking marbles he'd ever
seen. They looked made of rock. He also found a packet of
playing cards with women on the front who looked like they
were wearing long T-shirts and his father's boxer shorts.
These Aunt Clotilde took away, saying, "I'm sure they didn't
belong to Richard. Probably one of the servants left them
here by accident."

She said when she and her brother and sister were young
there had been Negro servants for every room in the house.
"But no matter how many servants she had, Mama would
never let them make her biscuits," Nanan said. "I can remember most clearly, Mama in her kitchen, surrounded by
the Negroes, standing back while the Mistress kneaded the
dough. She had a big bowl the size of the bathroom sink.
She'd stand there and fight that dough for, seems like, an
hour. Course, being a little thing like you"—she glanced
down at him—"I'd get tired before she finished. I'd pull on
her apron—women wore long aprons back then, long white
linen things, flax made from right here off the land, and on
Sundays, or when there was company, the aprons would have
ribbons running through the lace edging on the bottom.

"Where was I? Oh, yes. Anyhow, I'd go over and pull on
her apron and she'd say, 'Mammy, take Miss Clotilde out of

here until I get through my batter.' And Mammy would, too, lickety-split. All Mama's servants knew to obey right this minute, not that she was unkind, but Mama knew the way she wanted things done. If one of the servants didn't obey right now, that servant was gone the next day."

"Why wouldn't she let them make the biscuits, Nanan?"

"Because she couldn't be sure their hands were clean, Butt-head. The Negro is a germy race."

Thereafter, whenever Cato didn't see Willie Wooten, Cato thought he must be down in his shack on the other side of the chickens washing his hands. Willie's hands were almost white inside from all the scrubbing.

"Do you think your mama would let Willie Wooten make biscuits, Nanan?" he asked several days later.

"Boy, don't you know men aren't allowed in a proper lady's kitchen? Of course, I can't vouch for your mother, but I'd have thought even she wouldn't make your daddy cook."

Best of all in Clotilde Patout's house was a secret stairway that led from the closet in his room on the ground floor to the dirty clothes closet in Nanan's dressing room on the second floor, and then wound its way up to the attic. Cato discovered the stairs one afternoon when he was supposed to be taking a nap. Not knowing how else to amuse himself silently, he remembered the strange shoes he had seen there, slipped out of bed, and peeked inside. The closet smelled mysterious and faintly wooded. He went inside, sat down, and had just pulled on a high-buttoned boot when Clotilde Patout called, "Cato?" He hid behind the clothes. She opened the closed door. He pushed so hard against the back wall that the secret door, which had been stuck for years, flew open, and he fell backwards onto the stairs.

She let him know she didn't like children who snooped. She ate ice cream in front of him at supper that night and didn't give him any. But now that the stairway was open again, she allowed him to play inside. He spent hours going up and down, crawling out of the dirty clothes closet in her dressing room, jumping out from the curtain into her bed-room, yelling, "Surprise! Did I scare you?"

Once when Dr. Rodriguez came to examine Clotilde Pa-tout, Cato hid inside and watched. When the doctor was done, the old woman wrote out a check and handed it to him. Then the doctor took out a roll of dollar bills and offered them to her. She waved him away. The doctor went to her dresser, opened the middle drawer, and stuck the money inside. Cato crept back into the dirty clothes closet and down the stairs as silently as he could. When the doctor came down-stairs, Cato was waiting at the foot to say good-bye.

· 15 ·

One morning not long after, Cato peeked from the dressing room and saw Clotilde Patout in her rocker near the window. She was bent over, cutting something from a newspaper. "Cato, come here. I've got something to tell you," she said without turning around.

Crestfallen, he pushed the curtain aside and stepped out. "How did you know it was me?"

She waved her scissors at the dresser. Their eyes met in the mirror. He went over to her and leaned in. Keeping outside the heavy black border, she wacked off a thin strip of newsprint. It curled and dropped on the Bible in her lap.

"What you doing?"

"What's it look like, Stupes." She glanced at him sharply, then relented. "It's Sister's obituary I'm saving."

Her hair was down and bushed wildly about her shoulders. She looked different, strangely new, almost someone he could ask to play, like the 100-Year-Old Girl his parents had once taken him to see at a roadside stand where they stopped to pee, maybe when they came to Belmont from New Orleans. A short, frilly dress, a bow in her hair, and lots of thin, loose skin hanging off her legs above the knees, she sat very still in a little room behind a rope. On the table next to her, baby alligators squirmed in a jar biting the glass. He thought she must be very tired of just sitting there, but his mother jerked him away and put him back in the car with his father clutching the steering wheel, saying, "That's it. No more stops. I don't care how weak his bladder is." It sounded like a song.

The hair looked soft, inviting. He put out his hand to touch.

It was dry and dead as Spanish moss lying on the front lawn after a storm.

"Yours will be like that, too, someday." She turned the corner, trimmed down the left edge.

"No it won't."

"That's what I thought when I was your age. The Lord protects the innocent, I suppose." There was black ink on her nose. "Done!" she cried. The Bible slammed shut. "Now bring me my brush and I'll tell you."

Bristles up, a plastic comb stuck in its face, the brush sat in the place of honor on the dresser in front of the clock.

"Leave the comb," she added, seeing him start back with both.

He took heart and lifted the greasy black comb. White flecks and loose hair rained on a strawberry with black bead seeds.

"Go ahead. You can touch," she said, cackling when he cried out. "It's a pincushion, Stupes. I thought you knew." She always laughed like that when she fooled him and kept her eyes on his face until he joined in. "Pshaw, Boy." She dabbed at her eyes. "Now that thing's a buffer. Bring it. I'll show you." She took it from him, swung it briskly against her fingernails. "Women do this to make them look nice. See? Turns them pink." She held them up.

"Mama paints hers pink," he said.

"I know what your mother does, but in my day respectable ladies didn't paint. Give me your hand. Come, Butthead. Would I trick you?" She chuckled. He watched her and slowly held out his hand. The soft chamois pad swished back and forth. His fingertips tingled.

"Like it?"

He nodded.

"Put it back, but be careful. That was my mother's. I want you to respect old things."

"Daddy says things are not important, people are."

"Your father ought to know better," she said.

"Mama says so, too."

"No doubt she does, but then, she's never had nice things," then seeing she had gone a bit too far, "Anyway, women just repeat what their men say when it sounds good."

On the dresser scarf exactly where he had found it, he set the buffer down. A faint, sweet smell rose up. Uncle Richard, stuck in the mirror frame, held up a garfish. The frame was full of relatives. Clotilde had told him their names. Whenever he asked about anything in the house she would say, "That belonged to Charles—the one in the uniform, second from the left," or, "Lelia won it for elocution in tenth grade"—as though they were still alive. She wanted him to know family history. He'd rather have known what it felt like being dead. He addressed them silently, thinking one day they might look down from their silvery height and speak to this kinsman without gar, pipe, or wicker chair. Reaching the crest of the curved frame, going back down the other side, he searched for a flick of recognition from at least one pair of the fixed eyes.

She leaned forward. The rocker creaked. "Like 'em?" she said.

He shrugged.

"You don't know how fortunate you are, Butthead. Just think, you might have been a Mallard. Instead of your father, why, you might have gotten Willie Wooten. That should make you thank your stars."

"How come nobody likes them, Nanan?"

"I don't know. Some questions don't have answers. I don't like the uppity ones either. People ought to accept what destiny brings. All this nonsense about sitting in the front of the bus isn't going to change the color of their skin. But I'll tell you what, Boy, if I was one, I'd be the meanest Negro on the face of this earth. I wouldn't stand still and let people treat me the way they treat them." She leaned forward in the rocker, sizing him up.

"Now you listen to me, Boy. Someday The Oaks, all the

people on the land, and everything in it will pass to you. You will have to care for it after I am dead and gone. No one else shall. If Richard had lived, it would have been his, but I try to believe things work for the best. You are like Richard in some ways, but he had a wild streak that wouldn't break. He might have gone on dissipating, like Father in his last years, until there was nothing left, no trace of the family that has lived and died on this land for a hundred fifty years. Now that may be a burden you don't want yet, but it's a duty you can't escape. You'll grow into the role in time. You're not the sort to violate trust. People rise to the occasion when they are last."

He did not want to be last. If they disappeared, he would hide in the bamboo until they came back, or Willie Wooten took him away.

"Come here," she said, gruff.

"Did I do something wrong?"

She pulled him to her. He was enveloped in the faint sweetness he had smelled before. A cowbell tinkled nearby.

"I'm glad you're alive, Cato."

"I'm glad you are, too, Nanan." She laughed and released him. He wondered if he had lied.

Her mood changed. "And I'm glad your father was born," she went on, almost gay.

"Mama, too."

"Well, everybody has to have a mother, I suppose."

He pulled away. "Mama says you don't like her."

"She shouldn't say such things to you."

"Do you?" He touched the ink on her nose. She snapped. He jerked his finger back and giggled. "Do you?" he insisted.

"Sometimes people don't start off straight, Cato. A crooked beginning is hard to change, no matter how much you try. In case you didn't know it, neither your maw nor I is long on trying. Course, I could be, but your mama's a redhead. Redheads are stubborn."

"Me, too."

She studied him. "Your hair is almost brown now," she said, "but a true redhead, well, she won't take no for an answer. I ought to know. A redhead once came that close"—she held up an inch—"to getting her hands on my mama's nice things, not that she'd have had any use for them. That woman never drank tea out of china in her life. Sister and I knew the minute Daddy married her she'd make him sell The Oaks lock, stock, and barrel."

"What for?" he asked, eyes wide with wonder.

"To give the money to her pastor. She was a religious woman, always in church, if you call going to a meeting in a tin hut going to church. Honestly, every time you turn around the Protestants hatch a new religion. Your maw's a Protestant, isn't she, Boy?"

"Mama doesn't go to church. She says the people are hypocrites."

"She should try Catholics. Better class of people."

"What happened to the woman?"

"The Seventh Dayer? Went off to where she came from, tail between her legs—Texas, Mississippi, some faraway place like that. The moral of that story is watch out for redheads and don't let your menfolk mingle with foreigners. Remember that when it's your time to marry."

"I'm never going to marry."

"That's what most men think."

"If I did, I'd want her to be like Mama."

"Good Lord, the boy doesn't listen."

"Would you like her better if she changed her hair?"

"You miss the point. I'd like her fine in somebody else's family. Anyway, like her or not, I'm taking you to see her."

"You are?" he cried, greatly excited. "When?"

"Directly. Your father is coming to fetch us. A nuisance, busy as he is, but they've hidden the car keys from me and Willie can't drive."

"What if they catch me inside?"

"Guess they'll put you in jail." He backed away from the

rocker. She laughed. "Goodness, Boy, can't you tell when folks are teasing? Confidence, Butthead, that's what's lacking. Scared of your shadow. Rodriguez arranged it with St. Joseph's. He and your father think seeing you will cheer up your mother. I don't think it's wise, but they don't listen to me. Go on now. Wash your face, comb your hair. Patout will be here any minute, so move. We'll work on the confidence later." She threw back her head. "Ruby!" she yelled.

He did as she told him and when he had finished, quickly stuffed his pockets with things he hoped his mother would like—fossils found in the drive, the dried, brown crust of an insect still clinging to a twig—and headed for the front hall where the ceiling creaked to the old woman's movements above. Behind the closed doors of the parlor, the grandfather clock rasped, then struck the half hour. He went in, shut the doors quietly. The shepherd and his dog still clung together on either side of the thin crack. He squeezed between the chair and the wall. Lace curtains divided the front lawn by snow flakes and squares.

He had not seen his father in days. When Patout Minville called, usually the French woman or Ruby answered. This morning both had been outside doing chores and Clotilde Patout instructed him to answer. The familiar voice made his words stick. "Let me speak to Clotilde," his father said, angry. He immediately passed the receiver.

A turquoise sedan turned in the drive. Cato's heart leaped. The car stopped in front. Cato pulled the curtain back. His father slammed the door, went around the back of the car, and approached the veranda. An old blue windbreaker, the sleeves turned back, flared gracefully above his wrists. He was carrying a clipboard in his left hand, as he always did now that he was manager of the chicken plant. He held a large bunch of keys with his thumb against the board. He came up the steps. Cato saw everything he remembered: the wristwatch with its rusty face, the tan-colored band that matched the color of his father's hair, the way the pleats at his waist pulled apart, the small protrusion his father said was prosperity. His father was a beautiful man.

He ran to the door and opened it. "Hello, Daddy," he said, shy.

"Your shoes are caked, Cato, and for God's sake, find a pair of socks with elastic not worn out. Surely you have them? Every time I turn around I'm buying socks and underwear. And take the stuff out of your pockets. What have you got in there, rocks?"

When Cato returned, his father was depositing Clotilde Patout in the car.

"What kept you? Visiting hours will be over before we get there." He pushed Cato toward the other side, motioned him to crawl under the steering wheel, and sat down before Cato could move to the center.

"Don't be so rough, Patout."

His father slammed the door.

"He's got to learn to move when I say so, Aunt Clotilde. Energy, that's what he needs. I never saw a boy so dreamy."

"I think you might accomplish the same results more effectively in a different way." She raised her chin.

His father held his mouth as though he were trying to break a nut in his teeth. He drove past the pompom bushes, out the drive, and picked up speed. The old woman stared straight ahead.

"I don't approve of this visit," she said. They had just passed the town dump.

"I know you don't, Aunt Clotilde."

"Someone is too susceptible. I do hope nothing will be frightening?"

"Look, she's physically fine. No tubes, no machines, nothing like that. We've got to break this mood. St. Joseph's doesn't handle depressed patients. They won't keep her much longer. Rodriguez recommended a visit from Cato. He's a doctor—"

"I never believe what doctors say."

"Well, we're going, so that's that."

"Suit yourself. Never let it be said I interfere in your family, Patout, but you have left me in charge. I am the one who will suffer should he become distraught, so I would have thought you'd consider my feelings."

"I do consider your feelings. So does she, Aunt Clotilde. But she needs to see him badly. I'd take him myself, but I can't stay. I've got to get back to work. Please, will you do this one thing—"

"I'm in the car, aren't I?"

"Why can't you do it gracefully. What've you got against her? Do you realize you've never said one positive thing about anything we've done since we moved to Belmont?"

Cato looked from one to the other.

"May I suggest we change this conversation?"

"Fine, that's fine with me, Aunt Clotilde. I do appreciate all you've done. I didn't mean to—"

"Just drive, Patout. Don't run at the mouth."

Nanan had stiffened in her seat. She held her shoulders erect, clutched her purse. His father's face turned the color of ground meat. Heat came off his body.

They drove in silence. Cato did not move. He held his arms stiffly in front of him, trying not to kick Nanan, or brush against his father when they went around a curve. The car left the dirt road and swept onto pavement; a deep drainage ditch ran alongside. His father picked up speed. Clotilde withdrew the handkerchief from her sleeve, blew her nose, tucked it back in the cuff.

"Patout, I want you to know I am proud of you."

Gravel shot across the drainage ditch. Patout Minville straightened the wheels. They looked at each other. Their faces relaxed. Cato looked from one to the other. He kicked under the dash.

"Stop that," his father said.

"I never thought," the old lady went on, "you'd have that

little house built so fast, and here you are, already manager of the chicken plant."

Patout grinned. "I must admit," he said, "I like being boss."

"Yes, it presages great things to come."

"The plant's going to expand, maybe set up a smaller division in the next parish. I might make general manager someday, you never know."

"Now Patout, that's fine they want to expand, but I certainly hope you'll lift your horizons someday. You're young still, with a growing family. This smart little boy will be ready for college before you know it. He deserves the best education we can buy. Perhaps it's time you started looking around for a job with more prospects."

"But I like my job."

"One must reach for the unattainable and, if one is a Patout or Minville, the unattainable often comes true. It wouldn't hurt to ask around town. With our family's connections, you never know what might turn up."

"I don't know, Aunt Clotilde. Sophie's been mighty pleased with me lately. This is the first time since we married I've had a steady income, and—"

"Does she have so little ambition?"

"We have seen some lean times."

"I hardly think it manly to be led around by your wife, Patout. Besides, she hardly has had your advantages?"

"Advantages?"

His father was shifting badly. The car bucked as they approached an intersection.

"Advantages," the old lady went on. "Where did she come from? Who is she? Who were her people?"

"Please, Aunt Clotilde."

A car with a raccoon tail stuck on its antenna was coming from the left. Cato screamed. His father jammed on the brakes.

"What's the matter with you, Cato." His father slapped

his leg. "Get in the back. You almost made me have a wreck."

Nanan put her arm around him. "Advantages, Patout, you heard me right enough."

They went on and on. Now a tree loomed overhead. He wondered what his mother would say when she saw him come into the room. She would smile. She would hold out her hand. Cato, she'd say. Cato, my little man. She always said that. He was big now, but she still said that. He didn't mind as long as Mrs. Mallard's boys weren't around. Why did Nanan and his father have to go on and on? Nanan was saying his father did not make enough money to put him in military school, military schools built men. He thought of red jackets and long toy guns, a hat with a huge black plume, and a whistle. His father was laughing, out of control, saying, can you imagine him in military school? And she was saying it was part of tradition, fitting a son of the family, that was what was wrong with him, he had never learned discipline, and this time his father jammed on the brakes and they sat there on the side of the road, just inside the city limits, in front of a house where chickens ran around the backyard, and they spoke of nothing, and he wondered will I ever see Mama?

· 16 ·

"Why look who's come to see you, Mrs. Minville," said Miss Breaux, the nurse in a cap with wings. She poked a spoon down her patient's throat.

Patout pushed Cato forward. As though postponing what he must see, he approached the bed slowly, guided by strands of red hair on the pillow, and whispered, "Mama?"

A white arm flopped out, pulled him down. He straightened and wiped off kiss.

"Sticky. Medicine," said her mouth at the blanket hem.

Unkissed in a fortnight, Patout came forward, put his son aside, and leaned over a face turned away.

"Miscarriage affects some women that way, Mr. Minville. You really must try and be patient."

Patout made for the door, Miss Breaux in tow.

"I've got to get back to work," he said stiffly, stealing a glance at his wife. Her face was now turned toward the window.

"Oh yes, the chicken plant, isn't it?" Miss Breaux giggled, not because the plant was funny, but she was reminded of the house next door where an old colored woman painted faces on fence slats of people killed in car crashes all over the state. Beyond this exotic gallery and down a dirt road, Miss Breaux had done it for the first time in her life when fifteen years old, and she was in high spirits for other reasons today, chiefly having to do with the handsome fellow just spotted in the waiting room, but it was unfortunate she had giggled when her patient's husband said chicken plant, him being the manager and all.

"Oh, sir," she called him to make amends, "you've forgotten to give your wife her pretty flowers."

"Her son can give them to her."

"There now. Shall I put them in water? We've a lovely vase bought special in Woolworth's only yesterday."

"And how do you reckon to get us home?" Clotilde's head stuck through the door.

There was a slight commotion as he tried to get out. Clotilde didn't budge. Miss Breaux, waving bye-bye to Sophie and Cato, bumped into his back. "Oh, do pardon me," the nurse said.

"Rodriguez'll take you," Patout said.

"Oh, sorry, sir. He can't. His colored patient is having her baby early."

Clotilde jerked her head down the hall. Miss Breaux, in no uncertain terms, was given to understand the pleasure of her company was wanted no more.

"Well?" Clotilde said.

She and Patout were in the corridor outside the closed door. A card on the door said SOPHIE MINVILLE. A baby in blue matched one in pink on the opposite corner.

"My God, you'd think they'd have the decency," Patout said. He reached up.

"You'll have to come back and pick us up after your errands. Don't be long. You can return to the office later."

His hand fell back, the card intact on the door. "Oh God," he said, "why does everything have to be so complicated."

Down the hall in the orange waiting area, Jesus was indicating his bleeding heart next to the Coca-Cola machine. The sun shone momentarily, turning everything orange, including Pugie Reaux, who was rising from a plastic chair. Patout's face lit up.

"Why is that man lurking around here, Patout Minville. Did you call him?"

"Of course not, Aunt Clotilde, but he may be just the man."

"I won't ride with him, Patout."

He moved with the determination of a man freed from a meddlesome connection, guilty joy in his step for being rude to the old lady, whom he linked to the one in the bed, Cato between them.

"Howdy, Pat. How's the missus?" Pugie held out his hand as Patout came up. "You okay? Looking white around the gills."

Patout blushed hot, dropped keys, bent over and stuffed them in his pocket. Clotilde jealous as hell of Sophie. The tip of a key stuck out a hole in the leg. And vice versa. "Appreciate your stopping by, Pugie," he said. It would serve them both right if he walked off one day.

"Hey, boy, what're old friends for?" Pugie slapped him on the shoulder, shifted his gum.

"Look, I hate to ask. I mean, you're the only one who's so much as bothered to look in, but—"

"Shoot, man. Spit it out. Where you and the missus are concerned, what you need, just ask."

"Could you stand taking"—he jerked his head in Clotilde's direction—"and my son home? They're going to be kicked out in half an hour."

"Sure, Pat. No problem."

"I hate to ask."

"No apologies between friends. My pleasure."

"I'd hardly call it that."

A slow smile spread across Pugie's face. "Who her?"

"Yes, her."

"Hell, man, that old biddy don't bite. I been telling you that since we were—how old? Anybody wanna buy hubcaps real cheap?"

They laughed in a mischievous way. Patout's face flooded with memory.

"Get a load of that hat," Pugie said loudly. Miss Breaux put her nose in the air, walked by with a blue bedpan.

"Looks like she got a cob up her ass. Be seeing you, Pat." He sauntered down the hall.

"Later, Pugie."

"Yeah, later, Pat."

"Good morning, Miss Clotilde," Pugie said.

Clotilde glared with obvious distaste.

"Or is it afternoon?"

"Mightn't that orange spot provide a telephone? I suppose taxis still run in this town."

"Suit yourself, Miss Clo. No skin off my nose you take my ride or not, but it's going to cost you a mint. First floor, only pay phone in the building. Got any nickels in that old-lady bag?"

She hiked her purse under her arm, held on tightly with the other hand, and stumped away, nothing inside but a mended hankie with Sister's monogram, empty coin purse, and a torn envelope with things to pick up at the grocer last June. Lurching for the banister, she lowered herself slowly down the stairs, unaware that Pugie was watching the flat back of her head sink out of sight.

Without further to-do, Pugie put his hand on the door and pushed. "Howdy, Boy. How's your maw?"

Cato's mouth opened in a perfect "O."

"Well, Mrs. Minville, aren't we the popular one today," said Miss Breaux, carrying a Styrofoam pitcher to the bathroom.

"Get him out of here," her patient said.

"We're not going to send our guest away just yet?"

Sophie pulled the blanket over her head.

"Really, Mrs. Minville. Women have miscarriages every day."

"Get him out. God, the nerve of him. Cato, please, make him go." The room filled with muffled sobs.

Miss Breaux, pushed by small hands, reached up to secure her cap. Cato inserted himself between her and Pugie Reaux.

Pugie held him off like a troublesome dog and considered the lump in the bed. Then softly, with a trace of sadness, he said, "If you ever feel you need me, you just have to ask,

Mrs. Minville. I think you know you can count on me." The door sighed shut.

Miss Breaux collapsed in the easy chair.

With patient authority, Cato went to the bed, pulled back the blanket, put his arms around his mother, and let her sob.

When Miss Breaux left a few minutes later, they were still like that—the boy holding her, stroking her forehead, his mother sobbing—and she came out saying to the hall, "That boy's going to have problems later." Her cushioned comfort walkers squeaked to the nurses' station at the opposite end of the corridor.

Sophie stretched out her hand, touched his cheek. "My precious boy. It seems a miracle I could have had something as beautiful as you."

The boy's eyes shone.

"I used to talk to you when I was pregnant, did you know that?"

"Yes, Mama."

"I fancy you heard, even then." She made a face. He shifted her pillows.

"Want some ice?"

She shook her head. "Hold my hand. Let me talk. I haven't had anybody I could talk to in days. Sit still, darling. They'll come and take you away from me soon."

He waited for her to begin, but her eyes assumed a faraway look.

"Daddy brought flowers," he said, hoping to bring her back.

She peered at the mirror opposite the foot of the bed, flopped back. He pushed her hair from her face. It came away wet. Rain fell. They watched together through the huge window. She shivered. He found a plaid throw from home and spread it over her chest. "Do you hurt?"

She shook her head. "Who does he think he is, dropping by to see a lady he hardly knows? Smacks of a liberty. 'If you ever feel you need me.' How offensive! If he really knew me, he'd realize all I need is my son."

"Can you come home soon?" The boy's face, so like her own, was cut of all angles and trembling.

"I wish my father could see you, Cato. He's dead for all I know. Won't lift hand to pen. I had no family after he remarried. That's why I was happy when you came."

Clotilde stuck her head in. "Five minutes. I'm by the Coke machine. Mr. Reaux is taking us home. Get in the back with me, understand? We're not going to ride on the same seat with that man. Hello, Sophie." The head disappeared.

Cato looked at his mother. Her eyes wore the faraway look again. "Mama?"

Her name came across a great expanse of time and space. She remembered her mother's voice calling across the yellowed grass of their yard, down the red earth gully and out beyond the wide, flat fields gone to weed and full of snakes and all manner of silent, crawling things, until it came to her place under the pines where she hid afternoons after school. Her mother had been afraid of the field. She would not cross anything that covered her knees, she said, and she an American Indian, even if not full bred.

"Mama?"

What a pleasurable sensation—awakening to someone trying hard to get your attention. It made her feel like visiting royalty, going away into her own world and finding in that first, brief moment when consciousness pulled her back, the face of someone she knew, oh, all too well, frantic with fear in his eyes, that she, his beloved, had gone out of reach and left him alone forever. It always made her want to yell, Surprise!, but that would have spoiled the drama.

"Mama? I have to go."

There it came again, that name she must sometimes respond to, but wasn't it wearisome.

"Yes?" came out a long, expressive sigh, filled with despair for this house, this man, this life, the loathsome old woman who stood between them and a new life. "Yes, Cato?" Now she was fully awake. "Clotilde can wait," she said.

"Please get well."

"I'm not sick, darling. Just blue."

"About the babies?"

She looked at him sharply. "I expected you of all people to understand."

"Don't be angry, Mama."

Her hands picked at the blanket hem. The satin was frayed and opened. "You know I feel three children is more than enough."

"Can you come home soon?"

"If I could, I'd go down to the parking lot this minute, find a car with the keys inside, and head for New Orleans before anyone could stop me."

He lay down next to her, pressed his head against hers.

"My God, how does it happen? I spent the first eighteen years of my life trying to get out of a wretched little hole like this. You don't know how it scares me, Cato, coming into town on that back road, looking out the car window, seeing all those ticky tacky little boxes, knowing the people inside just live and die and they don't know what they're living for, and then when the car heads back the other way and we round that last bend and I see the box we're living in, I feel frozen with fear I'm just like them.

"God, I'm stupid. I don't even know what I'm saying. I just thought it would be different and now we're stuck in this one-horse town and your father acts like he's so damn happy. How can he be? He wanted to write poetry, be some-body, not manager of a chicken plant. People snicker behind our backs."

"No, Mama. I don't hear them. Please don't leave me."

"Clotilde Patout, richest woman in town, and her nephew builds on her front yard. Can't even afford a piece of land. I can't stand the smell of him when he comes home and lies in bed next to me. No matter how he washes, he smells of chicken. Burned feathers. Like dead people burning! Remember? You said that once. We're so alike. You hate him, too. I see it sometimes in your eyes. There now, oh darling, I didn't mean to scare you." She pulled the boy down on her chest and held him tightly. "Don't worry. I'm not leaving. It takes money to set up a new life. We're going to have to stay put as long as Clotilde Patout holds out."

"You'll take me with you?"

"Now what do you think?" She squeezed him tightly.

"Twins, too?"

"Bother the twins."

"Just you and me?"

She nodded, pushed him to the side. He was hurting her breast.

"Tell me a story."

"I'm exhausted."

"Tell me about the red window."

She caressed his cheek. He knew the story by heart.

"Go on, Mama."

"All right, but blow your nose first. Ouf!" she said as he slid off the bed. "Hurry. Clotilde's probably having a stroke." When he was settled, she began.

"When I was a little girl, I lived in a big, old house my great-granddaddy had built on the edge of town near a creek. The house faced the creek, because in those days before roads, everybody traveled by water, though the creek had gone dry long before I came into the world. Anyway, being a wealthy man, why, when it came time for great-granddaddy to build his house, he wanted the front to be especially grand, so he sent all the way to New Orleans for a ruby-red fanlight to go above the door. When I was a child I used to stand in the hall and gaze up at that ruby-red window by the hour. I thought it was the prettiest thing in the world, until I started school. The little boy and girl who lived next door, their family ran the gas pump and had all kinds of money, told everybody I lived in a house where the front yard was the backyard, and I went home that afternoon and threw a rock through the fanlight and made my mama cry."

His face was a mask of horror. "I'd feel bad if I made you cry," he said.

"You never will, Cato."

"Sophie Minville, let the boy go. The hospital wants us out now. They bent the rules as it is." Clotilde pulled the boy away.

"Good-bye, precious," she called. The door shut. It was then he remembered he hadn't asked what he must do about the broken figure in Clotilde Patout's parlor.

17

*E*arly in the morning on the day before Christmas, Françoise Fischler stood in the depleted vegetable garden at The Oaks and stared at a winter onion dangling in her hand. Ebbing life, the onion bore a strong and pungent smell that reminded her of her grandparents' garden near Strasbourg, where she and her brother had played long afternoons into the evening before the war.

She wondered if her brother remembered running through the onions to make them smell before going in at night, and immediately felt annoyed with herself for caring. Jean-Claude would not remember the childish prank. He scarcely recalled having a sister. Perhaps she should ask herself why this child-hood game still lived in her mind, but she knew why. It was a game they invented together, carried out in spite of their grandparents. She had loved her brother. Once they were the most important person in each other's life. She could not believe love would disappear without a trace, leaving only formal politeness in its place.

She lifted the onion and took a deep breath. There's something Egyptian about onions, she thought.

This was her second Christmas in Belmont. This year as last neither the land, climate, nor the people among whom she was living hinted of the spirit one usually associated with the season. The day was hot and growing hotter. On the other side of the chicken coop singing rang from a machete. No decorations had been put up. Even Cato, playing by the bamboo growing on the side of the Minvilles', seemed strangely unexcited for a boy on Christmas Eve.

He's nothing like Jean-Claude at that age, she thought. Always tense and unnaturally quiet, he seemed more so with his mother still in the hospital.

Françoise swatted a bug, caught a glimpse of red T-shirt in the bamboo, and looked away. He would hate his hiding place being discovered.

She threw bean poles aside, bent over and picked another onion out of the weeds. She was determined to bring cheer into The Oaks tonight. The child needed it. It would be good for all of them. She felt almost elated at what she was about to undertake, even if no one else cared. A shadow fell at her feet. She straightened, shielded her eyes from the sun, and found Willie Wooten waiting at the garden edge.

"Morning, Miss Fran-swaws Fishes."

She smiled at the charming absurdity he made of her name. "Good morning to you, Mr. Willie Wooten. I heard your machete. Cutting weeds?"

"Nome," he said, unhappy.

Now what, she thought.

"You starting up onions here?" Willie asked.

She laughed. "The reverse, actually. I'm pulling them up. I will undertake gumbo, a surprise for dinner tonight. It is Christmas Eve." She bent over and plucked another onion out of the soil.

"Miss Clotilde shore do love gumbo, Miss Fran-swaws," Willie said. "Bet she hadn't had any since she been sick, but you should of told me you was wanting onions. I do the digging around here."

She straightened at once. "I beg your pardon, Willie. I've seen you digging here, but I hadn't realized this was your garden." She held out the onions.

Willie stepped back. "No ma'am, no ma'am. You don't understand. This here's Miss Clotilde's garden. You take all the onions you want, Miss Fran-swaws, just leave the hunting to me. That's all, Miss Fran-swaws."

"Oh." She stepped out of the garden.

Willie took her place.

Françoise sat down on a tree stump nearby and watched. She would not have her festive mood ruined by ruminating on the man's byzantine manners. Surely that was what this was all about? Or was it something else?

"I been cutting me a branch off that old cypress stump Miss Clotilde's always trying to kill," Willie said.

Françoise searched for the proper response.

"Know what for?"

"Please tell me," she said.

"I been cutting a branch off that old cypress tree so my Lily can have a real Christmas tree tonight." He straightened for a moment, threw three onions on the lawn.

"Lily will be very excited, Willie."

"Yes, ma'am." He grinned.

Out of the corner of her eye she saw Cato steal out of the bamboo and run toward The Oaks. She was charmed by this child. Except for that first night when they arrived at The Oaks, he wanted nothing to do with her. Sophie Minville was continually putting fears into the boy's head about anyone he seemed to like. Françoise hoped to make friends with him one day. Her presence could make no difference in Jeanne's life, but there was a chance it might in Cato's.

Don't be ridiculous, she told herself. You've never been good with children. Cato hides when you come out. Had you stayed for Jeanne, it would have been disaster.

"Do you know, Willie. I have a little girl, too," she said.

"Yes ma'am." Willie did not look up.

Watching him work was hypnotic. Was it not fitting to speak of her daughter to this man who loved his?

"Jeanne was six when I left. She was beautiful. She lived in an institution. I used to visit her there. Once a week my beautiful daughter would climb into my lap, and the attendant would say, 'This is your mother.'

"One day I couldn't face it anymore. I got on a bus and left. It is my husband's turn to visit now. I hope he will. He always thought Jeanne was my fault. My only concern is that he not delude himself to the extent of not paying the institution's bill. They were kind to her there. It was a good dog pound."

Willie straightened and shaded his eyes from the sun. For a moment they looked at each other, then Willie bent over and began quickly to gather onions.

She stood up, relieved. She had not expected Willie to comment. It was enough to have spoken to someone of Jeanne. As she turned to go, Willie stepped from the garden, arms loaded with onions.

"Reckon this's enough for gumbo, Miss Fran-swaws?" he asked.

"Yes, more than enough, thank you, Willie." She took them, nodded good-bye, and started back to the house.

"Miss Fran-swaws?"

She turned.

"Reckon Mr. Cato'd like a tree like Lily's tonight?"

"That would be a lovely surprise, Willie."

"I'll bring it around back after a while," he said.

She continued toward the house. Cato appeared at the front door. He was carrying something in his hands. When he saw her, he ran down the steps and out into the yard. When she looked back, he had already disappeared into the bamboo.

Dear Brother, she wrote in her head. In ten years Jean-Claude had never answered her letters. She didn't know why she wanted to try again.

Dear Brother, she told him again, I am in a small town in south Louisiana, in the home of an old maid, one of the last members of her family. They were, I gather, an old, moneyed family. American aristocrats, I suppose one might call them. If you are still a Communist, perhaps you haven't the humor to enjoy the juxtaposition of those words. Not that Americans speak of class. They believe they have created a classless society. They refuse to measure people by breeding, manners, or accomplishment. No human quality beats money.

If you read any of the letters I wrote during the last many years, you know the essentials of my life since coming to America—that my daughter, Jeanne, is retarded, that Stewart, as you predicted, had as much feeling to offer as an adding machine. I saw it happening on the boat before my eyes, as soon as we left France. He seemed to drink in the accents of his fellow countrymen as they passed us at the rails. His thirst—

"What are you doing?" the boy said.

She turned around. "Writing to my brother."

"Your brother," he echoed and ran.

At the clothesline strung between sweet gums, she put down the onions, reached up, and felt the crotch of Clotilde Patout's pink cotton step-ins. The crotch felt damp. She picked up the onions and continued to the house.

As she neared the back door, Willie Wooten stepped out from behind a bush, holding a branch in one hand, the other behind his back.

"Reckon I could in-ter-es you in a dozen of the freshest, sassiest-looking eggs you ever saw?" He brandished a pot of brown eggs in front of her. The eggs were covered in filth and feathers.

"You should have been an actor," Françoise observed in her matter-of-fact way. "You always have to make a presentation."

"Nome. Never wanted to be an actor, me. I'd like to be a salesman, have a car, learn to drive, go all over creation telling people about the good things I's going to bring 'em, and how lucky they is I picked their house to stop at.

"I can just see them folks now. They's going to say, 'Get down and come up to the house, Mr. Willie. Been waiting for you and that magic catalog. Get down and come up and rest your feet. Whilst I's peruserating that little old catalog, I wants you to sit down and try some of my fresh pork sausage. I been saving back a piece just for you, Mr. Willie.'"

"Does that mean you want to come in and eat?"

"Wouldn't mind, Miss Fran-swaws. Cutting down Christmas trees's hard work. Course, I don't know what Miss Clo'd say."

"Come in then, Mr. Willie, if that is the only thing stopping you."

"Whatever you say, Miss Fran-swaws."

"Willie, there's nothing as irritating as people who don't stand up for what they want. I have never seen people like blacks down here. Ask what they want, they say, 'Why, whatever you want me to have.' "

"Yes, ma'am."

"Sit down, Willie. Give me those eggs." She put them on the counter and took out the frying pan.

"Where you want me to park Miss Clotilde's tree?" Willie asked.

"You were quick. I thought that was Lily's."

"Nome. I'll go on back and cut another for Lily after while. This one's awful pretty and full."

"Over there," Françoise said.

Willie put the branch by the back door and sat down as he was told. A daddy longlegs high-stepped off the branch, ran across the screen door, stopped in the middle of the top panel, and stood effortlessly upside down on the mesh.

Françoise placed the frying pan on the stove, peeled three slices off the bacon slab, and fried them, making sure the ends stayed limp. "Crisp bacon is for Yankees," Clotilde Patout said. Françoise wondered what category Clotilde put her in. When the bacon was done, she flipped it on a brown paper bag, and dropped an egg into the smoking grease. She put the egg and bacon in front of Willie, gave him a cup of coffee, took the dish towel off the corn sticks—still on the table from last night's supper—flapped open the lid of the molasses jar, and peered inside. The heavy odor was as breathtaking as a stable.

Willie giggled. "You shore don't like that blackstrap, does you, Miss Fran-swaws. Now that Black Velvet, he shore like his."

"Hers."

"Yes, ma'am," he chuckled. "Going to get me a brick out from under the house and pour blackstrap on it. You watch that cow eat it up, brick and all. That cow, he love his blackstrap, same as old Willie."

Françoise picked onions out of the steamy rinse water and threw them into a metal colander on the drain. While she refilled the sink with fresh water, she closed her eyes and blew a wet strand of hair off her forehead. It seemed impossible this was Christmas. A blue jay screeched in the crepe myrtle outside the window. The lid of the molasses jar made a tinny sound as it opened and closed. She turned the water off, began to wash dishes.

As she finished the frying pan, Willie asked, "Miss Franswaws? Do I presume too much to have the wherewithall to trouble you for another cup of that tasty coffee you makes so well?"

"One cup is more than enough, Willie." Clotilde Patout stood at the dining room door. "I've told you not to use my dishes for the darkies, Françoise. Scald them when he's done. Stack them separate in the corner. Don't forget. No telling what I could catch from Willie Wooten."

She marched through the kitchen, threw the Christmas tree out the door, smashed the daddy longlegs with the palm of her hand, and left the house.

Françoise watched through the window over the sink. When the old lady disappeared, she reached for the coffeepot. Willie was going through the door.

She kicked the door open and threw coffee after him. Willie seemed not to notice. He picked up the cypress branch, leaned it against the house, straightened the garbage can, and lumbered off in the direction of the chicken coop after Clotilde Patout.

"Didn't even have the guts to slam the door," Françoise said.

"What'd you do that for?" exclaimed Cato, who came in through the dining room unnoticed, and stood at her side, leaning against the door frame, resting his right foot on top of his left, staring at the smashed spider still kicking one leg.

"Why do you always stand that way?"

"I asked you a question first."

"Willie Wooten oughtn't allow your Aunt Clotilde to treat him so badly."

"Why?"

"He is a human being."

"Mrs. Mallard says Willie Wooten's just a nigger. Mama doesn't want me to speak to him because it'll make me talk funny, just like him."

"That sounds like your mother."

The boy's eyes widened.

"Before long you'll be going to school with black children, so you might as well learn now, they're no different from anybody else, just because their skin is a different color."

"I'm going to tell Daddy on you."

"As you please. I believe your father feels the same as I. If not, I have misjudged him. Go now. I will make gumbo. I cannot talk and make roux."

"Why?"

"Because I have never cooked it before. If I do not give it my undivided attention, I will burn the flour. Why don't you wrap your aunt's Christmas present?"

The boy was eyeing the spider's leg. "I don't have nothing to wrap," he said.

"Anything," she insisted. "I do not have anything. Is that true?"

The boy nodded. "Mrs. Mallard said Mama said Santa Claus wasn't coming until she came home from the hospital."

"But that has nothing to do with giving your aunt a present.

You must think of something. It will hurt her feelings if she gives you something, and you have nothing for her."

"Why?"

"Because she loves you, Cato. It is tradition to give Christmas presents to those we love."

"Do you love somebody?" He shifted to the other foot. "Who do you love?"

"I used to love my brother." She opened the cabinet to the left of the sink and took down a canister covered with flour.

"Do you love him now?"

"No." She pulled the lid off.

"I don't love my brothers either," Cato said.

"Be a nice boy. I must make the roux."

"Does your brother love you?"

"Go." She slammed the lid on the canister, threw flour in the frying pan.

"I'm thirsty."

She took a glass out of the sink, rinsed it, filled it with tap water, and handed it to the boy.

He backed away.

"You said you wanted it."

"That's Willie Wooten's glass," he said.

"Get out!" she said.

The boy opened the screen door and ran down the steps. She called to him, but he was gone. Her quarrel was not with that boy, she thought, and smelled flour burning.

18

"*H*e rambled, oh he rambled.
He rambled all around.
In and out of the town,
He rambled. Ooooooh he rammmmm-bled,
Heee rambulled, till the 'squitters cut him downnnn."

At the end of the song Willie Wooten leaned on his shovel, took the handkerchief out of his back pocket, wiped his forehead and across his eyes.

"Miss Sophie sure is off early this morning," he thought. Without turning his head, he could see the white woman getting into the turquoise car. She had on a yellow and black dress that crisscrossed low across her breasts. The skirt was so short he saw up her legs.

The woman got in the car. Started up and took off.

"Yes, sir, she sure is early this morning," he said and started to shovel again. "Reckon Mr. Patout ain't hardly up." He giggled and turned over the blade, and out fell a load of dirt.

"Damn it to hell, man, this ain't getting you no place." He threw the shovel down in disgust, lighted a cigarette, and squatted down on his haunches, with one hand dragging and one held out in front of him. "The thing to do is think, if you was that old lady, where you would've put it," a voice in his head said. It wasn't his own.

"I done tried that," Willie said.

"Try again," said the voice.

"No telling where that old lady might've put it. I've done dug up this yard all over the place. Only thing I know for sure, Miss Janice wouldn't have put it anywheres in the house cause Miss Clotilde would've eventually turned it up. And she didn't want her sister to have it no way. I'm the one she wanted to have it, me and Lily, not even Ruby."

"Morning, Mr. Pat." Willie stood up and tipped his hat. The white man had just come out of his house and was walking hell-bent for the black man, tucking his shirttail in.

"Morning, Willie," he said, looked around to see if anyone was in sight, unzipped his trousers and stuck his shirttail in. Willie knew if he did that to him, Patout Minville wouldn't like it one bit, but Willie's being a black man, Mr. Pat didn't have to worry. He knew that without being told, it was one of the unspoken rules he had learned even before he could speak. The ways of white people treating Negroes were different. Nobody held a gun to his head to make him observe them, but he did follow the rules. "I'm just like a mule with blinders on going up and down the field, and after a while I don't even know if anybody is behind with a plow. That Fran-swaws Fishes is right. 'Mr. Pat. You ain't good enough to lick my feet,' " that's what he'd like to tell him, was going to tell him, just as soon as he found that gold.

"Willie, I've quit my job," Patout Minville said, putting his hand over his eyes to ward off the morning sun.

Willie held his tongue.

"It was an awful place. I suppose you know some of the men who work there?"

"Yes, sir, Mr. Pat. Mostly they talk about the stink."

Patout Minville shook his head. "Oooff," he said.

"I know what you mean, Mr. Pat. You know I been wringing Miss Clotilde's chickens' necks since before you were born."

"Come on, Willie. You're no older than I am."

Willie Wooten laughed. "Just a manner of speaking, Mr. Pat, but you know what I mean. Sometimes, I been kept up nights after plucking those chickens. The smell of them feathers burning, that's something you don't soon forget." He talked on. The white man was after something. He didn't know what it was, but Willie could tell Patout Minville had something on his mind that he couldn't get out yet, so he kept on going to put him at ease till he could get the words out.

"I remember my mama talking about, when Mr. Lizzard was still up and about the place, how they had going on fifty-five chickens in that yard, back yonder. Mr. Lizzard he was great for fixing things with what he had. I wish he could have stayed alive longer, so I'd have known him as a grown-up man. Old Man Lizzard had a right good mind. You can tell because of some of the things left all over The Oaks, they just bear his stamp, like he done whatever it was yesterday."

The white man seemed surprised. "Like what, Willie."

"Oh, don't mind me, Mr. Pat. I'm just passing the day."

"No, it's really interesting. I didn't know him well either. Like what? That sort of thing interests me."

"Well, like back there in the chicken coop. Now most people, when they build chicken coops, they don't take into account the chickens' comfort. Oh, they give them a roof over their heads, and poles to sleep on, not too fat them poles have to be so the chickens can hold on. But mostly, all they got on their minds is dollar signs. They give chickens things because it's good for their pocketbooks, but they give the chicken the bare minimum. Now, you take Mr. Lizzard. You know what I found back there one day when I was collectin eggs?"

"No, what?"

Willie shifted his weight, held out his hands in front of him, and paused to emphasize his discovery.

"I found these little scraps of material with elastic sewn in top and bottom, a whole pile of them buried in the dirt on the other side of them fig trees where he had a garbage pile.

"I said to myself, Willie, what on earth is this for, man.

This little piece of material with elastic sewn in top and bottom. I scooped some of them up and took them home to my wife and I said, 'Ruby, look at these. What on earth you think they're for, I found them in the hen yard.' And my Ruby, she's crazy sometimes, but sometimes she has real good sense, she says, 'Them's coasters, dummy.' " He giggled. "She been so long with Miss Clotilde she talk like that. 'Coasters, dummy,' she said. 'I recognized them for what they is because Miss Clotilde she don't like to feel the cold ice tea glass in her hands, and I always got to put on these little blue and green socks, just like those.'

"So, I got to thinking about that. Why ice tea socks be back in the hen yard. After a while I figured it out. Mr. Lizzard, he must've used them little socks on the glass eggs so the chickens wouldn't get no shock when they sat down and felt something cold under their butts."

"Oh," said the white man. He looked away.

"Yes, sir, Mr. Patout, Old Man Lizzard was a right smart fellow. He knew them hens would lay quicker if they had something warm underneath them right away, first thing in the morning." The white man was disappointed, Willie could see.

"What in the hell you come out here for bothering me," Willie thought. White people didn't pick up on little things like that, you have to show them something big and flashy for them to sit up and notice. "Go on, man, I'm busy. I've got to find me that gold and maybe even one day I'll get down to finding that deed that's going to turn you out," Willie thought, but Patout Minville gave no sign he was fixing to leave.

"You smoke, Willie?" Patout said.

"Course I do. How long you have to stare at my mug to know I do," he thought. "Yes, sir," he said.

Patout took a pack of Lucky Strikes out of his breast pocket, held it out, then took a cigarette himself. He lighted his own cigarette and then handed the matches to Willie.

Their fingers worked carefully in conjunction so they did not touch.

"All so polite and easy, all so right and fine. Willie Wooten watch out. You might wind up doing time," the man sang to himself.

Both men took a puff on their cigarettes.

"Ah, Willie?"

"Yes, sir, Mr. Boss Man. That's my name," he thought. He said nothing out loud.

"You know Mr. Latouche's motorboat was found out in Vermillion Bay a couple of days ago, just floating on the waves. The anchor had been dropped, but Latouche was nowhere in sight. They think maybe he's drowned."

"Yes, sir, I heard," Willie said, wondering what that had to do with him. He waited for the white man to tell him.

"Looks like, if he's dead, Joy Rita Latouche's going to have a mighty hard time.

"I'm mighty sorry to hear that," Willie said. "Bout time that fat slob got her comeuppence," he thought. "She never let no black head lay down on her beds. Wouldn't even let 'em carry in the body when that poor little black child got run over front of her door."

"Well, I reckon you're wondering why I'm bringing this up."

"Take your time, Mr. Pat. That's all right," Willie said. "But I was wondering when you'd get round to the point," he thought.

"Well, I stopped in to see Dr. Rodriguez yesterday. I've been having heartburn and palpitations most every day for over a month, so I thought I'd get him to check me out."

"Un-huh," Willie said. He hoped he looked concerned enough. "Come on, Mr. Pat, nice and easy, spit it out," he thought.

"Anyhow, Rodriguez says I've just got to watch what I eat. Cut out the fats and don't eat so many acids. That'll be hard, Willie. You grow a mean tomato."

Willie laughed. "Thank you, Mr. Pat. I think so, too, if I do say so myself. It's the manure does it. You see, Mr. Lizzard, leastways, that's the way Miss Clotilde remembers it—"

"Yes, well, as I was saying, Willie, Rodriguez said there wasn't much wrong with me, except a little high blood pressure and too much strain from working over there at the slaughterhouse. You'd be surprised how much pressure there is in a processing plant."

"Go on, the way I hear it, you're always staring out the door," Willie thought.

"Anyhow, Rodriguez and I got to talking about first this thing and then that, and he mentioned to me about Latouche being gone and maybe drowned and how Joy Rita Latouche wasn't going to be able to run that hotel all by herself, and first thing you know, Rodriguez says to me, 'Patout, why don't you take it over? It would suit you better than the chicken plant.' "

"Lord, what a fool," Willie thought. "I knew you was going to say that, Mr. Pat," he said.

"How come, Willie?"

"Well, I was just thinking, Mr. Pat's a right smart fellow and mighty ambitious, too. It's a shame Belmont doesn't have a smart fellow like him to give it a real first-class hotel, just like the sign over the door says now, course it ain't."

Patout Minville grinned in relief. "So you really think it's a good idea?"

"Well, now—" Willie began. Patout cut him off.

"I must admit, at first I thought it was a lousy idea. But when I got to thinking about it more, I saw maybe Rodriguez's mentioning it was a stroke of luck. I could fix it up real cheap, I think—"

"Un-huh, this is where ole Willie comes in," the black man thought.

"Slap on a coat of paint in the lobby, do only a handful of upstairs rooms for now. With just one or two good men to help, we could fix the plumbing and patch the roof, I understand it leaks a bit. It wouldn't take much—" He waited for Willie to comment.

"I remember Miss Clotilde told me once about a ball she went to there where they had stuck sugar cane lined up all around the walls. She said that was the prettiest sight, Mr. Pat."

Patout Minville looked perplexed. "Cane would attract ants, wouldn't it? But we might put in some stands of bamboo in big red and gold Chinese pots, that'd give the same effect."

"Yes, sir, I reckon it would," Willie said. He noticed the "we."

"Anyway, I'm getting off the track. The point is, after we fixed it up, then I'd turn the lobby into a sort of art gallery and crafts shop, selling only stuff made in southwest Louisiana. What do you think about that?"

Willie could see the white man was excited. He'd never seen him look this way. His eyes danced and his skin went red, and he kept on running his hand through his hair. It stuck straight up on the ends. His eyes grew big. Any minute it looked like they were going to pop right out of his head, which bothered Willie Wooten because, for the first time, he saw how much Patout Minville looked like Miss Clotilde. He could hear her now. "Willie Wooten, after all I've done for you, you turn around and lead my nephew on. I never would have thought it of you. Where was your sense of duty. Why didn't you look out for my kin, you ungrateful man?"

"You say you're going to sell stuff, Mr. Pat?" he asked. "Forgive me, Miss Clotilde," he thought. "I wasn't aiming to lead him on when the conversation started out. I was just minding my own business, digging in the vegetable patch."

"Don't lie to me, Willie Wooten. I know you're digging for gold. Sister told you it was buried in the yard. You even think you're going to find a deed, saying your family had first rights to my land."

"Nome. I don't know nothing about no deed, Miss Clotilde."

"Yes, Willie, I'm going to sell things people around here make. We've got some mighty fine native artists in southwest Louisiana, only trouble is, they don't even know it. People making things out of cypress knees just to kill time. There's a woman down at the post office who does landscapes from popsicle sticks. We've got quilt makers, and one woman I've heard about over at the slaughterhouse made a whole dollhouse right out of doilies she crocheted together. That's the crafts part, but we've got artists engaged in fine arts hereabout, too. I know we do, only trouble is ferreting them out."

"Yes, sir." Willie looked doubtful.

"After all my family's done for your family," Miss Clotilde said.

"And I'd provide a place for them to exhibit right there in the lobby. I'd take a small commission, of course, to help with the electricity and the drinks. You'd have to serve coffee and Cokes to people when they came in, they'd expect that. But I wouldn't do like those gallery owners in New Orleans. I wouldn't cut into the artists' profits by half. You know, it would really help people out around here, especially the poor. Sometimes I think there's a correlation between being poor and being in touch with the creative urge, don't you?"

"Good grief," Willie thought. He laughed easily. "Mr. Pat, you're wading in over my head."

"No, come on, Willie. I want to hear what you've got to say. I've watched you. I know Aunt Clotilde trusts you to do things she wouldn't trust anyone else to do."

Willie Wooten looked down at the ground and poked at the upturned dirt. "Thank you, Mr. Pat. I appreciate your telling me that," he said. He could hear her again, coming in loud and strong. "Now's the time, Willie Wooten. Tell him. You heard what my nephew said. I trust you."

"Mr. Pat, it shore do sound good, but there's one thing I think maybe you had ought to think about."

"Yes, Willie?"

"Why, he's as trusting as a child," Willie thought.

"Well, I heard Mr. Tutie tell, pardon me, Mr. Pat, this ain't rightly any of my business—"

"Go on, Willie, don't be shy."

"Well, Mr. Tutie told his nigger the other day when I was over there"—he jerked his head in the direction of the neighboring farm—"borrowing a file. I took my shovel here over there. I don't know when I sharpened that blade last."

"Yes, and—"

"I'm getting there, Mr. Pat. Anyways, Mr. Tutie tole his nigger, him and me's right tight, that he wanted to lie fallow next year to save up the land, but he'd need a bank loan to help him out, but when he went to the bank, she wouldn't let him have money nohow. Not even if he put up the land. Money's tight."

Patout laughed. "Willie, set yourself at rest. I've already thought about that. Rodriguez says Joy Rita Latouche'll be so glad to be out from under the burden, he reckons she'll work out a lease with me at first, until it gets going good. I'm not going to take any salary. Anything I make will go to her to build up my equity in the place. Whatever the art gallery takes in, she'll take her commission right off the top."

The black man looked worried.

"I've had plenty of experience working on commissions before. Did right well as a salesman in the New Orleans–Mississippi Gulf Coast area once. I'm not worried," Patout said.

"This man is just determined to run headlong into trouble," Willie thought. "That place will eat him alive. Hadn't been any money made off that hotel since the war ended and all the men came home at once and started getting their wives pregnant and they didn't have any place else to go except that old dump."

As much as he begrudged the white man for all the trouble he caused the black—no white person ever tried to warn a black of oncoming trouble—Mr. Pat was, after all, Miss Clotilde's kin, and he owed her, yes, he owed her, even if she didn't like the color of his skin. "We's family, Miss Clotilde and me, even though it'd kill her to admit it," he thought.

"Mr. Pat," he said, "just one more thing, I think maybe you hadn't thought of."

"What's that, Willie?"

"Well, you heard about them civil rights marchers, them troublemakers over yonder in New Orleans?" He looked down.

Patout Minville looked away. "Yes, Willie, I've heard something about them."

"Well, Mr. Pat, I'm not saying it's right, or anything like that, but I'm telling you straight. It ain't going to be long before them troublemakers raise such a stink that Uncle Sam's going to come down here to southwest Louisiana, and you going to have to let niggers into that hotel of yours. And niggers, they don't have money to spend. You put one nigger in that hotel for one night, and you're never going to see a white face in it again."

"Thank you for speaking your mind, Willie. It's no wonder Aunt Clotilde loves and respects you," Patout said quietly.

"Hold on now, Mr. Pat. Don't you think that's going a bit too far?"

The white man looked up at him, surprised. It was the first time they had ever looked at each other squarely in the eyes. Patout was the first to smile.

"Yes, Willie. I'm sure you're right," he said.

The Studebaker drove up to the Minvilles' house. Sophie Minville got out. Her dress curled back and showed off her legs. Patout Minville looked at Willie. Willie looked away.

"I've got to help my wife take groceries in. I just want to know, are you in this with me? Aunt Clotilde says you're a mighty fine painter and carpenter."

"I appreciate that, Mr. Pat, but I've got me some trouble with my back right now."

"I'm sorry to hear that, Willie."

"Yes, sir, I shore do appreciate that. I hear Mr. Pugie

Reaux's got some right strong black men that lay in pipes and do a bit of roofing. You might check with him."

"Thanks, Willie. I enjoyed our chat." Patout started to leave.

"Any time, Mr. Pat. I enjoy a good chat myself," he said. "I ain't going to work for no slave wages, me," he thought.

· 19 ·

*I*n the entrance to Latouche's First Class Hotel Patout painted driftwood in the Mississippi River while a spider danced above his head on a cobweb between the chandelier and the wall.

"You know, Patout," Sophie said, "we should change the name to Minville's." She was standing at the top of a tall ladder with a paintbrush in her hand. There was paint on her face and hair. "Actually," she went on, "you should change it to Sophie's after all the work I've done."

"You call that work?" his father said, turning to look at the ceiling where she was painting. "I could have done it in half the time."

Her face fell.

His father outlined a fishing boat. "Maybe you mean dusting chandeliers?"

"Mama hasn't dusted the chandeliers yet, Daddy," Cato said.

His father laughed.

"Bastard!" she said. Her lips trembled. She looked as if she might cry. "Go check on the twins, Cato. Ruby's probably broiling them in the sun."

"Aren't we ever going to eat?"

"Cato!"

"Yes, ma'am." He went to the back of the hall and peered into the lobby. The big room seemed cold and wet and smelled of stale cigars. Defeated-looking sofas and easy chairs sagged in remembrance of previous guests. He had never crossed this sort of room without holding a grown person's hand.

"I asked you to do something, Cato."

"Yes, ma'am." He dove in, tripped, and lay in the gloom, sprawled on the worn carpet, smelling dust and cigars hammered in by three generations of Belmont feet. His mother and father began to argue. Dishes clattered to his right. "Okay, y'all ready to order now?" Fileene Ramirez, the waitress, said to the couple who'd come for lunch today. Cato couldn't hear what they said. No one knew he lay in the dark close by.

Poison gas attack! Lie down! Don't move until the white cloud passes. He pressed his ear to the carpet and listened for the sound of enemy feet transported through the earth's magnetic field into his supersensitive secret ear. He scarcely dared breathe.

Okay, men. Go in with swords drawn. Don't take off your gas masks.

"Ya want it with or without?"

"I can't do everything, Sophie."

"Whaaaaa!" (Enemy soldiers were running their swords through the twins.)

"Why you went and quit the plant—"

"Do you have pecan pie?"

"Bastard!"

"Bitch!"

Bombers droned overhead, now the patter, patter of helicopters coming to rescue him. He had to make it to the roof. He must dash for the stairs. He raised his head and stared into white jeans, red socks, and penny loafers.

"Where's your maw, boy?" Pugie Reaux shifted gum to the other side.

Cato traced a rose in the carpet.

"Don't tax yourself, kid. I'll find her."

"Pugie Reaux! That you?" his mother called.

"Y'all decent?" Pugie Reaux smirked and went toward the entrance. His muscles danced in the tight red T-shirt. He leaned against the door frame, crossed one leg over the other, and waited for the look of pleasure they would wear when they saw him.

"Howdy, Pugie. What you think of my mural?"

"Ain't that a pretty picture," Pugie lisped. Sophie laughed. For a moment Cato hated her.

"I don't want to interfere, Mrs. M., but you want your kid playing on that dirty carpet?"

"Cato!"

He sat up. His mother came to the lobby door and stood next to Pugie Reaux. She said something to the man, glanced at him, quickly looked away. The man's teeth flashed. His mother was blushing.

"Get off that floor," she said. "Go check on your brothers like I told you. Soon as we get home, you're taking a bath."

She turned. "Pat, I told you I couldn't keep tabs on the kids and paint and it's way past lunch. Can't you stop?"

"Not now. Got to finish this palette. The paint will dry out."

"I'd be glad to drive you and the children home, Mrs. M. I've got to go that way anyway, pick up my niggers for a job," Pugie said.

"Well, I don't know."

"Go on, Sophie. I'd be much obliged, Pugie. The kids are tired out, Sophie, too. We've been at it since eight thirty. I'll grab something here."

His mother looked at Pugie Reaux. "I'll get paint all over your new truck," she said, hardly more than a whisper. Her voice made Cato shiver.

Pugie Reaux just looked at her. A slow smile spread on his face. "Plenty more where that one came from," he said, not meaning that at all.

"Pat, I'll be back after the children's naps," she said, still looking at Pugie.

Pugie Reaux poked Cato in the back. "You heard your maw, kid. Move."

They found the twins parked in the sun outside the kitchen.

His mother pushed the stroller toward the truck. Pugie Reaux walked by her side. Cato followed. There was a wolf baying at the moon on the door of the driver's side. Cato followed his mother and the man around the back of the truck. On the passenger's door there was a hunter with a rifle in his hand, a dog at his heels, and a lurid sunset of orange, purple, red, and gold. "Pugie Reaux, Licensed Detective," it said under the hunter's feet and gave the telephone number under the dog's.

Pugie opened the door, helped Sophie in, handed her the twins one by one, and slammed the door. "You ride in the back, bugger," he said, mean and low.

His mother rolled down her window. "You'll like riding in the open, sweetheart," she said.

Soon they were in open countryside. The wind blew his shirt up his ribs, sun burned the top of his head. The bones in his rear jabbed him whenever the truck hit a bump. He watched for a while the road unwinding underneath the speeding truck, then stuck his fingernails into the rubber casing of the rear window and pulled himself up. Inside the cab his mother was speaking to Pugie Reaux. Then she looked at the twins, out the window, now back at the man. She did not turn around and look at him. She didn't really love him anymore. Pugie Reaux suddenly slammed his hand against the glass.

"Sit down!" his mother's mouth said. She pointed down. "Dangerous," the mouth said. Pugie Reaux shot him a look, slowed down. Cato sat down.

He must not make Pugie Reaux mad enough to stop. Pugie Reaux would grab him by the collar, yank him out of the back, and throw him to the ground. He was the kind of man who ran over you back and forth like in gangster movies until you were ground meat. His mother would cover her eyes. She wouldn't be able to look at something like that. She would feel the truck bump when it ran over his body, but she wouldn't scream. That would make the babies cry.

She hated when they cried. It made her nervous. The next day a cane truck would roll over him and pieces would stick to the tires and the next time they washed the truck he'd go down the drain and wind up in the bayou.

The truck stopped in the drive. Cato stood up. Pugie Reaux's head was close to his mother's. He was tickling the babies under the chin. They lay in their mother's lap. Suddenly Pugie Reaux turned and looked into Cato's eyes. Cato threw his leg over the side of the truck and ran.

"Cato!" his mother cried out.

"You want him?" Pugie Reaux said.

"I could throttle him when he does that disappearing act."

"I'll get him."

When Pugie got around to the other side of the house he saw only an abandoned doghouse, a wash line, and thick clumps of bamboo. The boy was nowhere in sight. He shrugged, tucked in his T-shirt, pulled his pants down so the waistband hung low over his hips, and walked lazily back to the truck.

As Sophie Minville handed the babies down, he saw the softly rounded tops of her breasts. He gave her his hand. She hopped out. They stood close together, bodies almost touching. He looked into her eyes, saw the heaving of her breasts.

"Lady, you look good enough to eat," he said in his husky voice.

"Oh, Pugie," she giggled, "I'm a fright."

Pugie pulled a gob of white paint out of her hair, took her by the shoulders and turned her around, picking paint out of her hair and neck. She blushed violently when she faced him again. They were standing nose to nose. Her eyes widened, her breasts heaved, but to her delight, he stepped away from her, took the stroller handle in his strong hands. "Shall we go inside?" he asked.

He was, she decided right on the spot, a perfect gentleman, not at all the way malicious gossips portrayed him. Pugie stood head and shoulders above most men in Belmont. That was probably why he was the target of clattering tongues. For the first time, she really looked at him, saw the strong neck, the determined chin. He had high cheekbones, lovely hazel eyes, really, almost the looks of a movie star and, at his age, hadn't gone fat around the middle. Nor was he sloppy with clothes, like Patout, who looked ten years older than this man. When someone stands out people are always jealous, Sophie thought. They're bound to gossip to cut them down to their own small size. Just as they do with me.

He carried the twins carefully up the steps and into the kitchen, put them down gently, and extended his hand. She laughed at this old-fashioned nicety, gave him her hand, mounted the steps, and disappeared inside.

Cato did not come out of the bamboo until Pugie's truck pulled away.

"Where've you been?" his mother asked. "You'll have to make your own tuna fish sandwich. I've already put the makings away. In the fridge, second shelf, no, wash your hands first. Why on earth did you disappear?"

She didn't press for an answer. He saw she knew why. She didn't look him in the face, got busy with the twins, went into their room, and put them down for a nap. She didn't return to the kitchen. He heard her bedroom door close, then the sound of a piano. "This is WWL New Orleans," the announcer said.

"Mama?" he called through the door.

"I'm asleep, Cato. Lie down. We're going to have to go back in a little while."

He waited for her to invite him in, but all he heard was the bed creak as she reached over and turned the radio down low. He went to his old room and looked in. There was a black mark on the wall near the crib where the head of his bed used to be. He had often stared at it mornings when he first awoke, imagining it a button he could press and blow up the world any time he felt like it, but never had. It frightened him. His father said it was the duty of Christian men never to get angry enough to hurt other people.

"Never hurt people, Cato, not intentionally," his father often said. "Even if someone does something that makes you really mad, turn the other cheek."

He walked to the crib. Andrew was asleep on his stomach, diapers pulled down so far that Cato saw the beginning of his crack. The other baby, Matthew, lay on his back half awake. His eyelashes blinked slowly, heavily. His tongue poked out the right corner of his mouth. Drool slid down his cheek.

"If either one of you goes near that button, I'll kill you," Cato said. Matthew opened his eyes wide and smiled.

"Did you hear me?"

The baby's smile disappeared. His eyes looked doubtfully at Cato. Cato picked a large stuffed bear off the floor. "All I have to do is smother you." He pressed the bear against the baby. After a while he lifted the bear. Matthew dimpled and made a soft, happy gurgle.

Cato drew back. Matthew whimpered.

"Go to sleep," Cato said. Matthew wailed. His twin awoke. Together they screamed.

The sound made him sick to his stomach. He put his hands over his ears and kicked the crib. They cried louder. Then he was crying louder than they, not knowing why, only crying, his body shuddering with the effort, his face growing red, as though a dam had broken in his soul and he must get out this water he had been saving inside himself for a long, long time, or else, why were his tears so hot.

"Don't you have any consideration for me? I can't even have ten minutes alone. What did you do to them, Cato?"

He couldn't stop sobbing to answer. She picked up the babies. They ceased crying.

"Mama, hold me," he whispered.

"Aren't you ashamed. You such a big boy." She yanked

the hem of her slip out of his hand, picked up the twins, and left the room. Cato lay on the floor by the crib, listening to the sounds she made getting dressed. The dresser drawers opened and shut with a bang. Water gushed in the bathroom sink. She slammed her plastic comb on the top of the toilet tank.

"You coming?"

He shook his head.

"Suit yourself, but take a bath."

Pugie Reaux's truck drove up. The back door slammed. The motor shifted into second. It went farther and farther down the road away from him. Then there was silence.

He stood up, went to the twins' room, and stood by the button. If he pressed it now his mother would stop, the whole world would stop. He seemed to be standing among line upon line of bodies stacked in neat rows, like in a vegetable garden. "Mama!" He looked toward the kitchen as though, because he had called her name, she must materialize in the doorway, one hand holding the swinging door open, but the door didn't move. He couldn't go into the kitchen to see if his mother was there. The door trapped children and tore off their fingers. For no reason and without warning, it went *whoosh,* and cut fingers off at the knuckles, that's what she said.

"O God, Great in His Glory . . ." he began as his father prayed at meals. He couldn't think what to throw in next. "O Great Swinging Door, please do not hurt me. I must find my mother. My mother cannot live without me. Mama!"

There was no sound. He had never been alone in the house.

He returned to the living room and lay down in front of the fake fireplace. The refrigerator kicked on, hummed. It made him uneasy. He remembered the broom in "The Sorcerer's Apprentice" and wondered if it would come alive, tear its cord from the socket, and march through the swinging door. He thought of escaping out the front and hiding in the bamboo until his parents returned, but instead, touched himself in that place, the mention of which made his mother frown and his father tell jokes, and felt comforted. He slipped off his pants, lay down, and touched himself again. The twin cats inside the fireplace arched their backs wickedly. His fingers smelled like the baking of bread. He stroked his genitals gently, as he sometimes did his mother's hair when she couldn't sleep and came to him in the night. She would sit beside his cot, and say, "Talk to me, Cato. I don't care what, just talk."

And so he would.

"Lily? Oh, Lily!" Willie Wooten's voice grew louder. He was passing in the yard, just on the other side of the living room wall. The boy kept still. There was no light in the room. He lay on the scatter rug with his head under the chair and waited for Willie to go away.

"Lily?" Now he called from the other side of the house near the coulee. He called again, his voice farther away, toward the cane field. He seemed to be headed for Tutie Romero's. Lily liked to play in his barn. Cato slept.

When he awoke, there was someone in the room. He opened his eyes and saw Lily standing over him. She took a spool out of her pocket and squatted by his side. He watched her. She paid him no mind. He was to her as inanimate as a pile of dirty laundry waiting on the scatter rug to be taken to the washateria. She drove the spool all over his body, starting where his underpants elastic had marked him with a thin, red line of heat rash across his stomach, traveled around and around the navel, like the traffic circle near Borden's Ice Cream Parlor, made a left turn and headed down the broad avenue of his right thigh.

He watched from underneath the wing chair. The travels of the truck made him drowsy and he said to her, "I am the mountains of Kentucky and the deserts of California, and right there, that hole in the middle? That's a great big hole full of mud and once you fall in you never get out alive. It's got the bodies of twenty-five people, two babies, and five tractor-trailers to prove it."

She giggled.

And then she came to it and her truck stalled. She held it up and tried to make the truck climb, but the truck stalled again, so she turned it to the side like the turn-key bridge over the bayou, closer down toward Belmont. And then, once the boat was through, she turned it straight down again and drove over, making revving noises as the people of Belmont make their cars do after waiting, with the motor turned off a long time, for a barge to pass, but he could tell from her expression she didn't think much of it as a bridge. He pulled up his pants and lay down again.

Yellow shades flapped against the window frames. The room grew dark. He closed his eyes and fell asleep once more. Lily sat beside him. When he awoke, she was picking her nose, wiping it on the scatter rug, and humming "Greensleeves" to herself. Rain fell faintly against the broad, tough leaves of the elephant ear just outside the front window.

"How come you know 'Greensleeves'?" Cato said.

Like a new heifer in a field, she got up, raising backsides first, pushing upright with her arms, went to the front door and made revving sounds while she looked around for a new route.

"Lily Wooten, you come out of there this minute. I'm going to get me a switch and come in there after you if you don't get your black hide outa that house this minute." The black man pressed his face against the window screen, then glanced uneasily in the direction of The Oaks.

"It's all right, Willie Wooten."

"Mr. Cato, that you?" Willie pushed his face against the screen. "You oughtn't done a thing like that, Mr. Cato, letting Lily in. What Mr. Pat and Miss Sophie going to say? Lily, you ain't heard me yet? One switch coming up."

Lily stood by the front door, running her spool along the molding, making soft engine noises as she went up the steep incline, then down, and headed across the great plains of the middle of the door, down, down, then headed across the tortured roads of the carpet design, where at length, the truck ran into Cato's foot.

Lily stood up, put the spool in her pocket, looked at Cato, a dreamy smile on her face, and began to urinate down her leg. Her father's voice went on and on filtered through the screen, now fading as he glanced toward the big house, then looked down the road for the turquoise Studebaker.

"Now, Lily," something, something, something, went the voice, ". . . been mighty nice to you, say good-bye . . ." something, something, on and on he talked. He and his daughter finished at the same time, then Lily walked to the kitchen and, to Cato's astonishment, out the swinging door.

"You all right, Mr. Cato? She didn't hurt you?"

"No, Willie." He got up and went to the window.

"My Lily's a strange child, but you sure know how to handle her, Mr. Cato. Now you sure she didn't cause you no trouble? Well, then, we'd best be running. What you tell Mr. Cato, honey?"

Lily stuck her finger in her nose.

Gently, Willie removed her hand and held it.

"What's wrong with her, Willie?"

"Dunno, Mr. Cato. Sometime God give people one child, sometime one and a half, like Lily. Well, you be sure and come up and visit at the big house soon. Miss Clo, she sure miss you."

"She said that?"

"She didn't have to, Mr. Cato."

Cato picked at a gob of dried varnish on the sill. "Mama says if Nanan really wanted me, she'd invite me."

"Honey, your mama just don't know Miss Clotilde. She don't give nobody a invitation, but I tell you what—how come Miss Clo make my Ruby dust your room and air the sheets every week? What you care if the bed be mildewed you don't hope somebody gonna sleep there again sometime?"

"She does that?"

Willie nodded. "Miss Clo told Ruby to keep your room ready for whenever you decide to come home."

Thunder rumbled. Lily whimpered.

"Well, we best be. Lily don't like that sound. Look like a heavy rain's coming. Be sure and shut the windows, Mr. Cato. Your daddy going to be upset he come home and find his new floors all wet. He's right proud of his new house."

Tutie Romero's cane waved frantically in the wind. Cato pressed his nose against the screen and watched Lily and Willie run out of sight. Black clouds scudded over the trees. He felt suddenly frightened, chilled. The day had turned green-black.

He ran to the twins' room, took underwear and pajamas out of his dresser, wrapped them in a towel and came back to the living room. There was a small dark spot in the carpet in front of the fireplace. He threw yesterday's *Belmont Crier* over it, gathered his belongings, and left the house.

Françoise Fischler opened the front door.

"Where's Nanan?"

She pointed upstairs.

He ran up the stairs and knocked. The door shut behind him.

It was the first time the boy had slept at The Oaks since his mother came home from the hospital.

· 20 ·

Sophie had known from the beginning it wouldn't work. Here it was late August, the Sugar Cane Festival a week away, nothing finished yet. Only Patout, who lived his whole life seeing things the way he wanted them to be, instead of the way they really were, still thought he'd be ready in time to make a going proposition out of that dilapidated hotel. What could she do? He wouldn't listen to her. A change had come over him since moving to Belmont. She hardly knew him anymore.

She cocked her head at the bathroom mirror. Yes, you look fine. Don't overdo it. Once a man notices you're taking pains, he knows he's got the upper hand, she thought and screwed on the other earring. Pugie Reaux was coming in a few minutes, bringing a man who knew about plumbing to check on the washing machine. She hadn't seen Pugie for almost a week, and was beside herself with excitement.

What she let Pugie Reaux do to her wasn't right, she told herself, but it wasn't right of Patout to treat her so unkindly. Sometimes he even forgot he was a man, letting days and weeks go by without touching her, giving her a kiss on the neck, when anything, anything at all would have done to show he was sorry for being impatient. Did he think she didn't know he was under pressure?

And when Pugie Reaux's arm accidentally brushed against her breasts, there in the cab of his truck, as he reached across to make sure the door was shut, and she thrilled to the feeling going across the tips of her breasts, she said to herself, There, Patout, I refuse to be ashamed. I've a right to a little pleasure.

If you won't give it to me, I'll get it someplace else. Besides, it was such a harmless thing—babies in her lap—why, the idea it could lead to something else. Only dirty-minded people, like those back home who blocked the high school prom, because if girls got into boys' arms for one reason they'd eventually find excuse for another, could think a thing like that.

She fished tweezers from the bottom of her makeup bag. Pugie Reaux was such a help. Not long after taking her home the first time, Pugie showed up again at noon and volunteered to drive her and the children out to The Oaks. Patout hesitated, but she shot him a look. They argued about it that night. It was his own damn pride, she told him. His pride always got in the way, even if it meant depriving his wife and children of comfort. He couldn't stand to admit he needed help, couldn't abide being beholden to anyone.

God, she hated that word. Beholden! How many times had she heard it, first from her father, now from him. Translate it fear. That was the truth of the matter.

You don't mean that, he replied, trying to keep his temper under control. She knew he knew he was lost if he gave in and yelled at her. Ashamed of himself later, he'd have to let her have her way. And of course, that was what happened. Now Pugie came to get her almost every day at noon, only Patout made her carry an occasional bag of tomatoes, shrimp, or wild duck to lessen the beholdenness to him. Lipstick capped her teeth. She licked them. They always were too big for my face, she thought. Now it was an accepted part of the daily routine. Get up early, go downtown, break her back moving furniture, ruin her hands in turpentine, and wait for a gorgeous man to whisk her away. She leaned into the mirror and worked on her right eyebrow. There were days Pat came up for air and remembered he had a wife and children who needed to eat at noon, but that was a rarity. He'd always been that way, able to go off in the clouds when he got excited about something and forget anyone else was alive. It was one of the most infuriating things about him. I don't know how you didn't see that in him from the beginning, she mouthed at herself in the mirror.

Nowadays, it was the hotel that obsessed him. Just like him—five minutes after saying he was ready to head home for lunch—to get hung up with porch squatters—the half-dozen old men inherited from the previous owners—and actually have the gall to look relieved when Pugie showed up. I'd make those filthy old men sit someplace else, she thought. I'd take away the rockers. If that didn't discourage them, I'd do what they did back home when the niggers took to squatting in the shade on the courthouse square every Saturday from dawn to dusk waiting for their kinfolks to finish spending nickels, I'd cut down the trees. Nothing is more stubborn than a Negro, but even they won't sit in the hot sun just to prove they can.

"Are you crazy? Cut down the trees and you take away the chief charm of this hotel. Where's your head?" Patout told her. That was the nasty-toned way he talked to her these days, as though he were the only one scared of what lay ahead.

There was a knock at the back door. She licked a finger and smoothed down the brow. Skin was red where she'd pulled out hair. Looked like a birthmark. If there was anything in the world she hated, it was a woman with a birthmark on her face. The tweezers slipped from her hand and clattered against the sink. Lord, Sophie, calm down. She checked her hem in the mirror on the back of the door. Patout was forever finding fault with her clothes, saying they weren't right for a woman her age, but it seemed to her that the new short length nicely showed off her legs, and besides, she wasn't old. He just wants me to feel as ancient as he feels, she thought. Older women didn't make demands, like afternoon rolls in the hay.

"Yes, what is it, Cato?" She loved sex in the middle of the day and there was a time in New Orleans when Patout obliged her. Well, she knew one man who'd leap at the chance to oblige her. "What?"

"Miss Françoise is here, Mama. She brought peaches."

Parallel lines formed between her eyes.

"Well, put them in the fridge, and don't forget to say thank you."

"She wants to talk to you."

"What for?" Hem's not even. Has to be redone. "Cato?" He hadn't moved. "Oh for God's sake, can't you ask her what she wants? Tell her I'm busy. I'm on the toilet. Tell her . . . oh, all right. Tell her just a minute."

She heard him walk away. What could that damnable woman want? She saw herself standing in the kitchen, rattling away, hands flying everywhere, touching her hair, her skirt, wiping imaginary crumbs off the counter, increasingly unnerved while the French woman sat there listening without saying a word. It was un-American, at any rate definitely un-Southern. Rude. That's it. The woman's rude, she thought, licking her teeth once more for good measure. One has a social obligation to keep the ball of conversation rolling, she quoted Mrs. Pasquale, the tenth-grade home ec teacher whose pronouncements on social graces, once upon a time, sent her classmates into gales. They could afford to laugh, they without squaw at home for a mother. She recalled their shining faces, their rampant high spirits with distaste.

She yanked her hair straight out from the crown, burst into tears, and cried as she ratted. When it was smoothed down, she turned this way and that. Certain her hairdo was perfect and her eyes not giveaway red, she opened the door and went out, saying Pugie Reaux's coming on the other side of this visit, get her out of here quick, you'll be safe before you know it.

Françoise rose.

Nodding, Sophie went to the refrigerator and looked in. "Peaches. How nice of you, or was it Aunt Clotilde?"

"They're her trees." The French woman looked at her in

that level, unsmiling way, calmly standing by the kitchen table, one hand resting lightly on its top, no movement betraying any awkwardness, as though she did not think it worth considering whether she had the right to be standing there in the Minville kitchen, asking to speak to Patout Minville's wife alone for a moment, not in the presence of her child.

"Oh, very well. Cato, why don't you . . ." The boy gave the French woman a sullen look, paused at the screen door, and looked back at his mother. She blew him a kiss. He smiled shyly, his face suffused. Why was her love for him mixed with pain? It wasn't with the twins. The screen door banged and she was left alone with the Fischler woman. "Mr. Reaux is coming to check on my washer and take us back to town to help my husband," Sophie said, barely concealing her irritation.

"Yes, I know."

"Well?" Sophie picked at the enamel on her left thumbnail. Two dollars she'd paid for a new brand that was supposed to last two weeks, and here it was, the day after, already coming off. Paint remover and turpentine, of course, had something to do with it. She must tell Patout he couldn't count on her any more to work like a field hand at the hotel. He couldn't expect to get all the work done free just because he had a wife. Her visitor's fingers moved restlessly across the tabletop. "What do you want?" she said, feeling suddenly alarmed.

"Mrs. Minville, I have seen a great deal of Cato since he stayed with us last winter." She looked around the kitchen, her head wagging ever so slightly like one of those mechanical dogs people put in the rear windows of their cars whose heads bob up and down when the car comes to a sudden stop.

What has he done now? Sophie thought, not understanding the direction Françoise Fischler was taking.

"I find him exceptionally bright."

"Thank you." Sophie was genuinely pleased. Such a relief

that was all the woman came to say. "He really is a handful, more than I can sometimes deal with. I'm sure you must have seen, too. He is a demanding child."

"He's always asking questions."

"Oh, more than that, much more, I meant. He just won't leave me alone sometimes. He's jealous of any time I take away from him. He resents his father, strangers, why, even the twins. I have to remind him I don't belong only to him. When you are a baby, well, that's all right, but now he's growing older and, well, it just wouldn't be right . . ."

"Yes, I've seen Cato's attachment to you. It's rather a terrible love to witness."

"I beg your pardon?"

"Perhaps I'm not expressing myself well, Mrs. Minville. Mine is sometimes textbook English. I only thought it odd, because of his love for you, that he's been spending so many nights at The Oaks."

"I am not strong, Miss Fischler—"

"You haven't been sick lately."

"—and, of course, he loves his Nanan, though I don't see how this is any business of yours."

"Miss Clotilde—"

"Don't tell me she's complaining. She made a point of asking me to send him over more often." She was shaking with anger. At any moment Pugie Reaux would arrive. She had to control herself; she could feel the onset of a headache. "I can't sit here. I must touch up my nails." She got up and looked around wildly.

"I believe your nail enamel is on the windowsill over the sink," Françoise said. Together they looked at the squat bottle with a red fingernail for a lid. Sophie snatched it, stood with her back to Françoise, and painted her thumbnail. Having something to do calmed her. She told herself she shouldn't be so angry at this woman. It wasn't her fault. She at least had the decency to remain silent while she gathered her nerves. It occurred to her that Françoise Fischler would make

a good female friend. She'd never known one to stand back
and give her enough distance, let her breathe. Not that she
had ever given women a chance. She didn't trust them, regretted it, but there you were. The women she had known
never measured up to her father. There now, had she forgotten? She still didn't know what this interview was about.

"If that's why you came over, because Clotilde told
you . . ." she began considerably softer.

"That's not why, Mrs. Minville. Clotilde Patout is en-
chanted with the boy. I came on my own. As I told you, I
am worried about Cato."

"Well, you needn't worry," Sophie said. "I'll keep him
home for a while."

"I hear him at night, Mrs. Minville. My room is across the
hall. Clotilde Patout has unsealed the doors into her late
sister's half of the house, so I can hear Cato if he has trouble
during the night. I do hear him. Lately, almost every night.
He lies in the dark talking to himself about things a boy his
age shouldn't worry about."

"Such as?"

"Death."

Sophie laughed. "It's obvious you don't have children.
They're obsessed with death."

"I have a child, Mrs. Minville. Cato's age. She's in a home
for retarded children."

She said, "I'm sorry. I didn't know."

"How could you have?"

Sophie sat down.

"It isn't only death," Françoise went on. "He seems obsessed with violence—guns, war, mutilating bodies. It's surprising from such a gentle boy. Have you thought he might
be unhappy?"

There was a stray in the backyard. It was thin and frightened and slinked along, tail between its legs. "He's always
been too sensitive," she began. "We've always tried to watch
what we say around him, but he can twist the most innocent

things into something horrible without my even knowing." The stray was looking longingly at the garbage can by the back door.

"I remember in New Orleans," she went on, "our landlord had a dog that always stood at the bottom of the stairs greeting tenants when we went in or out of the building. One day the dog died, possibly rabies. The Russells took it for an autopsy. When Cato asked where the dog was, Patout and I told him the truth. All the books say you should." She appealed to Françoise. "For weeks after, whenever we entered or left, Cato would throw a tantrum. I didn't know what was the matter. In time, he got over it, but it was another year before I found out he thought autopsy meant the Russells had cut the head off their dog. Maybe he thought they'd do it to him, too."

Sophie couldn't see the stray anymore. She listened. Something was coming down the road, possibly a truck. She cocked her head to the side. The sound came closer. Metal clanged, rattled. The cane truck drove by.

"I knew he didn't seem happy lately, but I thought it was because he doesn't have friends."

"I've wondered why I never see other children coming to play."

"We live too far out."

"Surely their parents would bring them?"

"They might bring them, but I'd have to take them back, and by the time Pat gets home with the car, it's dark. Patout doesn't like me driving out here in the dark. There's so much meanness these days." Sophie sighed. "Bringing up children isn't easy anymore," she murmured and glanced at the clock over the refrigerator.

"It never was," the French woman said.

Sophie cocked her head. Was that a truck coming down the drive? "Look," she said and her mood changed, "I appreciate your coming, but I don't know what any of us can do. I'll take him to Dr. Rodriguez and see what he says. In the meantime, if he upsets you at night, the best I can advise is close your door." She stood up, but the French woman did not take the hint. "Really, you must believe me, all boys his age think about death. They're little maniacs on the subject of killing. I suppose they never grow out of it, do they?" She tried to laugh. The French woman was not to be moved. "I'm sorry, but I've got to ask you to leave now. I think Mr. Reaux just turned in. He's taking me back to the hotel. Patout must think we've landed in a ditch by now."

"He also talks about other things, Mrs. Minville, things that are beyond his comprehension," Françoise added.

Sophie froze. The truck drove up to the house and stopped.

"Sometimes he pretends to be your husband. He seems to be scolding you for your behavior around other men."

"Really, this is too much," Sophie cried. "I don't know why you're telling me these things . . ." The door of the truck slammed.

"Perhaps you should stay home for a while." Françoise got up. "I was once married, too, Mrs. Minville, and I know the signs, even if Cato doesn't."

"What right do you have spying on me. Get out of here! Leave me alone!" she cried.

"I shall, but your child is suffering on your account." Françoise went down the back steps. Pugie Reaux was standing at the bottom.

He said, "Howdy."

She nodded her good day and walked toward The Oaks.

"Hi, gorgeous," he said, coming right in and heading for the washing machine. It quite took her breath away.

"Don't you know it's customary to knock before you come in someone's house?" she said.

He stopped suddenly, put his hands on his hips, and stared at her.

Why, the man could take out a knife and kill me right now, Sophie thought. It was part of his charm. That he came

into her house without asking, as though he had the right—
Patout never entered his own house without that hangdog,
meek kind of walk—made her feel hot between the legs. She
felt like throwing her arms around his legs and saying, take
me, I'm yours. She giggled. Whenever he was around, she
thought in scenes, like in a movie. It was a good thing she
was married. She could see why some women were pushovers
for a man.

"It's funny to hurt me?" he said, soft.

"Why no, Pugie," she said, genuinely surprised a man like
Pugie could be easily hurt.

"Then why say it?"

"I was only teasing."

"Fine. Go ahead. I've got better things to do than hang
around with a tease." He opened the screen door.

"Pugie, please! I'm sorry. Françoise Fischler's got me all
upset about Cato. That's why I snapped. Please, please
don't go."

"She comes over here, you go ape over your kid, and take
it out on me, huh? That the idea?"

"I'm sorry. Please," she said, no longer understanding what
her feelings for this man had to do with her son. Even if Cato
didn't like him, she would make him see Pugie Reaux was
no threat to her love for him. Cato would see it her way if
she asked.

The screen door thumped closed. "You gonna tell me what
this is all about?" he said in his husky voice.

"That Fischler woman said Cato thinks—"

"What does Cato think?"

"He's scared and having nightmares and—"

"And?" Pugie demanded. He watched her.

"She thinks I ought to stay away from you. People and
their dirty minds!" Sophie burst into tears.

And then he was kissing her and asking if she thought it
was dirty, this beautiful thing between a man and a woman

in love, and calling her baby, and pulling the straps of her sundress down, pushing his pelvis into her hard, until she fought him not knowing why.

He left her, went over to the table, picked up her bottle of nail enamel, put it down. "If you had a real man in your life you wouldn't need me," he said, his back to her. "But you don't, and I'm the best the town's got to offer. I'm in love with you, baby. I'd never hurt you. It kills me, a beautiful woman like you thinking she's gotta sacrifice herself for what people might say. It's not right, but I'm not used to arguing with a lady. I'll send one of my boys out tomorrow to look at your washer." He picked up his bag of tools, went to the door, and started down the steps.

"It's not because of what people think," she cried out. She ran after him, but he was already halfway down the drive.

She collapsed on the steps. After a while Cato came out and sat on the step above her. She leaned into his knees. He petted her hair. "Like old times," she murmured. It was a comfort to have a hand, anyone's hand, brush back her hair. "How do you always know when I have a headache coming on?" she said. He didn't answer.

21

*T*he situation was unbearable. It had been that way for years, but Willie was religious and without a reason sufficient in the Lord's eyes to wash the sin away, he couldn't justify leaving Ruby, even though someone with a lawyer for a sister-in-law in Chicago told him you couldn't leave a wife once she went altogether crazy.

When that happen, Lily and me shore gonna be stuck, Willie thought, dreading the already occurred, as people sometimes do when the truth is painful to face. Sitting on a stump near the veranda, he was waiting for Clotilde Patout and Françoise Fischler to come out. They were going to a tea honoring Sugar Queen contestants in town, and Clotilde had promised Willie a ride to the Queen Brown Sugar Parade.

I never should've married Ruby, he thought. He wouldn't have, if he'd known how superstitious she was, messing around with hairballs and entrails.

I was bewitched, he thought, disgusted, brushed a piece of bark off the seat of his pants, and sat back down.

Inviting as grass, four dark green rockers stood empty on the veranda. When Miss Clotilde had been sick, it was pleasant to sit there, but he wouldn't risk it now, not with the old lady running around good as new, and likely to come through the door any minute.

People said Dr. Rodriguez was a miracle worker the way he pulled Clotilde Patout through her strokes, but Willie knew it had nothing to do with the doctor and everything to do with Cato Minville living at The Oaks and the old lady having someone to love.

"Me, I know Lily's the only thing keeps me going," he murmured, and asked himself, half ashamed, how come he didn't get cracking, find the gold, and take his baby to a decent doctor in New Orleans?

Ruby, of course, dismissed the idea. She'd said it again last night. "Why you wanna waste time and money taking that Lily to New Orleans? You so hot to trot, why we don't all pick up and go to Chicago? They got doctors up there, and they know how to treat colored people right." She was always hollering about Chicago, like it was the promised land.

Willie shrugged. It was a lot of fuss about nothing. Nobody was going anywhere until he found that gold, and he'd begun losing hope lately. Felt none at all today. Felt different somehow. Uneasy. The top of his head tingled.

Must be the weather's about to snap, he said to himself, but there was no sign of rain in the sky.

If only Lily could talk. Like Miss Clo and Cato, they would sit back yonder on the porch in the evenings and tell stories, just him and his little girl. How he'd wanted that child. He still remembered the ordeal of her birth—Dr. Rodriguez showing up drunk, Ruby screaming for hours. When it was over, the baby's head didn't look the right shape. The forceps left black marks on either side. Rodriguez told Willie to sit and hold the baby's head until it went back into shape good, but Willie knew he didn't expect her to live. Willie'd never said anything about it to anyone. How could he, a colored man, go up against a doctor. That was something even white people didn't do.

Willie slapped an ant crawling on his arm. He supposed Dr. Rodriguez did the best he could. A decent man, one of the few doctors left who would come when you called, no matter who you were, and he didn't charge an arm and a leg if he knew you couldn't pay. Besides, Willie thought, he'd never had much faith in doctors. Like Miss Clo always said— what can you expect of people who get rich trading on other people's misery.

He took out his pocket watch. "Parade be half over by the time we get there," he mumbled. Ruby and Lily were already downtown, having left the house so early this morning he hadn't heard them go. He supposed Mr. Tutie's hired man, Demi John, gave them a lift. If he saw Ruby at the parade, he was going to give her a piece of his mind for leaving without him.

A truck was speeding down the road. As it went over a sandy stretch, it kicked up a great cloud of beige-colored dust. (The week before Tutie Romero had ordered sand to brick in his porch. The contractor's boy had stopped by the road to take a leak. When he got back in the truck, he threw the wrong gear, and dumped the load.) When the dust changed back to gray, Willie saw it was Pugie Reaux's truck heading for the Minvilles'. Wasn't the first time he'd seen that truck drive up after Patout Minville left for town.

Why, adultery would do for the Lord, he thought, but his shoulders sagged as soon as he had the thought. He doubted he could catch Ruby with another man. Most stayed clear of her.

As Pugie Reaux turned in, Sophie Minville appeared on her back steps.

Some men have all the luck, Willie thought. It was a miracle Miss Clo didn't know what was going on right down there on the end of her front lawn.

The door suddenly opened behind him. Willie rose and snatched off his hat. The foreign woman was standing there, observing him with the peculiar half-smile she often directed toward him. She looked toward the Minville house and frowned. "How long has he been over there?"

"Just drove up, Miss Fran-swaws."

"Heaven help us if Miss Clotilde sees him." She put down the heavy shopping bags she was carrying and held out two silver keys on a ring with a tab of yellow leather into which had been burned the initials "CP." "She wants you to get the car out and bring it to the front."

"Me?" Willie said.

"You."

"Miss Clo must be mixed up this morning. She know I can't drive."

"Willie, I had a stroke, not hardening of the arteries. I know Alphonse Romero's been teaching you to drive," Clotilde Patout said, coming out the front door and pulling on her gloves. She was wearing a navy blue dress with a polka-dot jacket, a pillbox hat with a small yellow bird stuck on the front and wrapped around with red tulle.

"Go on, take the keys, Willie. Go with him, Françoise. Make sure he finds neutral."

Willie stiffened. "I know neutral when I see it," he said, snatching the keys out of Françoise's hand.

"Back it up. Bring it around heading toward the road. Help me, Françoise. I swear, I never could wear a hat, me with only half a head," Clotilde Patout said.

Françoise adjusted the hat, stuck in the hatpin, and looked down. "You look very nice," she observed.

There was a glimmer of pleasure in Clotilde Patout's eyes. She quickly looked away.

Probably no one has told her she looked nice for over fifty years, Françoise thought. Her employer was not fashionably dressed, but she could hardly appear in public wearing a helmet hat, white boots, and a miniskirt without causing a riot. No, decidedly she is not chic, but she looks nice, almost handsome, Françoise thought.

Willie Wooten noticed it, too. He stopped by the corner of the house and shook his head. "Miss Clo, you looks good enough to eat," he said.

"Get out of here, Willie. Don't run over my shrubs. And put on a hat," Clotilde yelled, but Willie was already gone. "That man!" She giggled. "He enjoys things more if he thinks he's getting round me. Don't have the heart to tell him I asked Alphonse to teach him to drive."

"You did?"

"Of course. We have an emergency, we'll need a man who drives on the place. Patout's busy making a name for himself in town. Can't expect him to drop everything and come running every time we need a pound of beans. So I said to myself, 'Willie's always wanted to drive. Now's the time.' He turned forty-seven a while back. He's as mature as he'll ever be. I rang up, and Alphonse agreed to teach him."

"I could have, Miss Clotilde."

"That wouldn't have done." The older woman pursed her lips in distaste. They looked at each other. "You think we don't treat them right, but some things change slowly. You can't push people, Françoise Fischler. As long as you're living in my house, I expect you to respect my wishes."

The car jerked into view.

"Watch those preserves, Françoise Fischler. I intend to take first place." She stepped off the veranda.

Françoise looked down at the dingy backs of the old lady's shoes. Only the fronts and half of the sides were well covered with nurse's white polish.

"You'll ride in the back with me, of course."

Willie got out of the car, went around the back, and opened the door for Clotilde Patout. "Not bad, Willie," she said, bent over, and got in. He beamed.

Some time ago Françoise Fischler realized Clotilde Patout was a better woman than she made herself out to be. As the bony feet encased in the old-lady shoes disappeared into the back of the car, Françoise now told herself there was also something about the relationship between Clotilde and Willie she didn't understand. Clotilde often humiliated Willie, or would have, had Willie the pride of a normal man. Yet at times when Françoise would have thought him most affronted, he simply shrugged, or laughed, as though the old woman were acting toward him in some kind of grossly exaggerated way he found extremely funny. He was not, she knew, incapable of stubborn loyalty to Clotilde Patout, which, Françoise could only assume, had grown out of years and years of indoctrination by the Patout family—he, his mother and father before him, his grandparents before that, coming at length to believe their white patrons always had their interests at heart. At times, though, it was more than that. Love, you couldn't call it, at least not on Clotilde's side, or perhaps you could, if you didn't say it out loud.

Clotilde Patout and Willie Wooten were both staring. She gathered up the heavy shopping bag and hurried to the car. They drove down the drive, Willie riding the brake.

"A little faster, Willie." Clotilde Patout was in an expansive mood. After so much sickness and decades of living alone, she was well again, surrounded by people, some of whom, she'd begun to believe, possibly even cared for her. For a long time she had not been able to sustain the belief that her family's name counted for much in the community—two old maids, living alone, never going anywhere, all the family money gone long ago, people tend to forget. But after years of suffering the town's neglect, she was on her way into town to celebrate the sugar cane harvest and, just as when she was a child, one of her own kinsmen was running the show. She felt puffed up and proud. The Patouts and Minvilles had always been leaders of this civic event or that. In honor of the occasion, she felt duty bound to take first prize in the preserves contest.

Caught up in this festive mood, she checked to make certain her preserves were standing upright, patted the back of her head, and said to Françoise, "My dear, if you have never seen a colored parade, you are in for a treat. The white schoolchildren barely have the energy to pick up their feet and toot, but when little colored boys and girls play, they really play, and when they march, they strut. Why, sometimes they just stop and dance, right in the middle of the street, don't they, Willie."

"Sometimes they throw in a dance to change things up a bit, yes, ma'am, they do."

"White children only take band because their parents think

it's the thing to do. The Negro children put them to shame, don't they, Willie."

"Some folks do say so."

Clotilde Patout lowered her voice and addressed Françoise Fischler. "If we are forced to integrate, at least the public high school will have a decent band at last."

"The debating team at Booker T.'s mighty fine, too."

"That's enough, Willie. Look at the road, not in the rear-view mirror. For Heaven's sake, drive faster. We'll miss the parade."

"I going as fast as I can, Miss Clo." Willie did not take his foot off the brake. They inched down the drive toward the Minville house. Pugie Reaux's truck was out of sight on the other side.

"Why, look yonder. Sophie Minville's left her wash on the line. I declare, that woman hasn't got the brains she was born with. Doesn't she know about afternoon showers. She should've taken it in before going."

"She not gone, Miss Clo. I seen her on the back steps just a little while ago."

"Why, if my husband were chosen to host the Queen Sugar Contestants' Tea, I would think it my duty to be at his side."

"Mr. Minville probably had to be at the hotel early," Françoise said.

"Yes, that could explain it, although Patout's so busy, he's probably forgotten she doesn't have a way into town. Drive over, Willie."

"I wouldn't do that if I was you, Miss Clo."

"Whyever not?"

"Miss Sophie ain't expecting you."

"What does that have to do with the price of beans? Drive over there, Willie. I must try harder to be nice to that young woman, at least for today. I'll give her a lift."

"Willie's right, Miss Clotilde. If Mr. Minville drives out and finds her gone, he'll be upset."

"Nonsense! Good Lord, Willie, can't you go any faster? We'll miss the parade."

"That ain't my fault, Miss Clo. I been up and ready since dawn."

"Stop the car! Hop out, Françoise Fischler. Go over yonder and tell that young woman we're coming to fetch her. She can comb her hair and change her dress by the time Willie gets us over there. Tell her to put on something decent."

"Stay put, Miss Fran-swaws. That yard's right wet in the middle. Rain hadn't had time to burn off since yesterday."

"Willie, I told you to stop. Françoise, do as I told you."

Françoise opened the door. Willie slammed on the brakes, turned around, and glared as though she were a traitor.

"Miss Clotilde," she said, anxious, "wait here. I'll run over and tell Mrs. Minville that when we reach the hotel, if her husband hasn't already left to fetch her, we'll send Willie back."

"I swanee, was a lady ever plagued with such stubborn hired help? Will neither of you do as I say?" The old woman reached over and slammed the car door. The hat fell over her eyes. "Drive on, Willie."

Willie started up. The car turned slowly into the road and headed for the Minville house.

Françoise ran across the lawn. As she reached the bamboo, Cato appeared.

"Miss Françoise!" he called in a panic-stricken voice. He grabbed her hand and pulled.

The black sedan had reached the edge of the Minvilles' yard.

"Cato, let go of me," she said. "I've got to tell your mother Nanan's coming to take her to town. What are you doing here? Why aren't you in school?"

"I didn't feel good. Mama let me stay home," he said.

The sedan turned into the drive.

She shook the boy off and ran toward the house.

"Françoise!" the child screamed. She mounted the concrete

steps and lifted her hand to knock. Sophie Minville's name caught in her throat, as she looked at the naked back of a woman on which a man's hands were traveling up and down.

The brakes on the sedan squeaked.

Pugie Reaux looked up.

"Clotilde Patout is here," Françoise said.

Pugie Reaux pushed Sophie aside, went to the sink, opened the cabinet doors, and dropped to the floor. He put his head underneath the sink.

Sophie ran to the hall, went into the bathroom, and shut the door.

Only then did Françoise realize Cato was standing beside her, peering through the screen.

Clotilde Patout got out of the car and bore down on them. "What are you waiting for. Go on in. Did you tell her?"

Françoise nodded and opened the door for her.

Clotilde Patout raised her voice. "Sophie Minville? Get a move on. I've got to get my preserves downtown. I'm only going to wait a—" She stopped suddenly, seeing the man's torso extending from under the sink. "Who's that?"

Slowly, Pugie Reaux pulled his head out and gave her his handsome grin. "Howdy, Miss Clotilde. Long time no see."

Clotilde Patout stepped back. "What are you doing in Patout's house?" she said.

"He's got a little problem with his sink. Asked me to take a look."

"You stay away from Patout, Pugie Reaux. You got him in trouble once years ago. Don't think I've forgotten. Now go."

Pugie reached in his back pocket for his wallet, opened it, and took out a piece of gum. Slowly he unwrapped it, stuck out his tongue, and folded the gum into his mouth. Then he grinned. "No offense, Miss Clotilde, but Patout asked me here, and I aim to stay."

"Miss Clotilde," Françoise said, low, "Cato doesn't seem well. Oughtn't you take a look at him?"

"Where is he?"

"With Willie in the car."

"Yes, yes, I'll go." Without another word she turned and slowly walked to the car.

Sophie came out of the bathroom. She had been crying. Her face was a mess of red splotches. Her lipstick was smeared. "Why did you bring her here? She's going to turn us all out now without a cent. Where are we going to go? I thought you cared about my son?"

"Mama, Nanan says I've got fever. She thinks you ought to take my temperature." The boy was standing on the top step, talking through the screen door. As he spoke, Sophie burst into tears.

Cato went inside, took his mother by the hand, led her down the hall toward her bedroom.

"You'd better go," Françoise said to Pugie Reaux.

The horn honked.

"Tell them we'll be out in a minute. We've got to bundle up the babies."

"In this weather?"

"I don't give a damn what you say, just stall them."

She went to the twins' room, found the stroller, got them in. When she wheeled them into the kitchen, Sophie was sitting at the table. Cato was running a brush through her hair. Pugie Reaux was gone.

"We'll wait in the car till you're done," Françoise said, picked up the twins, and left.

"Cato, what are we going to do?" she heard Sophie say.

"It's all right, Mama. Everything's going to be all right," the boy replied.

They drove in silence into Belmont. When they reached the turn-key bridge, Old Man Boudreaux was standing in the middle of the road, waving his arms wildly over his head. Willie slowed.

"Drive on, Willie Wooten. Drive on, I say. Don't stop for

that fool." Clotilde Patout had never forgiven the man for vomiting on her running board one day in the late 1940s when she stopped to see what was the matter with him.

"The bridge is out!" Sophie cried. "Stop, Willie. We'll drown!"

Willie slammed his foot to the floor. It missed the brakes and hit the accelerator. The car shot forward. Sophie and the babies screamed. Suddenly the car jolted and stopped.

Clotilde Patout pushed back her hat and rolled down the window. "Stay there, Boudreaux. Don't come any closer to my car. What's the matter with the bridge?"

"Nothing. They got that colored parade going on up yonder. Sheriff Mouton tole me to wave y'all away. Street can't handle more cars up there. Go round by the new bridge."

"Nonsense. My cousin's hotel is on this side of town. We are not going to spend two hours doubling back and fighting traffic." She rolled up the window, leaned back. "Drive on, Willie."

"Yes, ma'am," Willie said. The black sedan shot forward, rattled over the bridge, then crawled up the bayou bank to Main Street. Ahead Sheriff Stanley Mouton stood in the middle of the road, holster protruding from his belt. He waved them down. Behind him was a teeming mass of parade watchers—men, women, and children in sundresses and overalls, eating cotton candy and waving little flags with a pelican on a field of blue, and, here and there, homemade banners that said, "Bon Ton Roulé," "Ti Coteaux Kiwanas," and the like.

"You may stop now, Willie," Clotilde said.

Willie stopped.

Down came the window.

Sheriff Mouton took off his cowboy hat, squatted. "*Mais*, Miss Clo, *Sha*, you looking good, huh?"

"Feel fine now, thank you."

"Y'all can't get by. We got us a parade."

"Ease back the crowd, Sheriff Mouton. When there's a gap in the floats, go out in the middle and direct us across. Patout's waiting with a hotel full of dignitaries, including the mayor."

"Miss Clotilde . . ."

"Don't argue with me, Mouton. Drive on, Willie." The window closed.

The sedan inched forward. People parted, shook fists, but Willie drove inexorably on, until the front fender touched the police barricade. He killed the motor, squeezed out, and sat on the hood.

"Can I get out and watch, Mama?" Cato's eyes glistened. His face was unnaturally flushed.

Sophie felt his forehead.

"Did you take his temperature like I told you?" Clotilde asked.

"Patout took the thermometer for the first-aid kit. I'll take it when we get to the hotel."

"Mama, can I get out and sit with Willie on the hood?"

"It's a parade for colored people, Cato. You stay in the car."

"Nonsense, Sophie Minville. This is the best parade of the year. I'll take him myself," Clotilde said. "Come on, Boy, climb over the seat. Take my hand." They squeezed out the door. Cato climbed onto the hood. Willie hopped down, helped Clotilde Patout up, then got back up himself.

The parade was going full steam. A loudspeaker announced the bands and floats. "Look out! Here comes the best band in Louisiana. I give you Booker T. Washington's award-winningest Marching Tigers. Let's hear it, folks!"

In the distance, growing louder every minute, came the throbbing of drums beating in double time. The crowd roared.

"Stand up, Mr. Cato. Stand up. You light enough. Won't make no dent."

Clotilde nodded. He jumped up, just in time to see two young women, carrying banners, high-step down the middle of Main. A few moments behind the banner carriers marched a squad of young girls in white satin shorts, red sequin jackets, and cowboy boots. They carried nothing in their hands, just marched, bringing their knees up high, reaching for their chins. Right behind them came Booker T.'s Marching Tigers. Suddenly the band swung into song, and the girls stopped dead, raised their hands in unison, kicked their right legs in the air, wiggled side-back-side, dipped, and turned, marching right through the band in double time, and the drums beat mercilessly on, rapid-fire, and Cato thought his heart would burst with the noise of life and spirit he did not know.

The crowd screamed.

Willie grinned.

Clotilde Patout shook her head.

The girls kicked again, dipped, turned, and high-stepped forward. And now came the band, all red-and-white satin and purple plumes, swinging their instruments right left, right left as they played. The faces of the crowd reflected in the bells, and the crowd let out a roar.

Queen Brown Sugar sailed by on a crescent moon. Her maids smiled out of stars and waved tiny magic wands.

Cato bent over to tell the old lady she was clutching his hand too tightly. As he did, the bird on her hat looked up at him, opened its beak, as though it would speak, and he felt himself slipping down. Then it was dark.

He did not feel the hands clutching at him, nor hear the alarmed cries, nor smell the half-eaten candied apple that lay on the pavement near his nose. Later they told him Sheriff Mouton pushed through the crowds, went out in the middle of the street, and stopped the parade, while the car spun across—this time with Nanan at the wheel—leaving Willie Wooten behind, for he could not sit in the back with white ladies. When he came to, his mother was saying, "Whew, it smells like a funeral parlor in here." He opened his eyes in the rose-scented room and looked into Dr. Rodriguez's eyes.

"Where'd you get mumps, Boy? Anybody else in your class had them?"

Cato closed his eyes.

"There's nothing more any of you can do here, so why don't you go downstairs." Rodriguez looked in the mirror over the cigarette-marred dresser, smoothed his cowlick, and saw the worried look on Sophie Minville's face.

"Cato's in no danger, Mrs. Minville," he said.

"Well, I for one need to go downstairs. All this commotion over Cato probably has made me too late to enter my preserves."

"When Cato wakes up, I'll make him apologize," Sophie said. The women glared at each other.

Clotilde Patout rose, headed for the door, seemed to think better of it, and ripped off her hat. She threw it on the empty bed. Her chin quivered.

Rodriguez put his arm through hers. "My dear, it's a normal childhood ailment. He'll be right as rain in no time. Shall I see you downstairs?"

Clotilde nodded.

"Mrs. Minville, just keep him covered. I'll be back soon to check on him. I'll have the kitchen send you something good to eat."

Willie Wooten was sitting on a stool outside in the hall. As they came out, he rose.

"Goodness knows I've tried to be kind to that young woman, James, but she has such a chip on her shoulder."

"Miss Clo—"

"How could she think I wasn't concerned about Cato?"

"My dear, I'm sure she realizes you are—"

"She thinks she's the only one permitted to love him. Wants the boy all to herself."

"Miss Clo—"

"What, Willie?"

"We going home soon? People round here keep asking me to carry bags."

"Not yet, Willie. Go downstairs to the kitchen. Ask the cook to make a nice tray for Miss Sophie," Dr. Rodriguez said. Willie did not move.

"Tell them to give you a sandwich, while they're at it," Clotilde said. "When you're done, wait there. Nobody'll bother you in the kitchen. We'll be along directly. We want to let the boy sleep a bit before we take him home."

"Yes, ma'am." Willie walked to the service door at the end of the hall and started down the stairs.

"Lord, they are so afraid somebody's going to ask them to do a little work," said the doctor.

"Well, I do think people have a lot of nerve. Willie Wooten has worked for me his entire life. Everybody knows."

They stopped in front of the elevator. She poked the button. The chains of the elevator clanked. Slowly the cage climbed.

When Willie reached the bottom of the stairs and went into the kitchen, he saw Françoise Fischler chopping scallions at a table near the window. She drew off a small stack from the large bunch of scallions in the center of the table, held them with her fingertips, and, like a professional cook, reduced them to a pile of green and white O's within seconds. Françoise Fischler wasn't much to look at, but she'd have made somebody a good wife, Willie thought. She was kind, too, although she tried to hide it. She and Miss Clo were both that way. I guess women alone have to act tough so nobody won't take advantage of them, Willie thought.

"How's Cato?" Françoise said.

He smiled. He had a funny taste in this mouth. Metallic-like. The French woman was looking at him. How wrong you could be about people, he thought. First time he'd seen Ruby, he had thought no angel in heaven was sweeter. And come to find out, she was good with a knife, and not for chopping no green onions with neither, he said to himself. And first time I seen Miss Fran-swaws, I said to myself, look out, Willie Wooten. That lady's going mean trouble. Come to find out, she's mighty nice.

"You feel all right, Willie?"

"I beg your pardon, Miss Fran-swaws?"

"What you want here, man? Anybody take up room in my

hotel kitchen better work, or git, quick. We got one hundred judges and a passle of ladies and gentlemen to keep in feed, so what'll it be, work or git?"

Willie glared at the head cook. "I come down here on orders from Dr. James D. Rodriguez. Y'alls to fix something real nice for the boss's wife. Right now. Soup, crackers, a little of that ambrosia I saw you stick in the fridge a minute ago. Put it on a nice silver tray. I'm gonna carry it up. Y'all suppose to feed me, too, but I can wait. Miss Fran-swaws'll fix me up with a right nice dinner when we get home, you can count on that. Better than anything you got here." He paused to let that sink in. His eyes stung. Maybe he needed glasses. He turned to the French woman. "I'm fine, Miss Fran-swaws, but Mr. Cato, he got the mumps."

"You ever had them, Willie?"

"Yes, ma'am. Seem like it, but I don't rightly recollect."

A noise caused him to turn and see Frank, his wife's second cousin, coming through the kitchen door with a green plastic garbage pail in his hands. The sun shone down and lighted the bucket. The color reflected on the man's white uniform.

"How you making it, Willie?" Frank said.

"Right pretty pail, Frank." He never knew what to say to his wife's family. They were slow country people. Most of them couldn't speak English well. He hadn't learned French, growing up as he had at The Oaks. The Patouts prided themselves on speaking English as good as anybody outside Louisiana.

"How's my cousin?" Frank asked. There was a watchful, almost contemptuous look in the man's eyes. All of Ruby's people looked at him that way, ever since the day he got taken in by her.

"Fine," Willie said.

"Y'all taking a little trip?"

"Trip? We ain't taking no trip. Where to? What with? Man, who told you that?"

"All I know's the other day Ruby done borrowed my suitcase."

"Heck, Frank, she just trying to make herself look big, walking down the street with a suitcase in her hand. Don't pay her no mind. She ain't going no place."

The head cook yelled. "You going to talk or work, Boy?"

"You tell Ruby if she not going no place, she better give me back my case. I wasn't planning on giving it away."

"I'll tell her, Frank."

Frank picked up a garbage can and went through the back door.

Willie shook his head. That Ruby. No, she wasn't going anywhere, not now, not ever, but, Willie thought, someday he and Lily were. Getting acquainted with Miss Clo's old car was the first step. He laughed. Someday, somehow, they'd get away, and the first stop was going to be New Orleans.

22

*U*nder a gigantic welcoming banner scripted in silver glitter, the entire female population of Belmont appeared that afternoon to be celebrating over petit fours and bourbon balls the picking of a new Sugar Queen, but that was not quite how it was. These were women only of a certain type and class, namely: women of money or family; women without fortune or background, but whose husbands had attained a certain rank through politics or professions—bank officers, independent insurance salesmen, owners of filling stations, that type of thing—and lastly, women of great physical beauty. All other women in town—the poor, the ugly, the black—were elsewhere on that afternoon, having understood all their lives they weren't uninvited, merely not expected to attend. (Each year an identical reception honored Queen Brown Sugar on the other side of town where, not wishing to be outdone, the black ladies not only matched the social winnowing of the whites, but added a further qualification based on the fairness of skin. By tradition, these teas were held one day apart to save the town from a white and a black young lady appearing on the same front page.)

Now into this mass of the town's nicer women descended Clotilde Patout and James Rodriguez. The elevator lurched and stopped. They stepped out and moved to the side to adjust to the deafening noise and survey for a moment the pandemonium in the lobby. There were ladies everywhere— in flowers and feathers and ruffles, even a fur or two jumping the gun, while on the chests of each hopeful and mama was a joint of sugar cane, a tiny bottle of Tabasco, and a miniature box of Morton salt entwined with a pink carnation. Here and there men sprinkled the room. The present and former King Sugars, each old enough to pass for his queen's grandfather and wearing a crown, representatives of Belmont's chamber of commerce and men's clubs, plantation owners, and smaller, but wealthy, cane farmers huddled together in knots.

In the midst of this abounding humanity a man could be seen bobbing in and out, shifting teacup one hand to other, picking up silver trays, putting them down, looking wildly about the room, smile stuck to upper teeth.

"There's Patout," Clotilde shouted in the doctor's ear. "And there's my cut-glass punch bowl. Oh, an ice swan!"

"Where? I don't see him, not in this mob, unless he's wearing high heels and pearls," Rodriguez shouted back.

"Don't argue, James. Come on." She seized his arm, dragged him into the crowd, straining to see if there were camellia petals in the ice cubes this year. "Patout! Yoo-hoo!"

He waved, motioned for them to stay put, trotted free. "Thank God!" he shouted. "Quick, over here."

He brushed aside a velvet drape and steered them into a small antechamber off the lobby where the noise was a manageable roar.

"Good to see Patouts and Minvilles running things again," Rodriguez said, shaking Patout's hand.

"Patout, you do me proud," Clotilde declared.

Patout leaned down, smacked her cheek, blushed hot.

"I told Patout this hotel was a brilliant idea." She patted the bun on the back of her neck.

"You did?" said the astonished doctor.

Clotilde said, "We been looking for you, Patout. Where've you been?"

"Me!"

"Is that punch spiked?" Rodriguez said, peering out.

"No you don't, James. You're going to get me and my preserves across that lobby intact. Get away from that curtain and sit."

The doctor sat.

"Where have you been? Where's Sophie? Damn it to hell, this shindig's been going an hour. A man can't function alone in there." Patout collapsed beside Rodriguez on the loveseat.

"Cato's got fever, a hundred and three. Fainted at the parade. Your wife didn't have sense enough to keep him in bed. Lord, Patout, do something about the heat in here." She waved at an elderly lady serving punch who had spotted them. "Fine, fine," she mouthed and jerked the curtain closed. "I wouldn't have lent you my best cut-glass bowl if I'd known Marybelle Dautrieve was serving. Breaks anything beautiful that isn't hers, right, James?"

"Now, Miss Clo, don't start on poor Marybelle. She came and brought a whole baked ham that time she chipped Mary Louise's cake stand. And don't worry, son," the doctor went on, "Cato's going to be fine. He's just got mumps. Both sides." Rodriguez puffed out his cheeks.

Clotilde opened her purse, took out kid gloves, and slapped them in the air. "Don't act the fool, James. Patout, if I were the father of a sick little boy, I'd want to go see about him."

"Where is he?" Patout asked, weary.

"Upstairs. Room Fifty. Isn't refurbished, but that was all you had left," Rodriguez explained.

Patout got up, pushed aside the curtain.

"Would you keep an eye out, Aunt Clotilde? Make sure people—"

"Patout, I'll thank you to remember I was brought up to hostess this sort of thing, not like some people I could mention."

He refused to rise to the bait. He turned to Rodriguez. "Where are they again, Doc?"

"Fifty. Room Fifty."

"Sophie, too?"

Rodriguez nodded. "Take your time, son. We'll handle things here."

"Thanks, Doc. You, too, Aunt Clotilde," he added lamely and went out.

Rodriguez shook his head sadly. "You know, my dear, I don't try to tell you what to do—"

"Then don't," she said, then added with malice, "If you ask me, all he has to do to find Sophie Minville is follow Pugie Reaux's trail. Haven't you noticed that man hanging around her, Rodriguez?"

"Can't say I have. Matter of fact, I heard she had a conniption when Reaux stopped by the hospital to see her."

"Perhaps I'm mistaken," she replied, doubtful.

"Pugie's devoted to Patout," the doctor went on. "And Patout to him. Now that I don't understand. Never was a Reaux in history worth shaking a finger at."

"Patout's probably flattered by attention from an all-around male like Pugie Reaux. It's Pugie's devotion I don't understand." She rammed a hand into a kid glove and began working down into the fingers.

"My point was with Pugie and Patout being such good friends—"

"I got the point, Rodriguez. You don't have to dot all the i's and cross all the t's," Clotilde snapped, then seeing she'd gone too far, "You of all people ought to know by now that sort of thing drives me wild."

The doctor rose, hiked his trousers. "How's about entering those blackberry preserves? Win a blue ribbon and I'll know I got you cured once and for all."

"You had nothing to do with my recovery, Rodriguez, so don't go taking credit where none's due. Come on. Into the fray." She was in fine spirits today. Nothing was going to bring her down. She grabbed the doctor's arm. They fought across the lobby and into the ballroom on the opposite side, where hundreds of half-pint Mason jars sat tagged and waiting. Glaring at a nearby judge until he thought better of saying the deadline had passed, Clotilde marched up, plunked down her jar, and watched him dip into watermelon rind preserves. There were three jars of pepper relish before he got to hers.

Meanwhile Patout was pacing in front of the elevators stuck on six and seven. Guests came up. He was forced to stand still and wait. He thought the man in the beige leisure suit was a sugar buyer from Texas. He didn't recognize the women.

"We having fun, no?" the man roared. The women giggled. "That's the way you Cajuns talk, no?"

"No!" They screamed with laughter. The sickly sweet odor of bourbon hit Patout in the face.

"Going to be a first-rate hotel when they're done, don't you think?" an elderly gentleman shouted at his wife.

Blushing with pleasure, Patout turned and gave his grin to the lobby. He had to admit he'd done a pretty good job. Of course the remodeling wasn't complete, not even in the lobby. Filthy carpet lay underneath the borrowed funeral parlor grass. The gilded mermaids scattered on consoles throughout lobby and smoking rooms smiled through grime, white plaster showed through cracks in their necks and broken-off noses, but no one could see them in the crush. Even the roaches were behaving. He fervently hoped they would stay under the moldings until the last white glove and flowered hat exited out the front. He went over, poked the elevator button, turned and faced the lobby.

His mural of the Mississippi shrouded in yellow mist would have made Turner proud. One day a magnificent ceiling would be swirling around the huge chandelier here in the lobby. He'd thought of Chagall, but as he was aiming high, why not Michelangelo? He climbed scaffolding, lay on his back, unbeknownst to the ladies underneath, and painted fat fingers and hairy legs in glowing blues and greens and fiery reds, as he had seen in *Life* magazine's coverage of the Paris Opera and a postcard of the Sistine Chapel saved these twenty years and only recently lost.

If only he had come home to Belmont sooner. His great mistake had been to fear compromise. Now he knew it was possible to experience all that life offered—accomplishment on a grand scale and the joys of being a husband and father. What liberation! He pictured Sophie as he found her in the back of that café. "I don't know where I'm going yet, mister, but the important thing is I'm going." Her determination charmed him. Glowing with renewed expectations, he felt seized with the need to tell her he'd found their destination at last.

"Mr. Pat?"

He turned. Willie Wooten was holding a silver tray.

"Do you know where Miss Sophie is at? I went upstairs just now to bring her food—ain't this a pretty tray—and she wasn't there."

"Cato was alone?"

"I don't know, Mr. Pat. All I know is I knocked and she didn't say come in."

"Why didn't you go in? She just didn't hear you. Here, give it to me. I'm going up, if the elevator ever comes." Patout reached for the tray. Someone grabbed his arm. The tray clattered to the floor.

"Oh, my," Margaret Richard said under her wide-brimmed hat. She stepped out of the wreckage.

Willie Wooten scowled.

"That's all right, Mrs. Richard. No harm done. Pick this mess up, please, Willie, and have cook fix another tray."

"He ain't going to like that."

"Tell him it's my fault. Miss Sophie's bound to be hungry. It's way past lunch. I'll go on up and tell her—"

"Mr. Minville, I do so want you to tell me about the arts and crafts shop you're planning for the lobby. I've been hearing so much about it," said Mrs. Richard, the wife of the owner of Belmont's largest furniture store. There were canvases languishing in her attic, paintings done some years before at the Art Students League when she accompanied her husband to a furniture convention in New York City and stayed to complete her month's course. Although paintings of the Statue of Liberty, Grant's Tomb, and Macy's from Sixth Avenue were the object of ridicule in class, she knew they would create a stir in her hometown and, better yet, they would sell.

"She ain't there, Mr. Pat."

"Excuse me, Mrs. Richard." Patout lowered his voice. "Do as I say, Willie. She just didn't hear you." He turned back to the waiting matron. "Now, what was it, Mrs. Richard?"

Just then Pugie Reaux sauntered down the stairs.

"Excuse me a moment longer, Mrs. Richard." Patout left the astonished woman and hurried to Pugie.

As president of the Belmont Garden Club, Margaret Richard had been prepared to offer up to two thousand dollars to assist Patout Minville in opening a shop dedicated to the furtherance of south Louisiana artists—the garden club had wanted to open such a shop for years. But seeing his attention so easily diverted from the topic at hand—and by the likes of Pugie Reaux at that—her opinion of him and the project underwent an immediate change.

"He was positively rude to me," she muttered, the blue feathers on her hat trembling. She felt herself a girl of four all over again, one who could never sustain enthusiasm for playing doctor if only her girl cousin, but not the boy, wanted to play.

She sat down on the nearest sofa, utterly dejected. Her canvases would continue to sit there in the dark for another ten years until at length, when she grew old and died, her son would throw them out when he and his wife went through her things and selected who would get what. Or perhaps they would split the paintings between Catholic Charities, the Salvation Army, and the Knights of Columbus rummage sale. The thought of her canvases in the rummage sale made her so sad that she got up, forgetting she had loaned two dozen punch glasses and promised to give Rachel Jones a lift home, and walked out.

"Look, I'm not saying you have to stop playing, but for God's sake, keep it under wraps," Patout was telling Pugie. "Howdy, Mrs. Richard," Pugie said as the matron left, fingering her pearls. "Imagine waking up in the middle of the night and seeing that on the pillow next to you. Whoo-ee!"

"Okay, Pugie? I can't afford to get the place closed down by the police. Not now."

"Sure, Pat, but you got nothing to worry about; Mouton's winning."

"Sheriff Mouton's up there?"

Pugie grinned. "What's wrong with that? Everybody in Belmont plays. Even your Aunt Janice. You talk about poker. That old gal used to play every chance she got. I went up against her once or twice at the church bazaar. Man, she liked to cleaned me out. Had the darnedest poker face, like that kid of yours."

"It's called being shy."

"Bet she had every nickel she ever won. Left a pile when she died?"

Patout flushed. Now he either had to tell Pugie it was none of his business, or reveal his family's financial condition. Life seemed full of small bogs into which he was always stepping. "Beg pardon?" he said.

"I said, your kid told me not to call Willie Wooten a nigger."

He had never noticed how muscular Reaux was. "Well, things have changed since we were young, Pugie."

"Man, you talk like you're a hundred years old," Pugie said. "Me, I just started to live. Looks to me like your kid's got ideas most folks don't take kindly to. You don't want people saying you're raising a nigger lover. That sort of thing's bad for business."

Seeing a flash of Pugie's white teeth—he really was a handsome devil—Patout put his hand in Pugie's and shook it, relieved to see his old friend going.

Pugie leaned in. "How's about a little game of poker ourselves, just for old times' sake, huh?"

"Mr. Minville?"

Patout turned and faced Françoise Fischler.

"Could you come to the kitchen? Willie and the cook were arguing, and the cook told Willie that Ruby's left him."

"What!"

"Ruby's cousin confirms it. The kitchen's in an uproar. The cook's angry. Willie's crying. He's afraid Ruby's taken Lily. None of the orders are leaving the kitchen. Can you come?"

"Pugie, could you do me a favor?"

"Shoot, man."

"Sophie and Cato are upstairs in Room Fifty. Cato's sick. I was on my way up to check on him and take something to Sophie to eat. Could you stop by, tell her I'm coming. It'll be half an hour at least."

"Sure, Pat. Anything else I can do?"

"No, we can manage. No need to stay. Just stick your head in and tell her, will you? She's probably wondering where I am."

"I'll do it. Remember, you get tired of serving cakes to old bags out here, me and the boys will be in Room Fifty-eight."

He hitched up his pants, then pulled them down low over his hips, winked at Miss Lizzardville, who got third runner-up in the Shrimp Queen contest and was odds-on favorite to be Queen Sugar before the evening was out, then went to the elevator, got in, and blew a kiss. The doors shut. Patout turned. Miss Lizzardville was covered with blushes.

"He can't resist, can he," Françoise said.

"Come on. Let's get things moving," Patout said. They headed for the kitchen. "Where did Ruby go, home to her mama?"

"Chicago," Françoise said.

"Chicago!" He stopped, thunderstruck. She might as well have said Ruby'd flown to the moon.

"She went off with a man from Alphonse Romero's farm who has a brother up there working in a steel mill, promised him a job."

He couldn't get over it. "Why, Ruby and Willie have been at The Oaks—poor Willie." He trailed off. What had come over him? The French woman was looking at him strangely. "Look," he said, "I'm not much good—"

"If you could just come in and say a word," she said.

"Look here, I must see about Cato. It can't wait. I'll be back in a minute, okay?"

"Okay," she said, not understanding.

Patout ran for the stairs.

· 23 ·

*I*n the time it took to race up three floors, his mood underwent a dramatic change. From the fear that propelled the first flight until he stopped to gasp on the third, he hadn't realized it was possible to feel so ashamed of himself. He sat down on the stairs, covered his face with his hands, and faced the awful truth. If he could not trust an old friend like Pugie Reaux, there was no one in the world he could.

The runner was torn from the riser. He stuck in his finger and listened to his heart pound. The day's excitement was upsetting his equilibrium. Wrenching emotion hadn't plagued him in years. He was settled, comfortably middle-aged. Such antics belonged to twenty-year-olds and women, like Sophie, whose thirst for excitement never abated. The certainty of that had made him link his life to hers, but damn it, he wasn't some kind of performing bear, hired to fuel her intensity. There were scuff marks on the walls. They would probably come off in an afternoon with a little ammonia, but the carpeting would soon have to go. Boredom was terrible for marriage.

Knowing where that thought was leading, he asked himself again how he could sink so low. He knew very well Sophie needed people more than he, yet he had left her virtually alone half of the summer and into the fall while he fell in love with this ridiculous hotel. If men only knew the responsibilities of marriage. He was obliged to set things right with his wife. There was even a certain comfort in the burden. Only a fool wouldn't admit it. His spirits lifted. Again he thought to tell her what he had discovered in the lobby, but he was less certain how it went. Giving himself another minute to rest before going on, he followed this train of thought further.

Two floors above in a darkened room his son lay and watched through his lashes the door from the hall slowly open.

"Psst, Sophie."

The light from the bulb in the hall shone in the boy's eyes. His mother's taffeta slip swished against her nylons. The scent of a flower sweeter than honeysuckle lingered near him as she went to the man at the door. The door chain dropped aside, rattled. The man leaned in. They put their faces together. The light shone in his eyes again. His mother returned to the bed and looked in his face, while the man shut the door. The room went dark. Cato could not smell her perfume anymore.

"Asleep?" Pugie Reaux whispered.

"Yes, but you can't stay." She put her hand on Cato's forehead. It felt foreign, not the hand of his mother. It felt like she was separate from him.

Pugie Reaux lifted his mother's hair, put his mouth on the back of her neck. A hand edged around her waist, grabbed her stomach. He pulled her against him.

"No, please," his mother said and closed her eyes. The hand moved up her body, stopped under her breasts. The thumb brushed back and forth lazily, a cat's tail issuing warning. Then they were gone to where he could not see. He turned his head slowly as though in sleep and found them again by the shuttered window. Pugie Reaux's shirt was open. His mother's blouse was hanging out of her skirt in the back. She whimpered. It made him feel she had locked herself away from him in another room, as she did when she got angry. He was certain he had done something wrong. He wanted to ask her how to behave while this thing he did not want to think about was happening, but he daren't until they stopped.

Meanwhile Patout had reached the fifth floor and was walking down the hall trying to find Room Fifty. There were missing digits on every door. A damn nuisance for the guests; surprising no one had complained. When he reached Fifty, he stopped and put his ear to the door. There was no sound inside, but why should there be? Cato was asleep. Sophie was probably dozing by his side, or maybe, famished, she'd slipped down to the kitchen. That sounded right.

He tiptoed away, but halted at the stairs. There was no point in not checking while he was here, but was it the right door? There were too many missing numbers along the corridor to be sure. He'd hate to walk in on guests.

Then he was standing in front of Number Five-cleanspot again. How do you do? Lovely weather. Oops, I'm sorry? Nothing worked. He raised his hand to knock, found himself silly, put his hand on the knob. The elevator door banged. Françoise Fischler stepped out, staggering under the weight of a tray. He hurried over, took it out of her hands. Milk, coffee, ambrosia, salad, a turkey sandwich, plate of bourbon balls, he ticked them off. "This could feed an army," he said.

"Sorry it took so long. Thanks." She collapsed against the wall. For a moment she looked as though she might cry.

"Look here," he said, "you don't want to get yourself upset. They play by different rules than us, you know."

"Yes, when they run off they take their children," she said, pushing off the wall.

"Beg pardon?"

"Nothing," she said, passing her hand through her hair. "I just feel sorry for Willie."

"So do I, but look here, you were up when they brought Cato in, is this right?" he said, lowering his voice and nodding at the door.

"Of course," she whispered back.

"Wouldn't want to walk in on somebody. I'd probably say something inane, like, 'Hello, hope you're having fun.' "

"That would be appropriate in certain situations," she said, laughter welling in her eyes.

He laughed soundlessly, colored. Their eyes met.

"It's been a success, hasn't it," she said. Her eyes wore a friendly expression. She told hold of the knob.

"After you," he said. She cracked the door. Rose-scented room spray invaded his nostrils. Dirt, shoddiness, the pretense of a boudoir passed through his mind. He coughed. Milk sloshed on the tray, soaking the paper napkin. Françoise Fischler gasped. He looked up and caught a flash of white. Someone had gone into the bathroom and shut the door. Sophie in her slip? Hard to tell, the room was so dark. What would she be doing in her slip at this time of day? He turned toward the bed. A shaft of light from the hall fell on Cato's face.

"I brought Mama something to eat," he said. It sounded like an apology.

The boy made no reply. His eyes were wide open, staring.

Patout stood there, puzzled, still as a deer blinded by headlights, noting incongruous detail: the shutters were inappropriate, travelers always wanted modern conveniences, but they certainly gave the room character. Pugie Reaux sat on the dressing-table stool. It might have been a seedy room in the Quarter, a stage setting for a play; the air was charged with atmosphere. Men didn't use dressing tables. He made a note to capture it on canvas before they fixed up the decor. What was Pugie Reaux doing in this room?

"Patout," Pugie said, soft. He rose from the stool.

"Pugie," Patout echoed. Alone with his wife and son? Sophie in her slip? "Weren't you going to play cards?" he asked, his voice hollow. She couldn't have been in her slip.

"Thought I'd better wait here till you came, in case your wife needed anything," Pugie said. "Man, you'd better put that thing down," getting no response, growing bolder, "You got enough there to feed an army."

Patout looked down, discovered the tray in his hands. No woman would do such a thing in front of her child. Certainly not Sophie. She loved Cato more than anyone in the world. There had to be an explanation. The coffee cup rattled in the saucer.

He led the way in, heading for a small table between the windows that looked the right size for a tray. Françoise was still hanging back, apparently afraid of stumbling in the dark. "There!" he said, voice loud, cheerful. Tray down, Gideon Bible on the floor, he bent over, threw it on a chair, and reached for the switch under the sconce. He swore softly. "That's more like it," he said when he had stopped fumbling and the lights were on.

"That you, sweetheart?" Sophie called through the door.

"Anyone else you're expecting?" he said, his voice unconvincing, bright. He hesitated perhaps a moment before turning around.

Pugie was outside in the hall, as though he had been passing, seen the door open, looked in. "Well, I got to get going. Remember, Pat, me and the boys can always make room for one more. See you folks later."

Galvanized to the spot, he flung out his hands, put them down. Françoise Fischler looked away. He followed her eyes to the bed. The boy his wife loved more than anyone, certainly more than him, was staring at the bathroom door. He was suddenly aware of the French woman.

"It's not what you think, Miss Françoise," he began.

"It's none of my business," she said.

"That man is my oldest friend," he said, addressing her but not taking his eyes off Cato. The boy wouldn't look at him. "Look, who can a man trust if not his best friend?" He was almost shouting.

She sat down on the edge of the bed. The boy squirmed away and pulled the sheet over his head.

The toilet flushed. "I'll be out in a minute," Sophie called.

"What are you doing in there?" he cried.

"Washing clothes! I spilled medicine on my blouse. If I don't get it out now, it'll never come out."

Torn between relief and doubt, he turned away from Françoise and the wounded lump in the bed and approached the bathroom, as the outer door opened and in walked Clotilde.

"Well," she said, as pleased with herself as though she had just finished gutting a chicken. "I told you I hadn't lost my touch." There was a blue ribbon pinned to her chest.

"Sophie? Shall I bring the car up to the back? You ready to go soon?" Patout yelled through the door.

"Ready in a sec."

"Come on, Aunt Clotilde. We're going home. You look worn out. Miss Françoise, will you keep an eye on things until I get back from The Oaks?"

"You're not giving her charge of petty cash?"

Patout dragged the old woman out. The outer door closed. Sophie emerged from the bathroom, eyes darting door to bed, a large wet spot on the front of her blouse.

Françoise rose. "You'd better see what you can do with him," she said.

"You're going to regret bringing my husband up here," Sophie said.

"I tried to warn you, Mrs. Minville."

"Get out!"

Françoise crossed to the door. When it closed behind her, Sophie went to the bed and crawled in.

· 24 ·

*B*ehind The Oaks in the distance under a chinaball tree, Willie Wooten lay on his back in his shack and wondered where his wife and Lily were. It was coming on to night almost a week after their disappearance. They would be out of money by now. How did they eat? If only she had left Lily. He would never see his baby again. Something terrible would happen to her now that she was alone with Ruby without him to protect her. He shouldn't have stopped until he'd found Janice Patout's money. All that talk about finding the money, taking Lily to a doctor in New Orleans, now it was too late. He turned on his side, put his palms together, cradled his head. The back of his hand felt cool on his cheek.

The evening was still, the air heavy with moisture from an earlier rain. Sounds carried a long way. A car drove up and stopped on the far side of the property. It must be the doctor. He always stopped to take a snort before coming up the drive to the house.

He looked toward the screen door. Under the table by the door a spool lay forgotten. He cried.

A few moments later the car started up again, seemed to stop closer. The doctor was checking on Cato. "Poor little boy," Willie muttered. Half the time Cato looked as mixed up as his Lily, torn like that between his mama and Miss Clotilde. "I tole her she ought to leave him alone. She ain't his mama." He began to cry again, wiping his nose on the back of his hand. His stomach growled. He observed the body hungry, but it seemed not something he felt responsible for. "I'm not to worry about a thing," he went on muttering.

"She going to help. I seen what she done. She talked to Sheriff Mouton. She call that help? I seen him shrug. He not going to waste his precious time looking for no nigger woman."

He cried. His body ached, but he couldn't make himself stop.

He considered whether to get up and fetch something to eat. Cornbread was in the pie safe, left over from the week before. If he went down to the big house, Françoise Fischler would give him a meal, but as he had, seemingly, for days—he no longer kept track of the time—he decided to stay where he was. The woman would see he'd been crying; also, his throat felt sore. His eyes closed. He grew quiet.

Across the abandoned pasture where fifty head of cattle had grazed in Lizzard Patout's day, beyond the vegetable garden, the clothesline, and the hen house, the lights were going on in The Oaks. The day was heavy, dark, and overcast. Farther down the long expanse of lawn, inside the Minville house, Dr. Rodriguez was pulling a tongue depressor out of Cato's mouth. He tossed it in the wastepaper basket next to the double bed, ruffled the boy's hair.

"Mumps aren't so bad if you get to sleep with your mama, eh, Boy?"

Cato turned his face to the wall.

Rodriguez fished around in his disreputable-looking bag and kept up the irritating chatter. "Yes, sir, swore I'd quit when the handle broke on this bag, but that day's come and gone and look at me, will you, still here, doctoring little boys, eh, Cato?" The doctor glanced at the door, brought out a bottle, threw back his head and took a long swig.

"What's that?"

"Medicine, my boy. Keeps me running smooth." The boy's eyes narrowed. Rodriguez stuffed the bottle in his bag, took out a thermometer, shook it. "That'll be our little secret, shall it, Cato?" He rammed the thermometer under the boy's tongue.

"Hush, Cato," Sophie said, returning to the bedroom. "Dr.

Rodriguez wouldn't hurt you. He's not rough like those new doctors downtown." She smiled sweetly at the doctor. Rodriguez beamed.

"Thank you kindly. Appreciate the words of confidence, Mrs. Minville."

"Sophie to you."

He colored slightly and took the thermometer out. "Bout one hundred." He shook the thermometer. "Looks like school for you Monday."

"Do you really think so, Doctor?"

"He'll be right as rain in no time, Mrs.—I mean, Miss Sophie. Don't you worry that pretty little head. You've got enough to fret about already." He stuck the thermometer in his bag and stood up. Sophie followed him out.

"Mama?"

"Just a minute, Cato." She hurried into the kitchen behind the doctor and closed the swinging door.

"I declare, I've never seen a family with so much trouble at once," the doctor was saying, his hand on the screen door. He lowered his voice. "Sheriff Mouton says it's only a matter of time?"

"Pat's trying to keep it open a few more days, but he can't make a go of it. Only two paying guests since the festival closed." She shrugged. "Would you want to visit this one-horse town?"

"Well, rotten luck, but something will turn up."

"It better. Pat's thinking about going back to New Orleans."

"Miss Clotilde will certainly be distressed to hear that."

"Thinks he might get his old job back. I'll stay, of course. Patout'll commute weekends. We wouldn't dream of leaving Belmont as long as Clotilde's alive."

"Glad to hear you say so. She's a mighty fine woman and a mighty fine friend. I'd hate to see her all alone in the big house again. You people have made a new woman out of her. I haven't seen her this happy since I don't know when.

Maybe not since her brother died. Let me tell you, that's a long time. That rascal in yonder had a heap to do with it. She's crazy about that little boy and, unless I'm sadly mistaken, he's crazy about her."

"Then why won't she help us?" she almost cried, and in spite of the frozen look on the doctor's face, went blundering on. "Couldn't you, I mean, you've known her all her life. We only need—"

"Young lady, she doesn't listen to me, never has. Just like her daddy." He pushed open the screen.

"Surely that's not true?"

Rodriguez grinned. "Oh, well, some slight exaggeration."

"She does listen to you then?"

"Of course. On occasion," he added.

"Dr. Rodriguez?" She clasped her throat, gave what she hoped was a helpless look. This was not going to be easy.

"My dear," he said, misunderstanding, "you don't have to thank me. I should thank you. Some people think I'm too old to be gallivanting around practicing medicine. Now not another word, you'll embarrass me." He tottered down the steps and headed for his car.

"Strange business about Ruby," she cried out.

"Yes, wasn't it." He opened the car door, threw in his bag.

She rushed down the steps. "Poor Willie. He's taking it hard."

"Willie ought to be glad to be rid of her. Ruby was a wild one. She'd have knifed him one of these days." The doctor started to close the door, but Sophie blocked his way.

"Patout says it's just Willie's pride hurt. Clotilde sent him to check on Willie day before yesterday. Nobody'd seen him for days," she went on. The doctor took his hand off the key. "Patout told him to quit moping, get up, and go back to work. Wasn't any use feeling sorry for himself. Françoise Fischler has had to do all his chores."

"Yes, even the good old niggers are being ruined by that nigger King coming around offering them the promised land."

Rodriguez tapped the steering wheel thoughtfully. "Take the child with her?"

Sophie nodded.

"Wouldn't have thought she cared. Willie's the one always looked after Lily, right from the moment she was born."

"Why, I'm surprised at you, Dr. Rodriguez. I couldn't live without my children, but Patout hardly knows they're alive."

"Spec you're right, Miss Sophie. I know one thing though— most children haven't the good fortune to have a mother like Cato's."

"Thank you, Doctor," she said, making herself out demure.

"I wouldn't say it if I didn't mean it, Miss Sophie. I've never seen a boy more in love with his mama," he said, not mentioning again the love the boy bore for a certain elderly lady just up the lawn. "Still," he continued, "Willie Wooten was proud as a peacock when I told him he had a baby daughter. It was right touching the way that nigger man cradled that baby's head in his arms day after day. No woman could have been more gentle. Course, it's a shame the way Lily turned out."

"Dr. Rodriguez, something is worrying—"

"You know what happened, don't you?" the doctor said, cutting her off. "Ruby didn't send for me in time. Her mama probably went to the traitteur and got a charm when they saw it was going to be a difficult delivery."

"Dr. Rodriguez, could you—"

"No, ma'am, I couldn't do a thing." He cut her off again. "By the time I got there, the damage had been done. These country darkies are mighty superstitious. Now and again I run across a woman thinks a charm got her pregnant." He shook his head.

"The hell of it is Washington expects us to send our little children to school with them. I tell you, I rue the day I voted for Eisenhower. He started this whole business, and now, whether they want to admit it or not, every white person in this country is wondering how far it's going to go and when it's going to stop. There's nothing wrong with wanting to be with your own kind. They don't want to be with us either."

"Dr. Rodriguez," she tried again, but there was no stopping him when he warmed to his favorite topic.

"You mark my words, young lady, one day people in Boston are going to realize they don't want their kids going to school with them either. It may take a while, but one day people will have had enough. Then we'll go back to the way this great country was meant to be."

"Doctor, I must speak to you," she blurted out. Rodriguez looked up, blank.

"Beg pardon?"

"Do you trust Françoise Fischler?"

"Good Lord! Is the woman stealing? I'd never forgive myself—"

"That's not it, Doctor," she cried before he went off again. He looked so comically relieved she felt a giggle rising, but got herself under control. "Whatever made you think that?"

"Miss Clo's been missing little things for months," the doctor said. He shook his head sadly. "Spec it's just lasting side effects from strokes. She'll never be a hundred percent again, you know, but I'm not about to tell her that." He pulled his foot in the car, put his hand on the key. "But why did you ask if I trusted Françoise?"

"I think she's been lecturing Cato about civil rights. Oh, no, he won't admit it. He's such a loyal child, but he's been having violent dreams about lynchings and I don't know what all. Last week at the festival Pugie Reaux told my husband that Cato told him not to say nigger." She paused to let that sink in. "I mean, who else could it be?"

"Mama?"

Cato's face was pressed against the screen door. Since the festival she could not move without his clinging to her. "Just a moment, Dr. Rodriguez," she said, irritated.

"No, I won't detain you. You need to get him back in bed. But rest assured, I'll look into this."

"I wouldn't want a word to upset Miss Clotilde," she said, meaning exactly the opposite.

"Of course not, my dear. I warned Françoise Fischler the day I brought her out. Told her not to poke her nose in family business. If she is polluting the mind of that young boy, why, she'll have to go. Simple as that, but I'll be discretion itself. Won't breathe a word to Miss Clotilde. I spec you folks want to handle this yourself." He drove off.

"Damn it to hell," Sophie muttered.

"Mama?"

"Can't I have one minute to myself?" she screamed.

Cato disappeared.

She dragged herself inside, went into the bathroom and locked the door. She sat on the side of the tub and stared into space. She didn't answer when Cato tapped at the door. She wasn't living just for him.

Patout would have to do it. He wouldn't like it, but she could make him. Tonight, before the old lady went to bed, she'd make him go up there and tell Clotilde her maid was polluting their son, lecturing on the rights of Negroes. Françoise Fischler would be gone before noon tomorrow. She hugged herself, looked down at the tiles. She had not seen Pugie Reaux for almost a week. Where was he now? Was he thinking of her?

She got up and looked in the mirror. She fished in her cosmetics bag, found her tweezers, and yanked a white hair out of her eyebrow. Cato knew she couldn't help flying off the handle now and again. She'd be a better mother if they didn't live hand-to-mouth. Cato knew. He was a good boy. If he just wouldn't get in the way.

25

*I*n deepening dusk Patout could just make out Françoise Fischler moving through shadows, scattering chicken feed. It didn't make sense, as much about her. Sophie at least had that right. The French woman was a mystery, unlike any he'd ever known, and full of contradiction. Anyone who'd grown up in a village as she claimed would have known chickens went to bed at the first sign of night. Yet, that was no reason to jump to conclusion. He could no more believe Françoise Fischler was a civil rights worker who'd come down South solely to make trouble for his family than he could picture a God who ran around the world peeking into mobile homes and cars, marking infractions in a little black notebook.

In spite of which, here he was, picking his way across the yard—when would he ever have time to collect the rubbish the workmen had scattered—going to persuade Clotilde to fire Françoise Fischler. He shook his head, ashamed of himself. He liked Françoise, it wasn't a question of that, but if he was going to leave Sophie and the children at The Oaks while he returned to New Orleans, eliminating her was one way of cutting down on the number of women who could get into trouble. Sophie and Clotilde battling was enough. Women beat all.

Françoise seemed to look up. He waved, relieved when she swung around without seeing him, and threw out more seed. In the long run, it would be best for her if she left. She had no real place here. No family, no old friends, no child. Cato could not be that for her. The boy actually disliked her— Sophie's fault for not watching what she said. Cato took everything to heart. Whatever Françoise Fischler was looking for, it wasn't in Belmont. He ought to know. He'd come looking himself, and now, as empty-handed as when he came, he was leaving no closer to anything, not even security, certainly not truth. She would keep looking and so would he. It was always surprising to recognize a kindred soul, even if only in passing.

He stopped and zipped the windbreaker. The nights were getting cool. And Sophie? he asked himself, followed immediately by the name of the man not mentioned in their house since the fair. He jumped a small drainage ditch and went on up the lawn, disappointed in himself. They were about to embark on a difficult period. There was no time for looking back.

He dreaded the coming separation, not knowing how long before he could come back for a visit, but Sophie agreed he must go. It would be difficult for her and the boys, but she would cope. She was a good woman, usually right about the big decisions in their life. If he listened to her, he'd never go astray, though he didn't always understand her motivations. This business with Françoise, for instance. She couldn't tolerate the French woman, never had, but she never did anything without having good reason. After all, his wife was upset, and it was a man's duty to remove the cause if he could, no matter how unpleasant.

He hesitated. Should he go up to the chicken yard and tell Françoise what he was about to do? It would only take a minute.

"Oh, what's the use," he said aloud, kicked a crayfish chimney, and continued on around the back of The Oaks. He let himself in through the kitchen.

The neatness of her small, cell-like room next to the stove pained him. The wardrobe door was ajar. Inside on the door hung one dress, two blouses, a skirt. No kind of life for a woman. There were no photographs, no papers he could see, no past, only the aridity of three changes of clothes. He might have understood if she were a man.

He went into the front hall, listened for a moment to the ticking of the clock, mounted the stairs and knocked.

"Come in."

He took off his hat and opened the door, wondering why electric alarms became so popular when the only sound they ever made was an irritating buzz. "Aunt Clotilde?" he asked.

"You weren't expecting the Queen Mother, were you?" She cackled. Her mood changed. She came to attention. "Is something the matter?"

"It's just—"

"Spit it out. I don't bite. If you showed more backbone, so would your son."

"I've come to talk about Cato."

The old lady patted the side of the bed. "Sit," she said. "What about him?"

Half an hour later Françoise carried in a warm glass of milk. She smiled. He looked at the floor.

"Go to bed. I shan't need you anymore," Clotilde said, taking the milk.

She looked at them, seemed about to speak, went out and shut the door.

"God almighty," Patout said.

"Nonsense, Patout, you have the right to protect your son. She knew better. I warned her myself. You can't change people's way of living that's been going on for two hundred years by just moving in and saying a few words. Change takes time. Anybody doesn't know that's a fool, and I won't have them living in my house. I'd rather find somebody new."

Patout got up, went to the back window, looked out.

"Something else you got on your mind?" she said.

"I've only had two couples since the fair." She made no response. "They ate peanut butter and crackers in their

room," he went on, "too cheap to spend money for supper.
I can't make a go of it on that, Aunt Clotilde."

"Rome wasn't built in a day, Boy."

"We're talking about a week," he said, nettled.

She lifted her chin.

He ran his fingers through his hair and shrank back to the
window. "I'm out of my mind with worry," he said.

"No doubt. I would be too if I had a wife and three children
to feed, but you should have realized it wouldn't be easy at
first."

"According to the books Mrs. Latouche showed me—"

"Who ever taught you to believe what you saw in black
and white? The hotel's had several suspicious fires. Now if
the Latouches would stoop to cheating an insurance company, what's to stop them from doing it to you? No doubt
Latouche will turn up dry as a bone one day, unless their
scheme backfired this time and he actually drowned. Good
riddance to bad rubbish, I say. I just feel sorry for the fish
that swallowed him."

"Nobody told me," Patout insisted.

"Should have made it your business to find out. Even if
somebody had told you, Patout, you wouldn't have believed
it. Trouble with you is you're so busy running around trying
to find good in people, you don't see evil right under your
nose. Now you take your wife."

"Leave Sophie out of it," he cried.

"Suit yourself." Her lips snapped shut.

After a while he said, low, "I've decided to go back to New
Orleans and try to find a job, maybe get the old one back."

Her mouth opened, she glared, then turned her head and
looked out the window.

"We're not going to leave you alone. Sophie and the children will stay. I'll commute, at least when I start making
money."

"Do what you like. You needn't think I can't get along
without you."

"All right then," he said, exasperated, "I'll put it on different terms. It would be a kindness to me if you would keep an eye out for Sophie and the boys, and could you help me with a little cash until my first paycheck? I'll send it back." He paused, relieved and half-ashamed, but Sophie was right. If the old gal loved Cato so much, why, she'd want to help out.

"So you're going," she said. "Hardly got here. Well, it's your business, I suppose. I don't give my blessing. I think you should stay and try to make a go of the hotel. I don't like quitters. Never did. And to think I sometimes fancied making you my heir. No, don't interrupt."

Patout swung back to the window and looked out toward the bayou and Willie Wooten's shack, remembering the newspapers pasted to the walls, whether for decoration or to keep out drafts, he didn't know. Whatever it was, it was pathetic. He wondered how Willie was and saw his own reflection in the glass. It was the figure of a pathetic man.

"Are you listening, Patout?"

"I always do, Aunt Clotilde."

"You are too much of a dreamer, Patout. I did have hopes, as I said, at one time of making you my heir, but I have decided now to wait and see. I'll either leave it to the church, or perhaps to Cato."

"Cato!"

"He's too sensitive and far too dreamy, but he is young. I have hopes of making something better of him, which brings me around to my proposal. I will continue to allow them to live on my land, but I want it understood that Cato is to spend most of his time here with me at The Oaks."

"Who do you think you are, taking my son, laying down rules? You gave me that land. It's mine!"

"If you'll check the records down at the courthouse, you'll see nothing was ever written down.

"I am prepared to lend you a small sum of money," she went on, "and will help them out for the first month, but after that, you will have to send money back to feed them. I told you long ago, I'm not wealthy, Patout. I can barely keep Willie, the cow, and myself in food, despite what your wife believes.

"Now once you are established and send for your family, the boy stays here. I will allow him to visit you in New Orleans on major holidays. Otherwise, you are to consider me the guardian of your son. I aim to make a man of him fitting to be the next owner of The Oaks."

He came toward her, shaking with anger. "I'm not going to stand here and take this. Tomorrow we're all clearing out. Going off and leaving you here to fend for yourself."

"They'll still be here in the morning after you're gone," she said, adding with malice, "You ask your wife if she has any intention of leaving Belmont."

"If you weren't an old lady," he cried, "I'd knock your teeth down your throat."

"Patout!" she called. "Come back here."

He slammed the front door, sat down on the porch swing, and buried his face in his hands. He had been sitting there for some time when the door opened and Françoise came out.

"Don't get up. I just wanted some air." She sat down on the steps, picked up a handful of pea gravel from the walk, and let it run through her fingers. "Is something the matter?" she asked at last.

"How do you mean?"

"I'm not an idiot. You were talking about me. Yes?"

"Aunt Clotilde has decided she can no longer afford to keep you on."

"I see," she said, seeing nothing of the kind.

"I am sorry, Miss Françoise. She'll give you a decent bonus so you can get started elsewhere," he said, promising himself he'd borrow it off Rodriguez if he had to, at least he owed her that. "References, of course."

"References?" she asked, surprised. "Oh, for this type of

work." She laughed. Laughter didn't suit her. She picked up another handful of gravel, looked over the lawn. Night had fallen. A frog croaked somewhere to the left of the porch. "Do you know, I didn't like it when I came," she said, indicating The Oaks—house, lawn, trees. "I thought it was too beautiful, phony somehow." She didn't go on.

"Will you stay in Belmont?" he asked, not knowing what else to say.

"Oh, no," she murmured. "You say I must go, so I must. I shall go someplace else tomorrow, and the next day, and probably the day after that. I'll keep going until I'm ready to stop for a while. I enjoy looking at lives in which I find myself. It's amusing to place oneself in context, then move on."

"It sounds lonely. Don't you miss belonging? Aren't you sometimes afraid?"

"I was once married, Mr. Minville. I have never felt such loneliness. Fear doesn't care whether it stays in one spot or moves around. As for belonging, what can I say, it usually implies rather boring responsibilities. I'm not a nursemaid of people or things." She got up, smoothed down her skirt. "Well, thank you for telling me, Mr. Minville. I shall act appropriately surprised when she tells me, no doubt in the morning? Good night."

No protestation? No need to shout recrimination? He wished she had not let him off so easily. He got up, feeling worse than before, and decided to take the long way home down the drive. He needed time to work off her presence. He turned around and saw the porch light fade. She had been waiting until he walked beyond reach of the light, into shadows.

He did not understand walking away from beauty, once acknowledged. Leaving The Oaks now pained him. There was an enduring quality to the evening. The vague longings of another human being filled him with awe.

"No matter what she says, she would have stayed if Clotilde would have let her," he muttered. "Everybody wants to put down roots sometime in their lives." He was grateful to Françoise Fischler. She had made him see going to New Orleans was a temporary answer. Someday, when he had enough money saved, he would return to Belmont. In the meantime, he'd swallow his pride so Sophie and the boys could stay. Sophie was good with people. With him out of the way, the women would have to rely on each other. They would work out their differences, grow closer, maybe by the time he got back for the first visit.

He turned into their driveway. The fluorescent light over the sink cast blue on the ground. Inside, slicking the hair off her forehead, Sophie appeared to be battling a pot. Sophie was not an observer. She was involved at all times—quarrelsome, puzzling, infuriating, affectionate, and loving. He could feel her; she was solid. If he suggested roaming the world looking in through windows into other people's lives, she'd think he'd lost his mind. Women weren't made for such things. They were physical creatures, not cerebral. She had her ups and downs, of course, but she understood life better than he. She said the important thing was to keep trying, and he was always happiest doing what she wanted.

26

"So?" Sophie said, her face all expectant.

"So that's that." Patout threw his hat on the kitchen counter and reached for her.

"Not now, Patout." She turned her back to him and picked up another pot. "Your supper's ready."

"That all the thanks I get for doing your dirty work?"

"That's a strange way to put it," Sophie replied. "Aren't you happy to be rid of a bad influence on your son?"

Cato felt a knot in his stomach. Seated across from him in highchairs, the twins were fingerpainting in oatmeal.

"It wasn't much fun, you know," his father said.

Steel wool scratched against cast iron.

Patout approached the table. Andrew and Matthew squealed.

"At least somebody's happy to see me." Patout bent down, kissed Andrew, and ruffled Matthew's hair. When he stood up, there was a wet glob of oatmeal in his hair.

Patout scraped a chair out, sat. "What's this?"

"Looks like eggs to me." His mother turned the frying pan face down on the drain, picked up a saucepan. It clanged against the faucet.

"I know it's eggs, Sophie."

"Don't start, Patout." Her voice was carefully flat.

"It seems to me you could exert yourself," his father went on.

"It seems to me you could talk for once. Tell me what happened. It's not like it doesn't involve me and the children."

She banged the pot on the counter and picked up the egg beater.

"She's going to fire her, of course. What did you expect? It didn't seem necessary to say it."

Sophie stopped scrubbing, left her hands in the soapy water, and looked out the window over the sink. Cato wondered what she was thinking. She sighed deeply. Her head tilted to the right. It always did that when she was thinking about something she liked.

His father had been shoveling cold eggs into his mouth. Now he tore off a piece of toast, reached for the butter. Cato put more eggs in his mouth.

"Why are you up?" his father said.

"Dr. Rodriguez said he's almost well." His mother picked up the bottle of dish detergent and squeezed some on her rag.

"Can't you talk? Does she always answer for you?"

The scrambled eggs were soft and wet on his tongue.

"For God's sake, swallow," his father said.

"Patout, please, let's go in the living room. It's hard on the children."

"Since when did you worry about that?"

She turned around as though he had slapped her, grasped the sink. "Don't speak to me," she said.

Cato shoveled in more eggs.

A baby roach scurried across the table. "Damn," Cato muttered. The boys in his grade at school now said damn, hell, piss, old cunt. He bit off a corner of toast. Another roach appeared. "Son of a bitch!" Cato cried.

Sophie whirled around.

"Tell your mother if she wants you punished, she'll have to do it herself," his father said.

Cato held the eggs and toast on top of his tongue, waiting for his father to remove his eyes from his face.

"Go on, Boy, tell her."

Cato spit the eggs on the rim of his plate.

"Our son has such fine manners." His father got up, took

a beer out of the refrigerator, and left. The twins began to scream.

The scrambled eggs slid down the rim and inched toward the center of the plate. When they reached the bacon ends, he lifted his eyes to his mother's, and searched for some sign that she wanted him to come to her, but she shook her head, as though to say, no, if you come to me now we are lost.

His father came back in the room. "Aren't you finished yet?"

"Yes, he's finished." His mother swiped the twins' faces with a wet cloth, extracted first Matthew, then Andrew from the highchairs, took them by the hand. "Put your plate in the sink, Cato, then you may go." She and the twins tottered through the swinging door.

Cato did as she told him. Then he went into the living room and lay on his cot. All week long she'd made him eat with them. She said his father might go to New Orleans soon. Who knew when they'd eat together again? So he'd go to the table, and suddenly his mother and father would start fighting, and he'd be caught in the middle, wishing he were with the old lady, or back in his bedroom at The Oaks, anywhere but here.

Sophie came out of the twins' room, went through the living room without looking at him, and into the kitchen. Cato picked up his comic book.

"Clotilde says you can stay here," his father was saying.

"That's big of her."

"Yes, isn't it?"

The refrigerator opened. The top of a beer can popped.

"He's to sleep at The Oaks. If we move to New Orleans, he stays. She has some weird idea of grooming him to take over."

Then his mother was crying out, greatly excited, "Cato! Cato! Come here! The most wonderful thing."

"Wonderful!" his father shouted.

"Of course, Patout, Cato can sleep there. You love it up

there, don't you, darling," she said as he walked in. "He has his own room up there. We don't really have room for him here. The twins are starting to get in your things, aren't they, Cato?" Cato looked from one to the other.

"And he loves his Nanan, don't you, Cato." He shrugged. She turned back to his father. "He feels sorry for her. You know how affectionate and sensitive he is. He likes to help her, don't you, Cato."

"You would actually move away and leave your precious son?"

"Of course not, Patout. I'm just looking out for the future. You haven't been able to give us any kind of security, so why not let Cato. And anyway, who said anything about my moving? I might stay right here."

"What about me?"

"We've got to consider the children, Patout. I mean, New Orleans is going to burst wide open. You hear them talking race riots on the news every night. Any day now there's going to be blood running in the streets of that city."

"Jesus, Sophie, have you no pride!" The beer can flew across the room, crashed into the cabinets and sprayed. His mother's mouth fell open. He held on to the spokes of a kitchen chair. His father went into the living room and turned on the television. Came hysterical laughter and applause from a game show. His father turned the volume as high as it would go.

His mother sat down and put her head on the table. Cato touched her shoulder.

"Don't!" She got up, went to the sink, turned on the faucet and ran cold water over her face. Then she dried it with the dishtowel left on the counter, wrinkling her nose as though it smelled. "Men can't face failure," she said. "They always have to blame it on someone else. Did I tell him to manage the hotel? So who's to blame when it fails? Why, me, of course." She laughed loudly.

"Mama, don't."

"You'll be just like him when you grow up." She cried great, gulping noises.

He got up and left his parents' house, stepped into the cool evening, and smelled at once the sweet and putrid odor of sugar cane being ground. He zipped his jacket, walked away. He quickened his pace, cut across the grass, and headed for the long drive that led to the big house. He could not bear the weight of her pain anymore. Coming in a depression in the yard where the weeds grew higher, he looked down for snakes, jumped across a wet spot, and hurried on, guided by the lights of the sugar mill twinkling on the horizon, off to the left of The Oaks. Above in the sky, a heavy black streak like a check mark led from the top of the smokestack into the limpid land of stars and moon. He stopped for a moment and gazed into the clear nothingness of the sky that shone with such tranquillity that he thought of it as home, then went on, and soon came to the drive.

· 27 ·

*I*t was only the first week of October, but the night before the weather had taken a sudden chill. Willie Wooten's shack was bound to be cold, set injudiciously as he had wanted it underneath those chinaball trees. Clotilde opened the middle drawer of her dresser, took out a cotton bodice, and lifted the pile of nightgowns. Only a five and eight ones were left in the wallet. When Rodriguez arrived, she'd ask him to take another forty out of her account at the bank.

She buried the wallet, closed the drawer, picked up the bodice, and returned to the bed. She peeled off her nightgown, unrolled the stockings she wore in bed. Elongated bosoms swinging, she turned and picked up the step-ins, gathered them neatly into her fingers. First the right, then the left foot went in. She stood up, pulled them over fallen hips and thighs, and put her hand in the small of her back. Cut in two this morning. Wouldn't support a thing. She collapsed and reached for the bodice.

"Nanan?"

"Just a minute." She pulled it over her head and smoothed it down. "Come in." Spreading the sheet over bare legs, "You're going to miss the bus," she said, patted around in the bedclothes. "Would you get me a slip? Middle drawer, on the right, next to the nightgowns."

He walked without energy to the dresser and opened the drawer.

"For heaven's sake, what's taking you so long. I'll freeze to death. Take one off the top." He closed the drawer, returned to the bed, and handed her a slip.

"You certainly do moon about." She held the slip up by the straps and looked for tears. It was one of her sister's— nylon, low-cut, covered with flimsy lace.

"That's why Sister was always cold," she announced. "Turn around." The boy went to the window and looked down the back toward Willie Wooten's. She smoothed the slip quickly over her hips. "You can turn around now." She went to the full-length mirror. "Not bad, when it's properly girded and supported," she said, pleased she still had her figure.

"Do I have to sleep here?" he said.

"You don't have to. I thought you'd be glad. Don't the twins get in your things?"

"Andrew threw my toothbrush in the toilet once," he volunteered.

"Seems smarter to stay where nobody can touch your stuff. You have your own room here."

"I don't want them to leave me."

"Your father's the only one's left, and he'll be back."

"Mama and the twins may go."

"Nonsense, Butthead. They haven't got the money for a hotel room big enough for all of them." Her eyes narrowed. "Did your mother say she was leaving?"

His inability to trust her rankled. "Go on. I've got to finish dressing," she said, impatient. He looked up, hurt, surprised. "Rodriguez will be here soon," she explained.

He opened the door, looked back.

"If you don't want to live with me, you can go. Nobody's stopping you."

"Mama won't let me," he said, eyes wide, dead in earnest.

Clotilde laughed. "Out of the mouths of babes." She sat staring at the door after he went out. He did not reappear. At length she stood up, grabbed her back, and sucked in breath. When the pain subsided, she crossed to the closet. The door opened. She turned around. The boy stuck his head in.

"We get out early. The teachers are having a meeting."

They looked at each other, she from her closet, he from the door.

"Do you want me to read to you tonight?" He rocked his right foot.

"That would be nice," she said, not moving.

"Good-bye," he said.

"Good-bye." He was gone. It seemed she was not yet to be kissed.

Black Velvet mooed outside under the window.

She sat down in the swan's neck rocker, leaned back, and closed her eyes. The French woman would be missed. There was pleasure in clean, repaired undergarments stacked neatly in drawers. Ruby had been such a mess. On the other hand, she'd never had a mania for order. French people were that way, always trying to show somebody up, making out they were better than you. That's what got Françoise Fischler in trouble. Still, she had to admit the woman made a difference in her life, though she wouldn't have told her for the world. People took liberties if they thought you needed them. She took the news calmly. Stood right there in the doorway two weeks ago not asking for an explanation, agreeing to wait until Willie got back on his feet, not asking for extra money. No doubt she'd been stealing eggs and selling them on the side. No telling what else. She would get Cato to help her with a proper going-through once the woman was gone. Black Velvet mooed.

She was unusually tired this morning, weary was more the word. As she thought of all to be done today—getting Willie ready for Rodriguez, doing his chores, calling in a grocery list, finding someone to bring them out, a real nuisance with Patout gone and Willie incapacitated—she suddenly felt the loneliness of her life closing in. She was terrified of getting sick. Black Velvet mooed.

"You can let the eggs sit there, that's not much loss, but you've got to milk that cow," she muttered. "It's inhuman,

her suffering like that." The milking was long overdue.
"Yes?" she said.

Françoise stuck her head in. "I'm ready when you are."

"Wait in the kitchen. Do not go over there alone. Can you
milk? No? Then telephone the Romeros. They can have what
she gives today."

The door closed.

"It's her own fault," she muttered. "I told her and told her
she had to respect my views if she wanted to stay here. Poor
little boy, wonder what he thought, listening to that trash.
He's guilt-ridden as it is without her piling it on."

As she grasped the arms of the rocker to get up, her old
friend Adeline Delahoussaye smiled, but Clotilde shook her
head. She lacked the patience to deal with Adeline today,
even if it had been a long time since she'd seen her.

She crossed to the dresser, twisted her hair into a bun, took
one last look in the mirror, went out, and began to descend,
so engrossed in her thoughts that she forgot to glance at the
picture of her brother, as she had every morning of her life.

She reached the bottom step, sighed. There was no time to
go back. A picture of Janice lay on the hall table. The *Belmont
Crier* used it for the obituary and had forgotten to return it
until now. She picked it up. Women were a nuisance. They
could never leave well enough alone. Of course it was Sophie
Minville who put Patout up to telling her about Françoise.
She knew Patout well enough by now. He never would have
had the temerity if Sophie hadn't pushed, which was reason
enough to reconsider. She could always watch the woman
when Cato was there, but there was nothing that could be
done if the woman was also a thief, and she had been missing
small things lately—her mother's gold thimble, a brand-new
box—not even opened—of her favorite bath powder, that
gaudy shepherd and dog figure Janice bought one year.

Clotilde checked her watch and pushed the kitchen door.
"We don't have much time before Rodriguez comes. Did you
get the things together I told you?"

The French woman nodded, picked up a bag from the table, and took the broom from behind the door. Together they went down the back steps and started across the yard. They crossed the vegetable garden, walking in the furrows, reached the chicken coop, and took a narrow dirt path that ran along the fence until they came out in an open field. Willie Wooten's house was in sight.

"I doubt," Clotilde said, stopping to catch her breath, "you have ever seen anything like the filth you are about to witness. For Willie's sake, I told Rodriguez not to get here until ten. If Willie recovers from this, he would never forgive me for allowing Rodriguez to see the inside of his cabin like that. No doubt," she went on bitterly, "you will blame me for the condition these people live in. Outsiders always do. But I did not know. Until last night I had never set foot in Willie Wooten's house, and I ask you, do I look like his wife?"

"I had not been thinking of whom to blame." Françoise shifted the groceries into her other arm and picked up the broom that had fallen on the ground.

"No? Well, you'll get around to it sooner or later, and when you do, I want you to remember, they choose to live like that. If I ever get my hands on Ruby, I swear I will knock some ideas of decency into her head. My God." She choked on her words, remembering the scene from the day before when she had gone—not having seen Willie for days—to the shack under the trees. Calling and calling his name, hearing nothing in reply, she at last climbed the rotten steps, opened the screen door and went in. She found him in the small back room that served as a kitchen, lying curled up on the floor in his own excrement and vomit. He was unconscious and lay with his hands holding his groin, flies covered the half-opened eyes.

She had found an old afghan, one Janice had made years ago and cast off, covering a makeshift sofa, pulled his body into the front room, and covered him. Then she went outside on the porch, sat on the steps, and vomited. She was too weak to get up, to cry for help, to go back to her house, to think. Sitting there, Willie Wooten lying silently a few feet away, she waited for hours. At nightfall she went inside and lighted a candle she found stuck in a beer bottle, put it on the windowsill. Then she left for the night, stumbling across the field, past the coop, reaching her own comfortable house at last, and going in by the front, so the foreign woman wouldn't hear. She wanted to think over what she had seen, and what she must do, before saying anything to anyone. She could not help feeling ashamed, and puzzled at why that should be.

"My God," she said again.

"I don't mind doing this alone," Françoise said.

"No, it's not proper. I can't allow you to go in alone," Clotilde replied. They went on and soon came to the shack.

Willie seemed not to have moved during the night. He lay on his back and breathed noisily.

The two women worked silently. Françoise carried pails of water up from the bayou, which curved just behind Willie's house. The bank sloped softly to meet the water there. Clotilde Patout took the pails out of her hands, and threw the water on the floor time and again.

When the house was clean, Clotilde ordered Françoise onto the porch, and removed Willie Wooten's clothes. She told herself it was Richard's body, Richard who was covered with mud, having lain on the bottom of the bayou for so many years, and she talked to him, and told him she was sorry they were only now finding his body after so many years, she hoped he hadn't been cold. Then she poured a bucket of water over the body on the floor, wrapped the lower part of the body in a towel, and called the foreigner back in. Together they moved Willie up to the sofa, covered him with a clean sheet and blanket, and went outside to wait for the doctor.

Rodriguez was not long in coming. He went into the house

for a moment, returned to the women. "He's dying," he said.

"Oh, he's been dead a long time, Rodriguez," Clotilde murmured.

The doctor looked at Françoise.

"He has mumps. Always dangerous in an adult, but I might have saved him if I'd known and gotten him to the hospital in time. I don't mean last night, Miss Clotilde, don't think that. He's been this way, I imagine, for over a week."

Clotilde got up and went inside. She stood at a distance from the sofa, but moved closer as Willie stirred. His lips moved. She bent over.

"Willie? Can you hear me?" She fancied he moved his head. "You've been a good nigger to me all your life. I'm going to see that you get a watertight coffin just as nice as the one I've ordered for myself. Don't you worry about a thing. And I'll make sure Lily—"

"He can't hear you, Miss Clotilde." Rodriguez stepped inside. "I think he's dead." She stepped aside. He squatted down, put his head on Willie's chest.

"Yep, he's dead."

"I've got to get back to my house and lie down."

"I'll go with you, Miss Clotilde."

"No, stay with Willie. I'll call the funeral home, tell them to send the ambulance." She jerked her chin in the direction of the porch. "Take her with you when you leave," she said.

"Shouldn't you reconsider? You're going to be needing help now Willie's gone."

"Let her stop and pack her things, but I don't want to set eyes on her again."

"Nanan?" Cato called from the porch.

Clotilde's face brightened. "No, don't come in here, boy. Wait outside. I'm going to need help going home."

"Please let me—"

"Do as I ask, James. Wait till the ambulance comes, then take that woman right out of my life as fast as you brought her in. No, don't put a sheet over him. He couldn't stand to have anything on his head, not even in summer. I used to tell him he ought to wear a hat." She went over to the sofa, looked down at Willie Wooten, then turned and walked to the door.

"Well, I guess I'm not going to have a cut-up yard anymore. It was Sister started him looking for gold. She thought it was a wonderful joke. I told him there was nothing buried in the yard. He didn't believe me. It didn't matter. It was the looking that counted. He mixed it up. Sometimes he looked for gold, sometimes it was a deed to The Oaks. I imagine he had heard that old saw about my granddaddy stealing part of The Oaks from his kin." She opened the screen door and went out. The boy took her hand. They went down the steps and started back across the field.

Rodriguez went out on the porch.

"I have lived here longer than any place since I was a child," Françoise said.

"Miss Clotilde's going to be needing someone, now Willie's gone. Let me talk to her, see if I can't patch things up between you two."

She shook her head.

"You'll miss the place. Didn't I tell you, this land gets inside you? And what about the boy?"

"Cato?" She looked across the field. Off in the distance the old woman and the boy were walking slowly and in single file around the chicken coop. Clotilde seemed to be having difficulty. They stopped. The boy took the gourd off the fence, gave her some water. Then he put his arm around her waist and supported her as they continued walking toward the house.

"He'll be all right," she said. "He has that one and his mother. He hardly knows I'm alive."

28

*H*e could not get out of his mind the things that happened that day, events that defied reason, twisted as they
were in the adult world. In expressionless faces turned aside,
in the order to hush and go away, he felt his oddity, knew—
as though he were they—the embarrassment of having a child
who could not understand without being told. "For God's
sake, do I have to dot all the i's and cross all the t's for you?"
was Nanan's way of putting it, but the questions would not
go away.

Each morning he awoke in Willie Wooten's shack with
Sunday comics pasted on the walls. He saw that thing lying
on the sofa wrapped in a blanket, heard it was Willie Wooten,
when it was not like Willie at all. Françoise Fischler was on
the porch, pushing the hair out of her eyes, then nothing.
Where had she gone? Why didn't she come back? Why did
she leave her clothes? Did his mumps kill Willie? The same
ones? Why did his mother make him sleep at The Oaks?
There was room in the double bed.

His mother said what with all her worries Patout being
gone and all, and not knowing where the next nickel was
coming from to put milk in the twins' bottles, he'd have to
help out, sooner rather than later. She couldn't afford to
love a boy who hung around doing nothing all day but asking why.

The disappearance of the chickens also worried him. He
hadn't seen them leave. Every day he went to the chicken
yard, stood in the middle, and waited for them to stop hiding.
The profound silence, smelling as it did of filth, chicken feed,

and dust, mocked him. He hid in the bamboo and tried to work it out. Had they marched in double file—as the children did at school to salute the flag—down the drive, into the road, and gotten run over, and people had taken them home for supper, because if you killed somebody's chicken, you had to pay a fine and most people didn't have money? But if this was so, who let the chickens out? It wasn't Willie. Willie wouldn't have left the gate open, flapping in the breeze as it did for weeks after he died until honeysuckle crept over and under the wire and strangled the gate, holding it down until it grew into the soil. It didn't squeak anymore. Planted the gate was now, part of the earth. Cato could not make it move, but it had not been open when the chickens left, of that he was certain.

Then one day as he stood in the chicken yard, a hawk descended in heavy weight, talons held under the great body as it landed in the top of a nearby tree. The wings rose up and back, cupping the air. Wings down, self-contained, the hawk watched for movement on the earth. He remembered Willie said hawks ate chickens, dogs, mice, and if big enough, stole babies.

After that, he only visited the chicken yard when he wanted Willie. He could feel the black man's presence in the yard. He talked to him, asked questions, described the condition of things, for Willie could no longer see for himself. The Hers sign Willie made was still up there, but the His had disappeared from the roosters' door. Willie said roosters had wicked natures. Nanan said wickedness was the nature of men. Certain changes in himself made him afraid.

One day he defecated behind a bush in the side yard. He did not plan it. He didn't think he could make it inside to the toilet. He wasn't afraid of anyone seeing. Nanan was in bed, his mother and the twins off for a drive. He'd seen Pugie Reaux's truck leave. When the filthy thing was done, and smoking in the cold November air, he ran away without covering it up, knowing they would blame it on a passing

Negro. Later it came to him that it was a good thing he'd
done, a kind of insurance. If they found the things he had
hidden in the bamboo, he could say he didn't know. They
would blame it on the Negro who passed through the yard.
Yet he was uneasy, always waiting to be found out.

One night Dr. Rodriguez stopped by to chat with Clotilde.
When Cato opened the front door, the doctor looked at him
strangely. He told Cato to get the decanter and glasses on
the sideboard in the parlor and went upstairs without waiting,
as though he wanted to talk to the old woman in private. As
Cato entered the bedroom, Rodriguez got up from the rocker,
poured dark liquid from the decanter into three small glasses,
gave one to Nanan, kept one for himself, offered the last to
Cato, held up his glass and drank it down, keeping his eyes
on Cato.

By the end of November life settled into a pattern. He got
up early, caught the bus to school, walked down the drive
just as Pugie Reaux drove in with a black woman inside. In
late afternoon when Cato returned, Mr. Reaux would already
have come to take the woman home, and he would find his
mother in the kitchen at The Oaks, cooking for him and
Nanan. Then he would take a tray upstairs, being careful not
to spill the milk, for Nanan laughed at him when he was
clumsy. He no longer stayed while she ate. She said nobody
could chew with that blank expression on his face, what was
the matter with him anyway? His mother would have his
supper waiting for him downstairs. While he ate, she washed
dishes, put away things, packed the leftovers for herself and
the twins. She didn't stay long. She didn't like leaving the
twins alone, even though they were taking a nap, she said.
Pugie Reaux's truck was always in the drive in the
evenings now.

She spoke once about his father while she was cleaning up.
Cato pictured his father backing down the drive, waving, the
sleeves of his windbreaker flared back. He could not visualize

the face. He supposed it must look sad. His mother said his father was fine, but having no luck finding a job. He did not write often. It was too expensive to call.

She worried about money. She slipped upstairs with the tray once to ask Clotilde for a loan, but the old lady recommended she apply for welfare.

"I can't do that, Cato," she said when she came down. "I can't stand in line with half the Negroes in the parish. I just can't."

"Dr. Rodriguez gives her money every week. He puts it inside a wallet in her dresser," he said.

"He's not giving her money, Cato." She laughed. "That's her money. Nanan always makes a great show of being poor, but the fact is, her sister left her money." She looked at him shyly. "Mr. Reaux told me Janice won it playing poker. Now don't look like that, Cato. He's your mother's nice friend, and one day soon she'll die and leave it all to you because you are such a good boy."

She gathered up her things, turned at the door. "I don't know how I'd live without you," she said, but she didn't hug him. She seemed to shrink from his touch, not like in the old days, when she came to him and sat by his cot in the dark late at night, drawing comfort from his caressing.

Yet, she looked happy. She went to the beauty parlor every week. Mr. Reaux took her. (Nanan would not let anyone drive her car. It sat in the yard until the battery went dead. The upholstery mildewed from the rains and a sudden heat wave one week.) She proudly showed Cato her pink fingernails. "Cherries in the Snow," or "Diamond Jubilee," she would say, holding them out for approval. She even had it on her toes. She giggled a lot. He joined in. She didn't like him to look unhappy.

"Mr. Reaux is such a help," she would say when they stood by the kitchen door saying good night, she carrying food in a container, he, standing on one foot, the other on top, listening to her talk and talk, until the sound and look of her stayed. When Pugie Reaux turned in, his mother would blow him a kiss, and go away.

One day the truck did not appear. His mother stayed longer than usual, glancing at the road now and again, talking to him, looking puzzled, until long after it was time for the twins to get up from their nap.

Often when he felt lonely, he would go into Françoise Fischler's room next to the stove. Everything of hers stayed where she'd put it. Nanan told him to close the door and stay out, one day the woman would send for her things. October, November, and now December was passing. A thin coat of dust covered the dresser and the night table, the sewing stand she had used as a desk. Sometimes he went into her room and drew his name in the dust. Wondering if she was dead, too, he got up the courage once to ask Clotilde Patout.

"For all I know she might be, Cato, and furthermore, I don't care."

"Did you want her to go away?"

"Yes, Boy."

"Why?"

"She encouraged Willie Wooten in the most shocking way," then seeing the boy wasn't satisfied, "Someday you'll know, not now," and she dismissed him with a wave of her hand.

In the evenings after Clotilde had gone to sleep, he wandered throughout the silent house, looking into closets, reading the French woman's diary, at least the parts not written in French, tried on Janice's old hats, played with the foreign woman's daughter, once he had read about her in the notebooks. When Nanan didn't fall asleep early, he would go in and sit by the side of her bed. She didn't talk to him much. Some days she thought he was someone else. When she was aware of him, she would tell him stories about herself. He was surprised she, her brother, and sister had also played in the bamboo until they grew too big to crawl through the tunnel. After, she would say things that made him sad. "All good things must come to an end. Regret is a terrible thing. One comes into the world and out again alone. I never learned how to forgive."

He felt these things were true, even though he did not understand. He watched her to see what was the proper emotion for him to have about those sentences she spoke in a low and ponderous voice, as though she were saying them into the iron caldron filled with rainwater in the backyard that once had been used as a goldfish pond. Deep from within came the voice. It was all he could do to sit there and wait to see what he was supposed to do.

She also recalled details about people long dead, "And my father shaved with an old-fashioned blade. Richard liked candied violets," pulling these things out of the air as though driven to tell him. He did not know what to do with the bits and pieces of her life, and forgot as soon as he heard them.

Sometimes she read poetry to him. One poem began, "*. . . the king of Cameliard, Had one fair daughter, and none other child; and he liked her a lot.*" Several lines down, wolves began eating children. Cato's particular dread was for the poem Clotilde loved most. It began, "*I hate the dreadful hollow . . .*" It was about a rich man who doesn't want his next child to be a daughter, then later, for saying such an ugly thing, he gets buried alive.

"*Dead, long dead,*" Nanan would whisper in her ominous voice, and look at Cato, her eyes growing wide. "*And the wheels go over my head,/And my bones are shaken with pain,/For into a shallow grave they are thrust,/Only a yard beneath the street,/And the hoofs of the horses beat, beat, . . ./Beat into my scalp and my brain . . .*" When she had scared him properly, she would laugh.

Once he came into her room and found her reading from the book, but there were tears in her eyes. She smiled when she saw him, closed the book, patted the bed for him to sit down.

"That was my own beloved mother's book, Cato. It's a great comfort to me. When one is as close to the boneyard as I, it is comforting to hear how it's going to be."

29

Christmas came and went, then his birthday. School began. A series of black women arrived, none of whom knew Ruby or Willie. They would hitch a ride out on the colored school bus, sometimes a beaten-up car would appear about sundown and take them away. He asked them if they knew where Ruby and Lily were, but they seemed not to want to talk to the boy. They never stayed longer than a few weeks. The Oaks was too far out in the country, they said, and she paid so little money they ate up their salaries in gas.

Now it was near the end of February. The redbuds and azaleas were already in bloom. Camellias lay face down on the ground turning brown. His father had not come back. His mother sent a telegram. After a week a letter came back. "Good news," it said. "I found a job at the Hibernia Bank. Rent takes most of the money. It'll be a while before I can get something bigger. Why don't you come and bring the twins for a visit, Sophie? I think I can swing it. Leave Cato in charge. How is the old gal anyway? Love, Patout." A twenty-dollar bill fell out.

"So what do you think, sweetheart? I wouldn't want to leave you here alone," she went on, "but I am about to go crazy. I never go anywhere, see anything different. No one to talk to. Oh, God, all our problems would be solved if she'd just go on and die." They were sitting at the kitchen table. He had just finished his supper. She was staying with him longer in the evenings these days. Mr. Reaux's truck did not come anymore.

"Don't look at me like that," she went on. "She's been

sick so long, why, she'd be glad to go. What good is her life? She doesn't get up. She just lies there and stares out the window. She's lost the will to live. I'm sure she would be glad to go."

"She has the mumps, doesn't she," he said.

His mother laughed. "What a strange child. Come here."

They went into Janice Patout's apartment, where they had lived when they first came, and lay down together on top of the chenille bedspread. When he said it hurt, she said, "Princess and the pea," got up, rolled the spread back to the foot. They got in again and stared at the watermarks on the ceiling.

He was careful not to touch her, unclean as he was, but she took him in her arms and rocked him back and forth, as she used to do so long ago before the coming of the twins. Slowly the world that had gone upside down began to right itself. It was late when she got up to go. "Darling," she said, kissing him good night, "could you ask Nanan for a little money. I could stay here longer if I could just get out once in a while. Get a baby-sitter. Maybe take in a movie. Could you do that for me? She won't refuse you."

The following afternoon he waited until she was asleep, opened the long middle drawer, and took out a twenty-dollar bill. It was easy. He told himself this was the best way. If she had been herself, she would have wanted him to have the money, but sick as she was, it would only upset her.

From then on, whenever his mother talked about leaving town, he waited until the old woman was asleep, stole into her room, and took money from the drawer.

He waited now, knowing she would die soon, but the days went by. Her condition did not change.

In the night when he lay downstairs in his room, he told himself not to be afraid. She wanted to go to that place where her brother and Willie Wooten had gone. He could not doubt that this was true, for his mother had told him so. "It will be such a blessing when she goes," she said almost every day now. "Old people have nothing but their memories. It is so painful when people outlive their contemporaries."

When Easter came, the old lady seemed to improve. She sat up in bed, her color returned, and Dr. Rodriguez said, if she behaved herself and didn't overdo, it looked like she might outlive them all.

His mother received another letter from his father, begging her to go to New Orleans. He couldn't get time off. He had found a bookkeeping job on Saturdays, which enabled him to send some money. She said, now that it looked like Clotilde would live forever, she had more than half a mind to go. What was there in Belmont for her? Just that shriveled-up old lady in the bed refusing to die. Cato would have to stay. There was no other way. Didn't he see if she stayed she would lose her mind?

"No, Cato, you must stay, no matter what. You're my only hope, darling," she said one afternoon when another letter came begging her to go. "If we leave now, why, she may leave everything to her church. Your father's not doing much. I can see through his letters. Same old thing. He's a teller at a bank. He probably thinks he'll get rich just by going in the vault and breathing the air."

He was not as careful as he had been at first when he took money out of the drawer. He took larger amounts, telling his mother the old woman was softening and wanted her cousin's wife to stay. His mother said she would as long as the money was forthcoming, but as soon as she cut her off again, she was gone in a minute.

And then one morning, under the pretext of looking at himself in the mirror, he slipped his hand into the middle drawer and found there was no wallet. He looked up. Clotilde Patout was watching him in the mirror.

"You're just like Richard," she said. "I suppose you were bound to let me down."

"Nanan—"

"I want all of you off my land by tonight," she said.

"Nanan—"

"Go on, leave me in peace." She turned her back to him and lay on her side.

"Nanan, please—"

"I'm tired. Leave me. You won't make me change my mind."

He walked to her bed, absentmindedly picking up a stocking from the top of the dresser.

He sat by her side until he heard her breathing deepen, then slipped the stocking under her neck and pulled until it was tight.

At three thirty that afternoon Rodriguez found them together. He went down to the kitchen and telephoned. Sheriff Mouton said he'd come right on out.

Well now, people said the whole thing could have been avoided and wasn't it a shame. Who'd have thought a little boy would do something like that.

It got under the skin, somehow, people said, it fairly crawled when they let themselves think about it, so after a while we just tried to put it out of our minds.

The church took up a collection to make up the difference from what was in Clotilde Patout's bank account and the funeral expenses. It was a right nice funeral, considering, but surprising to see how much in less than three years since her sister died customs had changed. They had an open casket, but nobody came. People are too busy anymore to go to wakes. They figure if they can make it to the church before the funeral home gets there with the body, that's enough, only there weren't hardly five people at the service even so. Only the Minvilles, the doctor and his wife, and Alphonse Romero went to the cemetery. When Lizzard died, they had to send back to the funeral home for more folding chairs. Times have changed.

Patout moved his family back to New Orleans, leastways,

what was left of it. The boy they put in the state mental hospital. Seems he was in pretty bad shape. Well, you can imagine, a thing like that. They thought for a while he might snap out of it. The Minvilles were real good about visiting at first. Old Dr. Rodriguez went a few times before he died, but the visiting back and forth's fallen off. You can understand how that is. The boy doesn't recognize you. Won't talk. Just stares out the window at the birds. They say he has a fit if he sees a hawk. We all felt real sorry for his parents, especially his little mama. Don't know what she would have done without her husband. He was the Rock of Gibraltar.

Patout Minville seemed surprised when he inherited The Oaks. Don't know why. In Louisiana you can't leave out next of kin. Clotilde Patout didn't even have a proper will. There was some talk for a while about them coming back here to live, but they eventually tore down The Oaks and sold off the land in parcels. Patout said he and his wife couldn't bring themselves to live there after what their son did to the old lady, but let me tell you, they made out. They drive a big car now, mix with the smart set, and send those twins to a swanky kindergarten in New Orleans. Doesn't that beat all.

Where The Oaks stood is now the fanciest neighborhood in Belmont. They got cul de sacs and big houses—mostly French provincial with English Tudor accents—sitting on little bitty lots, and great, gawky teenage boys play basketball on a concrete court about where the veranda used to be. Nobody knows where Willie's buried. Those wooden crosses they put up for black folks don't last long.